A RETURN TO DUTY

By William C. Hammond and available from McBooks Press

CUTLER FAMILY CHRONICLES

A RETURN TO DUTY

VOLUME 8 OF THE CUTLER FAMILY CHRONICLES

WILLIAM C. HAMMOND

Essex, Connecticut

An imprint of The Globe Pequot Publishing Group, Inc.
64 South Main Street
Essex, CT 06426
www.globepequot.com

Distributed by NATIONAL BOOK NETWORK

British Library Cataloguing in Publication Information available

Library of Congress Cataloging-in-Publication Data
Names: Hammond, William C., 1947- author.
Title: A return to duty / William C. Hammond.
Description: Essex, Connecticut: McBooks, 2024. | Series: The Cutler Family chronicles; volume 8
Identifiers: LCCN 2024006476 (print) | LCCN 2024006477 (ebook) | ISBN 9781493087341
  (trade paperback: alk. paper) | ISBN 9781493087358 (epub)
Subjects: LCGFT: Domestic fiction. | Novels.
Classification: LCC PS3608.A69586 R48 2024 (print) | LCC PS3608.A69586
(ebook) | DDC 813/.6—dc23/eng/20240229
LC record available at https://lccn.loc.gov/2024006476
LC ebook record available at https://lccn.loc.gov/2024006477

∞™ The paper used in this publication meets the minimum requirements of American National Standard for Information Sciences—Permanence of Paper for Printed Library Materials, ANSI/ NISO Z39.48-1992.

For My Cherished Granddaughter

Eva Victoria Hammond

Contents

CONTENTS

Author's Note

What you are about to read is a work of fiction. Not every character in the book is a real historical figure. But some are. Similarly, not every event transpired as depicted, or even happened at all. But some did.

As a student of history for more than fifty years, and a writer of historical fiction for twenty of them, I endeavor in all my novels to be true to history as far as plot and circumstances permit. The responsibility to "get it right" is daunting, especially for an author researching people and places with roots far removed from his native New England—places where history is often subject to speculation and interpretation. But having lived in New Zealand for six years now and having married a lovely Kiwi woman of British descent, I have taken on the challenge with gusto. My mission in this novel is twofold: to spin a good yarn and thereby entertain my readers; and to further expand the Cutler Family Chronicles to the Orient and introduce my characters and my readers to this part of the world and the threats it faced in the mid-nineteenth century vis-à-vis the United States and Great Britain.

I hope I have succeeded in fulfilling this mission. You be the judge.

William C. Hammond III
Puhoi, New Zealand

PREFACE

The year 1845 was a year of promise for the United States. Having defeated Whig candidate Henry Clay in the 1844 presidential elections, President James K. Polk, a man of vision and conviction, set about fulfilling the promises he had made in the Democratic Party platform. Many of those promises involved land: acquisition of the Oregon and New Mexico territories, settlement of the southern border, and establishment of the 49th Parallel as the boundary between the United States and Canada. Lower tariffs, expanded overseas trade, and Jacksonian principles in favor of slavery and against the national bank were also on the docket, to the delight of some and the outrage of others.

The outlook was not all rosy, however. Mexico resented America's continued meddling in its internal affairs and Americans settling in lands it claimed as its own territory, including what would soon become the state of California. And Mexico was not at all pleased by America's annexation of the Republic of Texas, which the Mexican government had warned would be regarded as an act of war.

In the United States, storm clouds were beginning to gather on the southern horizon, but save for a few extremists no one seemed to notice. The very notion of civil war between the united northern and southern states was anathema to most Americans, who simply wanted to get on with their lives and reap the benefits of prosperity and fulfill the nation's manifest destiny.

A trouble spot was brewing on the other side of the world as well, but since it had yet to directly affect most Americans, it too was largely ignored. The Opium War was strictly a British affair. The Honorable East India Company, a paramilitary organization established to carry out Great Britain's imperialist designs in the Orient, was championing the widespread importation and sale of illegal opium in China simply to address a crippling trade deficit that threatened to bankrupt not only the honorable company but Great Britain as well.

The Chinese emperor held a different view. He was infuriated by Britain's interventions and violations of Chinese law. He was further outraged by the adverse effects the flood of opium was having on Chinese society. Yet if piracy and smuggling were the inevitable consequences of the Chinese government's crackdown on the distribution of an illegal substance within its borders, most Americans could not have cared less. It was not their problem.

Such logic held sway for the moment, but not for long. The world was becoming a smaller place in 1845. As global trade expanded, merchants of many nations were willing to take extraordinary risks in Far East trade routes in return for extraordinary profits. Porcelains, silks, and black tea were much in demand in Europe and the Americas, and now that high-grade opium grown in the eastern provinces of India and smuggled into China was being added to the mix, profits were soaring. Merchants, pirates, and smugglers willing to defy Chinese government policy that forbade importation of the drug stood at the precipice. The stakes were too high, the potential payout too great, for nations and individuals to sit by and watch immense profits slip through their fingers.

Like every other global commercial enterprise, my fictional Cutler & Sons of Boston, Massachusetts, had to protect its interests in the Far East while expanding its customer base worldwide, just as it had been doing for nearly a century. But how far would individuals be willing to go in the pursuit of profits? To what lengths would the United States Navy go to safeguard the Far East waters through which their nation's ships plied their trade? And of equal concern, as it turned out: To what lengths would American merchant companies go to protect their crews and cargoes from the merciless pirates who haunted those waters?

These were questions that had neither immediate nor comforting answers.

CHAPTER 1

SYDNEY, NEW SOUTH WALES
September 1845

He stood by the window watching, waiting, aware of only the rhythmic ticking of a mantlepiece clock and the quiet ministrations of the servant cleaning at the far end of the parlor. As he replaced the bone china teacup onto the matching saucer he held in his hand, a motion on the flagship in the bay caught his eye. He turned from the window.

"I daresay the admiral is about to push off, Martha," he said to the middle-aged servant. "Will you be kind enough to inform Lady Anne?"

"At once, my lord," she replied.

As Martha hastened from the room, Richard Cutler smiled to himself. He was no English lord. Far from it. His bloodlines were far humbler than that. True, his great-grandparents had been English. A century earlier they had sailed from England to the village of Hingham in the colony of Massachusetts, where they had built a trading company and amassed a fortune from the production and distribution of sugar and molasses, and eventually, of West Indian rum. It was an enterprise passed down to three generations of Cutlers. Although the revenues generated were considerable, because they had been obtained by hard work and risk-taking they were of minor interest to those of a more genteel nature who had garnered such wealth as the result of a birthright.

While Richard Cutler had no claim to England's peerage, the man he had spotted through the window currently being conveyed by a ship's cutter to Government House certainly did. As, by right, did Richard's wife, Anne, the gentleman's sister.

He heard footsteps hurrying down the front stairway, and moments later Anne Cutler appeared at the open doorway. "Where is he?" she asked excitedly.

"Still a way off, my dear. Come see."

Richard drew aside the tasseled damask curtain to reveal the long, thin peninsula that crooked northward along the eastern edge of Sydney Harbor from South Head, where Government House was located. The view reminded Richard of Nantasket Peninsula near his home in Hingham Bay, Massachusetts. At the peninsula's northern tip, at the entrance to Sydney Harbor, stood a signal station and lighthouse. To the south, in a protected area of the peninsula called Watson's Bay, a squadron of ship-rigged vessels rode at anchor. Most were frigates, a blend of sail and steam power, unassuming save for the seventy-four-gun Third Rate flying the broad pennant of a Vice Admiral of the Blue. Pulling away from that behemoth was a ship's boat propelled by ten oarsmen. At the moment, it was passing before a moored twenty-gun sloop-of-war. High up on the sloop's ensign halyard fluttered the stars and stripes of the United States of America.

"There's Reggie sitting next to the coxswain in the stern," Richard said, pointing at the oncoming ship's boat.

"Wonderful!" she cried, clasping her hands to her breast. It was her first glimpse of her brother in nearly eight years. "Richard," she said, "I am going back upstairs to freshen up and make certain Jamie is dressed. Do send word the moment Reggie arrives!"

"Of course, my dear," he called after her as she scurried away. Not since their blissful reunion in Auckland after being separated for more than a year in the wilds of New Zealand had he seen her so animated.

Richard took a moment to check his own appearance in a wall mirror. His captain's uniform of buff trousers and blue coat was not his own, and it showed. The clothing belonged to John Sloat, captain of the sloop-of-war *St. Louis*, loaned to Richard during the voyage from Auckland to Sydney. Although the two men were equal in height, Richard had yet to regain the weight he had lost during his time in the bush, and the uniform was far too loose. Nevertheless, he was grateful to have it.

Otherwise, the mirror confirmed that he looked passable. His face was thinner than it had been before the shipwreck, and the deeply etched crow's feet around his hazel eyes showed his fatigue and the stress he had suffered. His queue was gone now, his chestnut hair cropped short. His square Cutler jaw bore scars earned during that year in the bush with his surviving crew and the Maori natives who had befriended them. He thought of them often, some of his happy memories of that time. And of one Maori native in particular, a woman of great beauty and passion who had saved his life, if not his virtue, more than once. He turned away from the mirror to forestall the rising tide of fond but painful memories and busied himself by brushing the arms and front of his uniform coat. After a final glance through the window, he stepped from the lounge into the front hallway.

The knock on the front door brought the same well-dressed servant out from the kitchen to answer it. "Let me, Martha," Richard said. "Go upstairs to Lady Anne and Jamie." The servant nodded her understanding and started upstairs as Richard stepped to the door and opened it.

"My word!" a deep voice resonated in the hall. "Richard Cutler, I presume? Here, at long last? I had thought that you would bypass Sydney and sail straight for home! So glad you decided to stop by for a visit!"

Faced with the man's imposing height and bearing, the majesty of his gilt-edged blue uniform, and his lofty rank, Richard's instinct was to salute. Which is what he did.

Reginald Blount Sedgewick Brathwaite removed his bicorne hat, revealing a full head of perfectly groomed tawny hair. "We'll have none of that, my dear fellow," he chuckled as he tucked his hat under his left arm. His cut-glass accent marked him clearly as being a member of the English aristocracy. "We are both off duty. What is more, we are family."

Richard smiled, grateful for the immediate bond with the brother-in-law he was meeting for the first time. The two men shook hands warmly.

"We are indeed, Reginald," he said.

"Reggie," Brathwaite returned with a smile. "Do please call me Reggie. I have heard a great deal about you," he added. "From Anne, of course, and from George and Cassandra. They have sent glowing reports from Washington. So have your colleagues at the Navy Yard. They were most distressed to learn of your disappearance and pleaded with me to do all in my power to find you. As I did. As we all did."

"I know," Richard said, "and I thank you. I also thank you for sending a dispatch to Washington about my reentry into the world of the living."

"Of course, of course," the admiral said dismissively. "No doubt your government has already notified your family in . . . Boston, is it?"

"Close. Hingham is just south of Boston."

"Ah, yes. Hingham. I should like to visit there someday. Now then, might I inquire as to the whereabouts of my sweet sister? I am keen to welcome her to Sydney."

"Your sweet—and only—sister is up here, Reggie," a voice called out from above them. "And on her way down."

Anne Cutler descended the wide, curving stairway of Government House as though she was entering the grand embassy ball in Washington where she had met her husband. Her long auburn hair was swept up in a becoming chignon, accentuating her delicate facial features. Richard had no idea where she had managed to procure the primrose yellow dress she was wearing. But it suited her. And despite all the privations she had suffered during their separation, she was still a handsome woman.

"Anne!" the admiral breathed as brother and sister walked toward each other, their eyes smiling as they embraced. "My dear little sister. It has been far too long. I thank God to find you alive and looking so fit. You are a walking miracle!" He kissed the crown of her head.

"Far too long indeed," Anne agreed. She backed up a step and looked up to meet his steady gaze. For several moments they stood there staring at each other, both remembering happy days of childhood at their parents' estate in England. The spell was broken by the sound of footsteps on the stairs.

"I say, what have we here?" Brathwaite exclaimed when he caught sight of the toddler and the young woman carrying him down the stairway. When they reached the bottom stair, the woman carefully set the neatly dressed little boy down on the hallway's marble floor. He stood there blinking curiously up at the tall, magnificent stranger.

"Meet your nephew, Reggie," Anne said with a flourish. "We named him James, after his grandfather, but we call him Jamie. He'll be two years in a couple of months, and as you can see, despite our perils he is a strapping young tyke." She gestured toward the brown-haired woman holding Jamie's hand. "And may I also introduce Miss Rachel Brown. Rachel is English by birth, and she has been a godsend to me since the day she joined the Wesleyan mission to which I was brought half-drowned and barely alive. I could not have survived without her. Happily, she has agreed to accompany Richard and me to America, and to live with us there."

Brathwaite took Rachel's hand in his with a courtly bow. "I am pleased to make your acquaintance, Miss Brown. Thank you for your care of my sister and my nephew. Your kindness shan't be forgotten, I assure you."

Rachel offered a graceful curtsy. "It's my honor and privilege, my lord."

Brathwaite smiled, nodded, and turned back to Anne. "We have much to catch up on, my dear. I suggest we get right to it. I believe we will enjoy luncheon together here, at Government House?" Anne nodded. "Excellent. This evening," he continued, "we shall take tea with Governor and Lady Gipps at their residence." He pointed in the general direction of a grand Gothic Revival mansion located not far away on Charlotte Street. "Is that your understanding as well?"

"It is," Anne agreed.

"Splendid. After dinner we can enjoy a stroll outside while we talk. The gardens here are stunning whatever the season, and if the birds behave themselves, you'll find it quite serene." As if on cue, a cacophony of maniacal laughter erupted in the gum trees outside the open parlor windows. "Crazy birds, those kookaburras, but quite harmless, I assure you! Nothing like the sweet songbirds of New Zealand, are they?"

"Nothing at all like them," Richard laughed. "We were a bit startled at first, I admit, but we're quite accustomed to the noise now."

"Tomorrow," Brathwaite continued, "I must tend to official business during the day. But I should very much like to host evening tea here at Government House. I have already sent word to the staff to be prepared."

He looked at Richard. "Are there men among your crew you might wish to invite?"

Richard nodded. "There are two. Jack Brengle, my executive officer, and Jonty Montgomery, the only one of my midshipmen to survive our ordeal. They were both instrumental in keeping the rest of us alive, though the truth is, all the survivors played key roles. I am personally indebted to each and every one of them."

"Then, by God, we shall invite the whole lot. And Miss Brown here, of course. Let us add Captain Stoat and his officers to the mix, and we shall have a delightful gathering. Good food, wine, beer, and rum. And if I know Governor Gipps, some fine music as well. These poor cuds deserve a fair bit of rest and relaxation!"

Anne reached out and squeezed his arm. "That sounds divine, Reggie."

"It will be, Anne," Braithwaite promised. "I shall allow only the best for my sister and her husband." He turned his attention to Jamie, whose eyes were drooping in anticipation of his afternoon nap. "I will see you and Miss Brown aboard my flagship before the week is out, Jamie," he said as he tickled the boy's back. "If you are to become a naval officer like your father and uncle, it's time you start learning the ropes!"

* * *

Lunch was served in a private alcove off the main dining room on the first floor of Government House. The guests enjoyed a simple but savory meal with excellent wines imported from France. As they ate, they engaged in small talk suitable for the occasion until Richard could no longer resist asking a question.

"Forgive me, Reginald, but I must ask, did the negotiations take place? And if they did, in your estimation did they go as well as expected?"

He was referring to the reason he and Anne had sailed to the Great South Sea two years earlier. As a naval commander whose family was profitably engaged in the Oriental trade, especially the trade routes linking China to Batavia and the islands of the East Indies, Richard had been the logical choice to add his ship, *Suwannee*, to three vessels of the East India Squadron under the command of Commodore Robert Strong. Their mission was to sail to Sydney to conduct negotiations with the British. Ostensibly, the negotiations were to arrange favorable trade agreements with New South Wales and other British colonies in Australia. A secondary—and ultimately more important—reason was to secure the use of Royal Navy bases in the western Pacific and thus to advance American interests in that region. In return, the United States was prepared to pledge not only favorable trading terms but also to support the Royal Navy in its ongoing struggles with Chinese pirates and smugglers. As the sister of two men important to the mission—one the commander-in-chief of British forces in the region and the other the British ambassador to the United States—Anne Braithwaite Cutler's inclusion on the American side of negotiations was deemed advisable by the American president and his cabinet. The squadron was nearing its destination when a rare off-season cyclone struck with such fury that it blew *Suwannee* off course onto a shoal off the western coast of New Zealand. The American frigate foundered, and most of her crew perished.

Brathwaite took a sip of wine before answering. "The negotiations did take place, Richard, and whilst you and Anne were sorely missed, they were quite constructive. I am most impressed with your Commodore Strong, an excellent commanding officer and a fine fellow. I found your Mr. Livermore a bit off-putting, but I must admit that he is a skilled negotiator who did a good job representing your interests. At some point during the next few days, I shall sit down with you and review the details."

"I look forward to that," Richard said.

"I should think you would," Brathwaite said with a wry smile. "Your family stands to make out quite handsomely as a result of the negotiations. But it is a good agreement that will work in our mutual best interests. Which is why I signed off on it with only minor modifications."

"Have the terms been officially endorsed by your government?"

"My understanding is that they have, Anne. Sir Robert Peel and Lord Palmerston"—referring to the British prime minister and his foreign secretary—"have given their blessings, so Her Majesty the Queen and Parliament will fall in line. You will find out for certain when you arrive in Washington and Richard is able to debrief his superiors." He looked at Richard. "If you wouldn't mind, Richard, I have a packet of dispatches for you to deliver to Secretary Bancroft."

"Of course."

Brathwaite hesitated, then: "There is much in those dispatches you will want to discuss with the Navy secretary and with your family."

"Such as?"

The admiral answered with a question of his own. "What do you know about the outcome of the recent war between Great Britain and China?"

Richard shrugged. "Very little, I'm afraid. I heard about it before I sailed in *Suwannee*, but I doubt even the British authorities in New Zealand know much more. As I recall, it involved the smuggling of opium into China from the eastern provinces of India. The war is over now, isn't it?"

"Officially, yes. The Treaty of Nanjing ended it several years ago. But though the battles are over, the scars remain. I have procured some back issues of the *Sydney Gazette*. It's a reliable newspaper and it covered the war quite thoroughly. You would do well to look at them. They make for interesting reading."

"And your tone makes for interesting hearing, Reggie," Anne said. "You sound quite mysterious. Is there something you are not telling us?"

"There is a lot I am not telling you, Anne. But as I indicated, you should hear it from your own government rather than from me. I have included in the dispatches a summary I wrote for your eyes only, Richard. Wait to read it until you are at sea. I think you will find it helpful."

Richard and Anne exchanged glances, then Anne said, "I'm sure he will, Reggie. And by all means tell us when that will be. When are Richard and I sailing to America, and in which ship?"

"Not *St. Louis*," Brathwaite said. "As I believe you already know, Captain Sloat has received orders to sail to Monterey, California, to join your Pacific Squadron. We are hearing reports of what is being hailed as America's 'manifest destiny.' That destiny, it seems, is to expand American territory across the North American continent from the Atlantic to the Pacific. I suspect that will happen eventually, and I further suspect that

Captain Sloat's sailing orders to California have more than a little to do with that so-called destiny."

Anne arched her eyebrows. "California? Is that not in Mexico?"

"It is, for the moment," her brother acknowledged. "But who knows for how long? The British government believes war is imminent between Mexico and the United States. Perhaps it has already started. I don't understand all that is involved, but the gist seems to be that most citizens of Texas wish their territory to be annexed to the United States. The Mexican government, not surprisingly, opposes such a move. It has never accepted the document signed by General Santa Anna in 1836 that recognized Texas as an independent republic. Perhaps you remember hearing of the battle at the Alamo? Santa Anna contends that he signed that document under duress while he was a prisoner of the Americans, and the document is therefore invalid."

Richard pondered that. "I wonder what role our Navy would play in such a conflict—assuming there *is* a conflict," he added quickly.

"A minor one, I suspect," Reggie said. "Mexico does not have much of a navy, although I understand that Texas has a decent one. If your ships can stay out of range of shore batteries, there should be naught for your Navy to do beyond offering logistical support to your army. The war will be waged on land and will likely involve capture of the capital at Mexico City to settle the matter." Brathwaite sighed audibly. "Your country is on the cusp of greatness, Richard, if it can avoid untimely entanglements.

"Putting Mexico aside for the moment," he continued, "I fear what would happen in a conflict between your northern and southern states. And I don't see how such a conflict can be avoided. The two regions seem to have little in common. The northern states have industrial superiority while the southern states have military traditions and know-how. Tensions are rising, and there is much at stake, especially for the South, whose economy relies on slavery, a practice outlawed elsewhere in the civilized world. If war should come, the United States would be ripped asunder." He shrugged. "Then again, what do I know? I am a simple British sea officer who has little practical experience with American internal affairs. As well as with Americans in general, although the one my dear sister decided to marry seems to be a fine chap."

Anne took Richard's hand in hers. "And so he is. Which ship, then, has the dubious honor of taking us to America, Reggie?"

Brathwaite cleared his throat. "My apologies. I digressed. You and *Suwannee*'s crew will be aboard *Alarm*, a light frigate that is being provisioned as we sit here. She is the swiftest vessel I have. She has twice made the voyage to your naval base in Portsmouth, Virginia, and both in record time. Captain Bennan is a gentleman and Royal Navy to his core. He will see to your every comfort, I assure you. For starters, he insists that you and Richard take his cabin."

Anne smiled happily. "That is most accommodating of him."

"When do we weigh?" Richard pressed.

"On Saturday week, nine days from now. We'll have you reporting to Secretary Bancroft at the Navy Yard quicker than a Yankee Doodle can sing 'God Save the Queen.'" His eyes lit up. "I say, here's something you may not have considered. Your new Navy secretary, Mr. Bancroft, has been in office less than a year and has already authorized the construction of a naval college to be located in Annapolis, Maryland, on Chesapeake Bay. It will be based along the same lines as what we project for our own Royal Naval College. I can see young Jamie enrolled there in a few years' time. And the college won't be far from your home in Alexandria."

The admiral drained his cup of tea and, after checking to ensure his guests were finished with theirs, said, "I suggest we go outdoors. It's a lovely day, and I am quite keen to learn more of your adventures in New Zealand. From what I have gleaned thus far, it is a fascinating saga. Precious little is known about New Zealand even here in New South Wales." He snapped his fingers. "Have you considered writing your story down and having it published in New York or Boston? Perhaps even in London?"

"I had not considered that possibility," Richard said flatly. "I am not a writer. What's more, I have precious little time to devote to such an endeavor. Anne is the writer in the family." He looked at his wife. "Perhaps she would consider it."

"You will have plenty of free time on your voyage home," Brathwaite said enthusiastically. "Give it a go, won't you, Anne? For my sake?" He added jokingly, "I trust the details are all aboveboard and in good taste, and will not embarrass the family!"

CHAPTER 2

Not for many years had there been such a family gathering. As summer's heat and humidity yielded to autumn's refreshing cool temperatures, twenty-three members of the Cutler family—three-quarters of the Cutlers residing in eastern Massachusetts—descended on the picturesque seaside town of Hingham, birthplace of Cutler & Sons. Featured prominently on Boston's South Shore, Hingham had since the early 1760s served as the family seat in North America. The family members seated today in William Cutler's house were in essence the American shareholders of a privately held global shipping company. Most of them were senior members who for years had enthusiastically and gratefully been taking care of business in North America, England, the West Indies, and, more recently, the Orient. But several younger members of the clan were now coming into their own, and their perspectives on the future of the business were not always in line with those of the older generations.

Two events of consequence had drawn the family together. Philip Seymour, the director of Cutler & Sons, had disappeared at sea a year ago while on assignment at the company's Far East headquarters in Batavia. Since neither wreckage nor bodies were found, the ship was presumed lost and her crew declared dead, in accordance with maritime law. Philip's devoted aunt, Lavinia, now aged eighty-one and the sole surviving member of the second generation of Cutlers in America, was still so beset by grief over her nephew's death that the rest of the family had considered either postponing the gathering or persuading Lavinia to remain at her home in Duxbury with Philip's daughter Lucy, his only child, who had announced she would not be attending even though the family was gathering in part to honor her father.

Lavinia, however, would have none of it. Because the family was honoring her nephew, and because the main topic of discussion would be the future of the company to which he had devoted his life, she saw it as her duty to attend. She took her seat in the well-appointed drawing room looking every bit the family matriarch.

There was some good news to report, most of it already known to the family. Richard and Anne Cutler were alive and well, and on their way home from New South Wales in a Royal Navy frigate. Word had arrived from Secretary of the Navy George Bancroft a week ago that HMS *Alarm* should soon be raising the Virginia Capes, almost two years after Richard and Anne had sailed for Sydney in *Suwannee*.

Months of anxiety with no word beyond the communiqué from the Navy Department that *Suwannee* had gone missing and was presumed either lost at sea or washed up on some distant shore had almost killed Melinda Cutler, Richard's mother, who fell into such despair that her family and friends feared for her sanity, if not her life. Her distress was short-lived, however. A woman of character, Melinda had emerged from the abyss and taken up her usual duties, but without the support of her beau, Harlan Sturgis, a local businessman and erstwhile acquaintance of Melinda's late husband. With hardly a fare-thee-well to anyone, Sturgis had up and left for parts unknown.

"You're better off without him, Melinda," Diana Cutler Sprague had told her several days after Sturgis left. Diana, the sister of Melinda's deceased husband, James Cutler, had long served as the voice of reason and calm within the family. At fifty-five, she showed many of the physical attributes she had inherited from her mother, Katherine. "If I am being too blunt, I apologize, but I must say that I never trusted or particularly liked the man. He could turn on the charm, but only when he needed to be charming. Or so it seemed to me. I am not saying he didn't care for you—I mean, he appeared to, but Peter and I always questioned his motives. We never felt comfortable in his company, and we never understood what he was doing here. Harlan didn't fit in with the rest of us, and

I believe he knew it. I believe he felt the walls closing in on him and left. Peter agrees with me, and as a district judge he is an excellent assessor of character. Richard didn't trust Harlan either. He confided that to me before sailing to Java and asked me to keep an eye on him. And on you."

Melinda had sighed. "Perhaps you and Richard were right, Diana. Perhaps I *was* played for a fool. I certainly agree that Richard will be relieved to see Harlan gone. And you are not being unnecessarily blunt, my dear," she added. "You are being honest, and for that I am grateful."

When all those attending the gathering had arrived in the two-story gray clapboard house on Ship Street and greeted one another, a tall, distinguished figure stood up from his seat by the large bay window. Through the diamond-shaped glass panes behind him, the harbor at the foot of the hill glittered in the sunlight. In the distance, a fleet of small boats rested at anchor. Beyond them, on the mud flats on the far side of the harbor, clusters of people probed the mud and sand to extract the succulent shellfish that fetched a handsome price in local taverns and markets.

William Cutler cleared his throat to attract everyone's attention. "Good morning," he said. "Thank you all for coming today. Adele and I welcome you to our home." He smiled down at his wife, a sweet-faced woman with white hair neatly pinned up under a lacy cap. The lovely French aristocrat who had stolen young William Cutler's heart long ago had aged gracefully. Just as the French Revolution was erupting, she and her mother and sister were saved from the guillotine by William's father, who spirited them away from France to America in the Cutler schooner *Falcon*. "Please be seated."

As people took their seats, William adjusted his silk neck stock and smoothed back his thinning hair. At sixty-three, he was the firstborn child of Richard and Katherine Cutler and had served as the face of the family business for most of his adult life. Cutler & Sons business had taken him three times to Batavia, and on additional occasions to the family's sugar plantation and rum production facility on Barbados. The *Boston Traveler* had billed his marriage to Adele Endicott as the social event of 1809. A man of few pretensions who practiced modesty and frugality despite his considerable wealth, William Cutler's interests and influence extended far beyond Hingham.

Before continuing, William nodded briefly at his sister Diana and his wife sitting next to her on the sofa, then lifted his gaze to take in the entire assemblage—everyone present linked by blood, marriage, or destiny. "We are gathered here today to remember the life of one brother and to celebrate the deliverance of another. As you know by now, Richard is on his way home to Alexandria. He is bringing with him his wife, Anne, and their son, Jamie. From what we understand, all three of them are well and in fine form." At the mention of her grandson's Christian name, Melinda Cutler clasped her hands together and bowed her head, moved that the boy had been named after her late husband, who had died while on active duty shortly after the British burned Washington in 1814.

"So, there is indeed cause for celebration today," William went on. "Exactly when Richard and his family will be sailing to Hingham I cannot say. But if I know my nephew, he will send word after he has landed in Virginia and will sail to us as soon as duty permits. I doubt it will be later than year's end."

"A perfect Christmas gift for us all," Joseph Cutler shouted from the back of the room. Joseph, the only child of John and Cynthia Cutler, had grown up on the Cutler plantation in Barbados. He had drifted in and out with the tides of indifference and self-doubt, lacking any interest in the family business, until Katherine Cutler convinced his parents to allow twenty-two-year-old Joseph to come to America in 1809. To the relief of his parents, he made a fresh start in the one pursuit that seemed to motivate him: mathematics. Joseph began teaching at Derby Academy, a Hingham coeducational institution, where he quickly became a respected and popular member of the faculty.

His remark sparked vocal agreement. "It would indeed be that, Joseph," William shouted into the hubbub, speaking for them all.

"Now then," he said as the room quieted. "Since we don't yet know what Richard's decision might be, we can only speculate. Will he and his family visit for a short spell and then return to Virginia? Or will he settle in Hingham and do as we all hope he will and assume the directorship of Cutler & Sons? He would have to resign his commission in the Navy to do that, of course, and that will be no easy decision for him. Nor would he be the first one in our family to put love of country first. His decision, I suspect, will turn on where he sees his primary duty. Whatever his decision may be, we are bound to honor it.

"Philip, God bless his soul, would be the first to understand," William continued. "Under his tenure as director, Cutler & Sons increased production of sugar, molasses, and rum, and opened many new markets in the Orient and elsewhere. Our company's earnings have risen to new heights as a result, a dividend you have no doubt noticed in your recent distributions."

Under normal circumstances the contemplation of their dividends would have lightened the mood. Today it did not.

"But we must not rest on our laurels," he continued. "We must not become complacent. Under no circumstances should we take our good fortune for granted. As Philip's untimely death confirms, danger lurks whenever and wherever our ships put to sea. The pending conflict with Mexico may be of grave concern to us as Americans, but as owners of a shipping enterprise we have other concerns. We can supply what the military needs from us from our warehouses in Boston and Baltimore. No, our primary concern is not war between our country and another. Our primary concern continues to be what it has been since our earliest days: pirates. Pirates in the Indies, pirates in the Mediterranean, and now pirates in the Orient. I had my first taste of these scoundrels as a young man in the Sunda Strait. They are a particularly unsavory lot.

"For as long as anyone here can remember, pirates have been the bane of legitimate shipping interests, which is why Philip mandated that our merchantmen be armed with the best weapons we can procure from our Navy and our foundries. I agreed with Philip then, and I still agree with him today. So does our government, and for good cause. Our country's economy depends in large part on trade, both for the goods we produce and those we carry on behalf of our clients." He paused to once again clear his throat. "I have said enough. No doubt you have questions."

To no one's surprise, the first question came from Thomas Cutler. The only son of Caleb and Joan Cutler, Thomas had learned the business from his father, who had directed Cutler & Sons until his sudden death eight years earlier of a heart attack. Thomas still lived in the old family residence on Main Street with his wife, Hester.

"Cousin," Thomas said to Will in a voice that carried across the room, "it could be a long while before we have the issue of corporate governance settled, even if Richard does decide to jump ship on the Navy. Assuming that is the case, will Cutler & Sons continue to be managed in the interim in the manner it is today?"

William nodded. "Unless there is opposition to what I am doing, yes. I will continue to assume overall responsibility for operations, here and abroad. Ben Cutler"—referring to Joseph Cutler's English cousin in Barbados—"will continue to oversee production and trade in the Indies. Pieter De Vries will remain at his post in Batavia. Although he is not a Cutler, he is doing a splendid job there, and I see no reason to change course. Ben, as some of you know, is seriously considering a move to Batavia to serve as Pieter's second-in-command. I am encouraging him to do so for reasons that I am sure are obvious. If any of you disagree, however, please speak your mind. Differences of opinion are encouraged here, as you know."

Zeke Crabtree stood. The only child of Agreen and Elizabeth Cutler Crabtree, since leaving Derby Academy he had served Cutler & Sons as a foretopman on one of the company's merchant brigs. Whenever the subject of promotion was broached to him, it was politely turned aside. It was life in the forecastle, not on the quarterdeck, that Zeke desired. Nonetheless, after a decade of putting into ports both lovely and squalid, he had decided to swallow the anchor and pursue his first love, teaching. "Mine is a simple question," he said. "If Richard were to decline our offer, what then?"

William smiled thinly and shrugged. "I have no specific answer at this time. Nor will I until we have hard facts before us. If Richard sees fit to decline our offer, Cutler & Sons will continue to prosper nevertheless. We are most fortunate to have talented people in our midst to assure our future." His gaze flickered briefly over to Thomas Cutler.

"William," Peter Sprague said, "on a different subject, what of the situation in the Dominican Republic? Anything new to report? Should we be concerned about our interests there?"

Twenty years earlier, the powerful *criollo* class in the Spanish colony of Santo Domingo on the Caribbean island of Hispaniola had overthrown the crown government. Soon after that Santo Domingo united with its neighbor Haiti to bring all the island under Haitian control. Despite two decades of prosperity, Santo Domingo was now seeking independence. Its government had severed ties with Haiti and declared the new Dominican Republic a sovereign nation. That did not end the matter, however. Wealthier Haitians, many of French extraction and merchants by trade, vehemently denounced this move and began stirring up trouble. The Spanish in Cuba and other West Indian islands saw an opportunity to regain what they had lost and started meddling in the internal affairs of the new republic, determined to see it restored to the dwindling Spanish Empire.

William considered his answer for a moment. As the early autumn sun streamed in through the open French doors and windows, the women began to fan themselves and men unbuttoned their collars and removed their coats. A servant brought in pitchers of chilled lemon water.

"Only a fool would deny it's a worry, Peter," William finally said. "Much of our trade in the Indies passes through Port-au-Prince and Santo Domingo. Much of the island's wealth is tied to shipping companies—our own and others. If the Spanish follow through on their threat to blockade those ports, neither country has a navy to stop them. The Monroe Doctrine may in theory prevent any European power from intervening in the affairs of the Western Hemisphere, but it's a moot point if the United States is preoccupied with Mexico and sends our Navy there. So we are left, once again, to our own devices. And since Spain seems unconcerned with doctrines of any kind, there is always the risk of one of our merchantmen running afoul of a Spanish man-o'-war." He sighed. "All this serves to underscore why Cutler & Sons needs Richard's naval experience and connections in addition to his business acumen. Regardless, we have met threats of this sort before, many times, and we will do so again if we must. Agree, Peter?"

"Agree," Peter said.

"Other questions?"

There appeared to be none.

William's gaze swept the room. "Then you all have deliberately left the sword of Damocles sheathed," he said dryly. "We have not yet touched on China, and we have not yet discussed the catastrophic influx of opium into our own country. Much of this opium is brought in by American merchantmen, some of whom we know and respect. I am ashamed to report that in 1840 alone, 24,000 pounds of the stuff entered the United States, a shocking amount of it through Boston." His words were met by rigid stares and silence. "Apparently, the lure of easy money is too enticing an incentive, whatever the social and medical consequences of the scourge. What are federal and local authorities doing about opium? I am ashamed to say, not much. They are imposing tariffs on its importation, is all. And they are using the proceeds from these tariffs to fund public projects such as schools, libraries, and hospitals. An admirable use of funds, you say? Well, yes, it is, but at too high a price, in my estimation. New schools and hospitals do not offset the consequences of allowing the use of such a drug to proliferate within our borders and poison our citizens. The threat starts in China, where opium smugglers have turned to piracy. The pirates attack our merchant ships and hold their crews and cargoes for ransoms that our government refuses to pay."

"Do you think that might have happened to Philip and his crew, William?" Diana asked. "Is it possible they are being held captive somewhere in China until ransoms are paid?"

"It is possible," William allowed. "I can get very little information from the government regarding the matter. It may be that a rescue attempt is in the works that we know nothing about. More than a year has passed since their ship disappeared, and we have not been approached for ransom payments. If they do have Philip, and they know who he is, they may turn to the family when they accept that the United States government will not pay ransoms for its citizens under any circumstances."

Diana nodded. "Then we may still hear something. There is still hope. I insist that there is still hope that he's alive."

"Keep that hope in your heart, Diana." William smiled kindly at her. "These things can take time, often a lot of time, and we will continue to keep open all lines of communication. But for now let us return to the subject of opium." William went on, "I must reiterate that our long-standing policy remains very much in effect. Simply put, no Cutler merchant vessel, now or in the future, will participate in, or profit from, the procurement, shipment, or sale of opium. However lucrative the opium trade may be, it is evil and not for us.

"Think about it. Why are Chinese authorities so intent on suppressing the smuggling of opium? Why did Emperor Xuanzong order twenty thousand chests of opium in Canton seized and destroyed despite having been warned by the British that doing so would be considered an act of war? The chests were British property stored in a British warehouse. Why did the emperor do that? I submit it was because he had witnessed the devastation to his people and his economy from the ill effects of opium. War with Britain could do no worse. He fought a war to stop opium from destroying his country. I ask you: Who was in the right here, Britain or China?"

William Cutler's voice rose in volume as he spoke. "It falls on us to do everything in our power to steer this nation clear of the opium trade, save for medicinal purposes. Lord Palmerston agrees, despite the complicity of the British East India Company in the trade. The prime minister is prepared to sign what amounts to a military alliance with the United States to address the threat. Whatever our differences may have been in the past, the governments of both nations agree that our futures are best served by the obliteration of this scourge. It is our duty and our responsibility to set the example. So I pledge to you here, today: As long as I am responsible for the affairs of Cutler & Sons, and as long as I draw breath, no Cutler or anyone associated with this family will ever participate in the illicit trade in narcotics!"

William Cutler sat down to general applause but an undercurrent of quiet grumbling among the younger members of the family. Though not best pleased by this show of displeasure, William had expected it. When profit crossed swords with principle, profit was a hard thrust to parry, especially when so much money was at stake. The importation and use of opium was not illegal in the United States. But William was convinced that would change, and when it did, he was determined that his family and their business would not be on the wrong side of history. Not on his watch.

CHAPTER 3

WASHINGTON, DISTRICT OF COLUMBIA
October 1846

Anne Cutler stood at the bow of the single-masted vessel, gripping its forestay as she listened contentedly to the symphony of sounds she had known since her childhood: the rattle of the halyards, the snapping of luff, the splash of wavelets against the prow, the gurgle of whitewater rushing aft along the hull, and the cries of gulls overhead. As the vessel sailed on, carried by the incoming tide and a strengthening southwesterly breeze, a riot of fall colors was everywhere in evidence along the banks of the Potomac. She glanced up to see puffs of sugar-white clouds scudding across the sky and breathed in the earthy scents of land. Would she ever again regard land as nondescript? No, she vowed, she would not. Today, at last, she was nearing the end of the fifteen-thousand-mile voyage that had taken her from Auckland, New Zealand, to Sydney in New South Wales, and from there across the Indian Ocean, around the Cape of Good Hope, and into the Atlantic Ocean on a course to the Norfolk Naval Shipyard in Portsmouth, Virginia. Home.

Sighing contentedly, she pushed still further away the hard memories of what had followed after the wreck of *Suwanee* and her concerns about what had actually happened to her husband during their year-long separation in the New Zealand bush. There was something he wasn't telling her, something that made him stiffen whenever she broached the subject. Whatever story remained untold, it was likely not one she wanted to hear. There was a reason why Richard's experiences remained a mystery. But as she had done since their reunion in Auckland, she forced herself not to dwell on it. His love for her was never in question, and he was as loving and attentive to her as he had ever been. They were on course to start life anew together, and if her instincts were correct, that new life would include a baby brother or sister for little Jamie.

She sensed more than heard his approach along the deck and closed her eyes when he settled a light woolen wrap around her shoulders. She longed to turn around and take him in her arms. But she dared not. This was a naval vessel, and one adhered to certain protocols. The young midshipman in command and the two sailors sitting next to him by the helm were no doubt watching closely.

"How sweet of you to bring me a wrap," she murmured. "But really, I don't need it. It's glorious up here."

"It is that," he agreed. They stood side by side on the foredeck enjoying the colors of the Maryland shore after so many months of blue seas until Richard broke the silence. "We are almost home, my love."

"I can hardly believe it. Our lives shall be quite boring after the excitement of the last two years."

Young Jamie appeared in the cockpit, looking tanned and hearty after spending months at sea, followed closely by the watchful Rachel.

"I must go aft," Anne said. She released her grip on the stay and turned to go.

"We haven't much time now," Richard called after her. She raised her right hand in acknowledgment.

Six sharp clangs of a ship's bell rang out. Three o'clock in the afternoon. The terrain was becoming increasingly familiar to Richard as the vessel knifed through the river waters on a comfortable broad reach. Already they were passing simple wooden dwellings he recognized from previous turns on the river. He could see a mile or so ahead where the river swerved to the northwest. Once they rounded that bend, they would see in the distance the Palladian-style mansion of Mount Vernon, the former plantation of George Washington. Beyond that, to port, the brick buildings and towering white steeples of Alexandria would loom, and across the river to starboard the silent brick majesty of Georgetown. *Here I am at last. Coming home to a place I feared I would never see again!*

"Excuse me, Captain. A word, if I might."

Richard turned to find the young midshipman facing him. Despite his slight build and youthful features, his attention to his duty and his craft shone through. Though command of a packet boat was hardly a prestigious assignment, the midshipman conducted himself as though he were in command of a ship of war.

Richard returned the salute. "Yes, Nathan, what is it?"

"We are approaching Washington, sir. My question is, would you prefer to dock at the Navy Yard or across the river in Alexandria? Earlier, you expressed a preference for Alexandria. Is that still your preference?"

"It is, Nathan. I realize that puts extra work on you and your crew." Warping a vessel in and out of one wharf simply to cross a river and repeat the process could be a sea officer's nightmare. "I apologize for the inconvenience, but I need to see my wife and son secured at home as soon as possible."

"I understand, sir, and I am honored to oblige you. Once I am at the Navy Yard, would you like me to deliver the dispatches from Admiral Brathwaite to the secretary? Or would you prefer to bring them yourself tomorrow afternoon?"

"You deliver them, Nate. That will give Mr. Bancroft an opportunity to scan through them before our meeting. I will bring my personal dispatches with me."

"Very good, sir. And shall I inform the secretary that you will be there tomorrow at four bells in the afternoon watch?"

"Please. And please extend my apologies to the secretary for the short notice. Those dispatches are rather important."

"Aye aye, sir. Should there be a change of plans, I shall inform you personally."

"Thank you, Captain." Richard said with a slight emphasis on the rank. If the midshipman felt self-conscious about being addressed with that lofty title, he did not show it. He offered a crisp salute, turned on his heel, and strode aft.

* * *

At three bells the next afternoon, six sailors tossed oars and sat rigidly as a clinker-style ship's boat glided soundlessly toward the dock where Richard Cutler stood waiting. A sailor on the forward thwart fended off before securing the small craft to a bollard with a clove hitch.

The cutter's burly coxswain offered a smart salute. "Welcome aboard, Captain," he drawled. "Bos'un Wickens at your service. Is there business pending ashore? Or shall we cast off straightway?"

"Cast off, if you please, Mr. Wickens," Richard said. He handed the boatswain the brown leather satchel he was carrying before stepping down into the belly of the cutter to take up position at the stern sheets. As he took his seat and waited for Wickens to take the tiller, he glanced at the red brick townhome on Queen Street that had housed his father and mother before it was passed on to him. It was there, in the master bedroom on the second floor, that his father had passed away in dignified agony.

Richard felt a strong sense of déjà vu. Two years ago he had made the same trip, walked into the massive four-story gray stone building that housed the Navy Department, and followed a Marine sentry down the long, cavernous corridor, his footsteps echoing on the marble floor. The oversized wall paintings depicting U.S. Navy single-ship engagements in four wars were the same. The one difference this afternoon was the lettering on the heavy oak door at the end of the hall. It read not "David Henshaw, Navy Secretary," but "George Bancroft, Navy Secretary."

Richard was ushered into a spacious but sparsely furnished office whose one nod to unconformity was a bookcase that dominated the east wall and served as a backdrop to the cherry wood desk sitting on an elegant Oriental rug. Neatly arrayed cloth- and leatherbound books filled the six shelves, clearly the cherished property of a bibliophile. And indeed, Bancroft was well known in academic and social circles as a well-read champion of secondary education.

A side door opened, and an African American youth in smart livery stepped into the room. "Excuse me, Captain," he said deferentially, "Mr. Bancroft will be with you shortly. He desires me to ask if you would care for a cup of tea or coffee while you wait."

"Coffee, thank you . . . Thomas, isn't it?"

The young man gave him a startled look. "Yes, sir. My name be Thomas," he said, the polish of his cultured tone compromised by his surprise. "How'd you know?"

"Two years ago I was in this very room with Secretary Henshaw. You came through that same door to serve us. You are not about to serve me that same coffee, are you?"

"Good golly no, suh! Never in my life would I do such a thing as that, suh," he said, beaming broadly. "I do remember you. I remember you well. You be Captain Cutler, and you be a legend in these parts."

"Am I indeed? Why so?" Richard expected to hear an exaggerated account of his shipwreck.

Thomas took a step closer. "Why, because of your family's sugar, suh. Best quality of anyone's acquaintance." He took another step closer and said, "But what people hereabouts *really* like is the rum your family makes!"

Richard grinned. "Have you sampled it?"

"Me? Oh my goodness no, suh. Not yet, anyways. My momma says I be too young for that. But sure as I'm standing here, it's something I'm looking forward to!"

Richard laughed. "Well, Thomas, your momma is right. She has raised you well."

"Yes, suh. She sure has tried to do just that."

The main door to the office opened and a tall, thin man entered. His three-piece dark brown suit, stark white shirt, and black cravat gave him the look of a professor. His short-cropped brown hair and mutton-chop sideburns were threaded with strands of gray and white. Richard judged him to be in his mid to late forties, a decade or so older than himself.

"You two know each other?" the man asked.

"We're old friends," Richard confirmed. "We go back two years. At the time I thought Thomas was a fine young man. I still do. You are fortunate to have him in your employ."

"I agree," the man said shortly. "Especially when he stops chatting with my guests and starts delivering the coffee." The man pointed at the side door. After Thomas had closed it behind him, the man's gaze swung to Richard. "I'm George Bancroft," he said. "Welcome home, Captain." They shook hands.

"Your wife and son are doing well, I trust?" he asked with what sounded like genuine interest. He motioned toward two deep-seated leather chairs, and the two men walked over and sat down.

"They are, sir, thank you," Richard said as he casually crossed his right leg over his left.

"And you are happy to be home?"

"Indeed yes. After all we had been through in the bush and the long journey home, we arrived to find our faithful housekeeper Abigail preparing a feast on impossibly short notice. And then, after supper, the delight to slip into the bliss of crisp, clean sheets and goose down bedding. I don't wonder that both Anne and Jamie are still asleep."

Bancroft chuckled. "If so, it's a rest well earned."

After a brief silence, Bancroft added, with a twinkle in his eye, "I very much look forward to hearing your story, Captain Cutler. Rumors abound here in the capital, and I understand that some of it may be quite scandalous."

Richard blinked at that remark, though he realized it was spoken in innocent jest, and immediately began busying himself with the contents of the satchel he had brought with him. From it, he removed three journals and handed them over. "It's all here, sir. As much of it as I could remember, which is most of it. The writing kept me occupied on the voyage home."

"I can imagine," Bancroft said. He took the journals and flipped through the pages of the first one. "I suspect this experience and the conclusions you draw from it will be of considerable interest to President Polk and his cabinet."

"That is my hope and intention, sir. You will also see in those pages my strong recommendation for two promotions. I would greatly appreciate these promotions being acted upon as soon as proper channels allow."

"Just so? Promotions for whom?"

"The first is for my executive officer, Jack Brengle, to the rank of captain. The second is for my only surviving midshipman, Jonathan Montgomery, to the rank of lieutenant. In addition, all my crew, alive and dead, deserve official recognition. We experienced hell together, and we relied on each other in ways only desperate men can understand. Every hour of every day was devoted to one objective: getting to the next hour and the next day alive."

"Quite," Bancroft murmured.

"During the cruise in *Alarm*," Richard went on, "I gathered my crew together to review and write down the name, rank, and service of every member of *Suwannee*'s two-hundred-man crew, paying special attention to commissioned, warrant, and petty officers." He pointed at the journal now lying on Bancroft's lap. "It's all in there, sir. Every name and rank and service in *Suwannee*. I am indebted to all these men. But were it not for the leadership and heroism displayed by Mr. Brengle and Mr. Montgomery, none of us would have survived, myself included."

"I see." Bancroft reflected for several moments before commenting. "Commendable words, Captain Cutler. Commendable words indeed. Most unusual words for a ship's captain, I must say. However, considering what you and your men had to endure on the other side of the world and the obstacles you had to overcome, I believe I can say with some confidence that your recommendations will be followed to the letter."

"I am grateful, sir. Thank you."

"You are quite welcome." Bancroft held up the other two journals. "Do these two volumes contain the full story of what happened to you on that island?"

"Yes, they do," Richard told him.

"Impressive. If you have no objections, I will read them and then share them with the president."

"I have no objection, sir, if you think the president would find them worth reading."

"I daresay he will." As if seized by an irrepressible urge, Bancroft opened a journal and began reading. "Yes, I am quite sure he will," he murmured to himself after a few minutes. Following a respectful interval, Richard said, to break the silence, "I understand from Admiral Brathwaite that Mr. Polk supports your call for the creation of a Navy College in Annapolis."

Bancroft closed the journal. "The admiral is correct. Such an institution is long overdue. If the United States is to fulfill its promise, we shall need young men of equal promise to lead our ships and sailors into diplomacy. And into battle, if that should prove necessary. Men like the members of your crew."

Before Richard could respond, Thomas reentered the office and deposited a tray containing a silver coffee urn, silver pots of sugar and cream, and porcelain cups and saucers on the highly polished oak table between the two men. With a practiced hand, he poured two cups of fragrant coffee, then placed the sugar and cream close to Richard's setting.

He looked at Secretary Bancroft. "Will that be all, sir?"

"Yes, thank you, Thomas. You may go."

Thomas bowed formally and made to leave. When Richard called out to him, he turned around.

"Yes, Captain?"

"I have enjoyed seeing you again, Thomas, and I have enjoyed discussing affairs of the world with you."

Thomas gave him an appreciative smile. "The pleasure was mine, Captain," he said before closing the door behind him with a gentle click.

Into the ensuing silence Richard said, to return the conversation to where he believed it had been heading, "I take it, Mr. Secretary, that our government is pleased with the Sydney Accords?"

Before answering, Bancroft took a sip of coffee and placed the cup back on its saucer. He contemplated the cup for several moments. "By all accounts, yes, our government is pleased. As a result of these agreements, we have opened new markets in Australia, and no doubt in New Zealand, on terms favorable to the United States. As for Asian markets, especially Canton and the so-called Five Ports, we have access to Royal Navy bases for our naval and merchant ships. Of equal value, for the first time we have the use of warehouses on Hong Kong in which to store our goods. The Treaty of Nanjing ceded Hong Kong to Great Britain, a monumental boon to the British, and now the Sydney Accords have made it available to the United States. Further, though at war just a few years ago, Great Britain and China are now cooperating with each other and with the United States to remove the scourge of smuggling and piracy from

Asian waters. It is in our mutual interest to do so. Today, the possibilities for trade in the Orient seem endless, especially now that China has finally opened its borders to trade with the West." He stopped and lifted a hand. "But mark well: not all that glitters is gold."

"I'm afraid I don't follow you, sir."

Bancroft gave him a sharp look. "My meaning is simple, Captain Cutler. Eighteen twelve was not so long ago, and the wounds left by that war remain raw. Great Britain and the United States are on friendly terms today, but we cannot be complacent. We can hardly be considered happy bedfellows. As we speak, Captain Lee and his West Point engineers are constructing yet another fort, this one in New York Harbor. When finished, it will join the string of other fortifications recently constructed along our Eastern Seaboard. Should you ask why we are constructing these forts, there can be only one answer. They are intended to defend our coast against the only European power with the wherewithal to threaten it. That nation, of course, is Great Britain."

Richard narrowed his eyes in thought. "Then . . ."

"Then," Bancroft answered the unspoken question, "the Sydney Accords, beneficial as they are to both parties, are not an alliance between two nations of like minds, but are instead an example of two nations safeguarding their own national interests. Such is the way of the world, alas." When Richard did not reply, Bancroft went on. "Look at it this way. The British in Asia may want to buy what we have to sell, but what they truly want is our assistance in clearing the sea lanes of pirates and smugglers."

"Is it not in our own national interests to do that?"

"Of course it is. It's high time we did something about these pirates, and now we can. After the humiliating losses the Chinese suffered at the hands of the British during the recent war and the harsh terms the British imposed on the emperor at Nanjing, there is no one to control the pirates; they have become international thugs. The emperor has formally requested the United States Navy to lead the charge against them, so to speak."

"I had heard that." Richard thought for a moment, then: "Tell me this: Are American merchantmen trading in those waters treated the same as the British?"

"By the pirates, yes. By the Chinese government, no. But you are thinking of your family's ships. You will be happy to hear that the United States now has its own trade treaty with the Chinese emperor. Have you not heard of it?"

Richard shook his head.

"It was signed by Caleb Cushing—like us, a son of Massachusetts—at the Imperial Palace just last year. The Treaty of Wangxia—forgive my horrible pronunciation—confers on American merchants the same benefits that their British counterparts enjoy. Americans also enjoy a sort of 'favored nation' status. But that status does not protect our merchantmen from piracy. For the time being, at least, *any* vessel or sailor sailing in Chinese waters under a Western flag is at grave risk. In the longer term, the risks are even greater. Opium is flooding into Europe, and the United States is at risk as well. I say this only to you: I am disgusted by our government's blasé attitude toward the threats that opium poses to our society. It appears reluctant to do anything beyond imposing tariffs on its importation. I find that reluctance shocking to the extreme. Some members of the Cabinet agree with me. But our hands are tied, at least for the moment. Britain maintains her empire through trade, and trade requires the exchange of goods.

"The British East India Company, with the full support of the Crown, is attempting to control trade going from the West to the East. The trouble is, the East does not want what the West has to sell, while the West wants what the East has to sell, especially black tea, and the East demands silver in payment for its goods. The outflow of silver from London has all but drained the Exchequer and threatened to bankrupt not only the East India Company but Great Britain as well. The East India Company decided to balance the books by trading in opium. The Chinese have no use for English woolens or machinery, but in countries with impoverished populations such as China there is always a demand for opium. The Company cultivates poppies in Bengal. Opium is made from these poppies and sold in the open markets in Calcutta, a major trading center on the Chinese border, or smuggled in bulk into China. The preferred method of payment for the opium is, of course, silver, which is then used to repay the Company's massive debt to the Crown.

Along the way, inevitably, some of the opium manages to find its way into Europe and the United States, where demand for the stuff is growing in leaps and bounds. You look puzzled, Captain."

"I *am* puzzled, sir," Richard confessed, "and I'm afraid the more you try to explain all this to me, the more puzzled I become."

"I apologize," Bancroft said somberly. "You are freshly home, and here I am firing broadsides at you. But did you hear nothing about the Opium War when you were in Auckland? Did you not discuss it with your brother-in-law in Sydney?"

"I did hear of it, yes," Richard acknowledged, "but not to any great extent. Governor Fitzroy was vague on the root causes of the war between Britain and China, how the war was conducted, and what the treaty means for the empire. I believe he is somewhat at sea himself but is loath to admit it."

"Rest assured, he is not alone there."

"As for Admiral Brathwaite," Richard continued, "he confided in me a little, and I sensed he had a good command of the issues involved, but I had the sense he was not telling me everything. I assumed everything would become clearer to me in due course."

"Which it will, no doubt."

"Yes, sir."

"With much more to follow."

"I would expect so, sir."

Bancroft drummed his fingers on a knee, momentarily lost in thought. "Well," he said at last, "I hope what all this means is that the United States and Great Britain both come out of this well and on good terms."

"That is my devout hope as well, sir, for reasons I am sure you can understand. Please God the guns in those forts are never fired in anger."

"I doubt they will be fired at the British," Bancroft said seriously. "But we Americans might end up firing them at each other if the differences between our northern and southern citizens cannot be resolved."

"I pray to God that never happens," Richard said softly.

"As do I," Bancroft agreed with equal solemnity. Suddenly his face lit up. "Enough gloom and doom, my good man!" he exclaimed. "Let us put all this behind us for the moment. I have a proposition for you!"

Richard eyed him guardedly. The last Navy secretary's proposition had left him shipwrecked in New Zealand. "A proposition, sir?"

Bancroft slammed his right fist on his desk. "I propose that you write a book about your adventures based on what you recorded in your journals. You have already done the hard work. The reading public is keen for this kind of story, you know, and yours would be like no other. You would have no trouble finding a publisher!"

Bancroft seemed not to notice Richard's lack of enthusiasm at the prospect. "I myself have written a book," he continued. "*The History of the United States*. A bit of light reading for the American public."

Richard grinned. "Is it being published, sir?"

"Indeed."

"By whom?"

"Little, Brown."

"Little . . . brown?"

"No, no. Little, Brown is a publishing company in Boston, not far from where you and I went to college as sons of John Harvard. It is a well-established business, and I can highly recommend it to you. So, what do you say? Will you do it?"

"I'm not sure what to say," Richard said, surprised by Bancroft's suggestion. "I can say that Admiral Brathwaite suggested the same thing to Anne and me while we were staying with him in Sydney. Anne has already put pen to paper. She writes a far better hand than I."

"All the better. I suggest you two write the book together. That will increase its appeal and attract female readers. Think on it! Naked savages and all that! Helpless little woman in the wilderness! Ha! Readers will devour it!"

"It will take time," Richard hedged, thinking to himself that Anne was the least helpless little woman of his acquaintance.

"You will have the time, dear man. I will see to that. And you will have your wife at your side. I hereby order you to take an extended leave from the Navy. With full pay. What you do on that leave, and its duration, are both entirely up to you. By God, if anyone has earned that privilege, you have. Should you decide to write your story, you must talk to Richard McDonough at Little, Brown. A fine gentleman who knows his business and is also possessed of exquisite literary taste. Indeed, he was the first in the firm to champion my submission.

"Now then," he said before Richard could respond, "I suggest we hale Thomas back in here and send him down to the wine cellar. A toast is in order. I fancy a claret."

CHAPTER 4

The warm, southeasterly breeze soothed the seaman's sunburned skin as the tropical sun weighed heavily on his eyelids. The gentle sway of a laden merchant brig under full sail was lulling him into stupor. With an effort born of necessity, Ben Stokes shook himself alert. He was off duty, and under normal circumstances he would be free to go below for a much-needed rest. But he refused to do that. It was hot below, and these were not normal circumstances. As placid as those sparkling turquoise waters might appear, *Boston Maid* was sailing in the South China Sea, a hotbed of piracy, and until the rocky peaks of the Paracel Islands were left astern there could be no rest. His responsibility as first mate of this Cutler merchant vessel was here, on deck.

He jerked at the touch of a hand on his shoulder, then laughed at his nervousness. "Morning's blessing to ye, Noah," he greeted the foretopman. Then he saw the furrows of worry on the lanky sailor's brow as he scanned the sea off to starboard. Stokes followed his gaze. "What do you see, Noah? Something bothering you?"

Noah Wright ran his tongue across his chapped lower lip. "Don't much like the look of them junks there," he replied, pointing ahead off to starboard where two sizable three-masted vessels with reddish-brown trapezoid sails were cruising. One junk was heading westward toward the eastern entrance to the Sha Tau Kok River, which together with the broad mouth of the Pearl River and Shenzhen Bay separated the land mass of Hong Kong from Guangdong, a mainland province infamous for harboring pirates. The other vessel had come off the wind and was sailing southward, apparently on a course of interception with the American brig. "You see them?"

"Hard to miss 'em if you're payin' attention," Stokes said as the first vessel disappeared behind the high, jagged hills. He swung his spyglass to the left. "Look yonder! Here comes another!"

A third snub-nosed junk had emerged from behind the western end of the island on a course aimed at *Boston Maid*. "They be war junks, I reckon," Wright remarked.

Stokes took a closer look through his own glass. "If so, they're more likely government ships. Pirates aren't known for vessels that size."

"Could be," Wright said, though his tone suggested he didn't agree.

Stokes slowly lowered the glass and glanced up at the brig's two pyramids of sails, their billowing canvas starkly white against the cerulean sky high above the topgallants, and farther up to the ensign of the United States fluttering atop its halyard. Ahead, to port, he could just make out the almost imperceptible dot on the horizon that marked Pratas Island.

"What do you think, Ben?" Wright pressed.

"Not sure," Ben replied carefully. He peered once again through the glass. "Are the guns loaded?" he asked perfunctorily, already certain that the four 12-pounder guns, two per side, would be ready for action.

"Loaded and primed, round shot in the forward two, canister in the aft two."

"Very well. Stand by. I'll have a word with the captain."

Stokes collapsed his glass and strode aft, feeling the eyes of the eighteen-man crew upon him. Many of these men were standing no more than an arm's length away. Stokes kept his own gaze fixed ahead until he was at the binnacle where Edward Walsh, the ship's grizzled master, held court standing next to Second Mate Russell Crain at the wheel.

Stokes stepped close. "You've seen them?"

"I have," Walsh replied casually. A man of few words and a deceptively slight build, he had, like Stokes, a career-defining portfolio of blue-water sailing experience, a penchant for defying the odds, and a heart of oak. A former gunner's mate on *Constitution* and a man born to the sea, Walsh was a master of the difficult art of employing artillery on a heaving deck. Which was why, years earlier, Cutler & Sons had given him command, at the age of twenty-nine, of a merchant vessel in the perilous but highly lucrative Far East trade routes. He had been working these waters ever since, amassing a tidy fortune while ably serving his employer and his crew.

"Shall I send Matthew up?" Stokes asked, nodding toward a sharp-eyed able-rated seaman currently standing next to the mainmast. The "up" he was referring to was at the peak of the highest mast, which afforded sweeping views of the surrounding waters. "Maybe he can see something from up there that we can't see down here."

Walsh shook his head. "Not likely, Ben. No, we'll hold our course and await developments. If those fellows are pirates, and my gut tells me they are, we can't outrun them. The only way we can outmaneuver them is to do what they can't do: sail close to the wind." He calmly continued weighing the pros and cons, talking more to himself than to Stokes. "One thing is certain: trying to outrun them would take us further out to sea, and for what purpose? Those junks may not be able to maintain our course, but they'll follow us to the ends of the earth if they want our cargo bad enough. Greed is the Achilles heel of those scoundrels, and we shall use that against them. But by God this is one cargo those bastards are not going to get." He nodded once, firmly. "So, we'll show them our heels and play the fool until they believe the game is up. I'm betting they don't know we're armed, and I want to keep them in the dark for as long as possible. If my hunch is correct, this engagement will be brief."

Stokes did not look convinced. "I reckon they have twice our weight of shot," he cautioned.

Walsh grinned. "I reckon thrice. But we've been up against worse odds and won. The Chinese may have fast vessels, but both their ships and their guns are inferior to ours. They lost every battle they fought against British ships in the recent war. And the junks in that war were government ships and a damn sight better than what we see out there." He paused. "Don't run out the guns just yet, Ben. Leave them hidden under the tarps until you see my signal. Then unleash hell."

Walsh nodded, his confidence regained. "Aye, Captain."

A half-hour later, what the three junks had in mind was becoming clear. The vessel to the east was closing fast in pursuit, despite the crew of *Boston Maid* clapping on all available canvas. To starboard, the second junk had rounded the island of Hong Kong and was drawing sufficiently close for those on the brig to make out her high bow and forecastle and her even higher poop deck supported by a horseshoe-shaped stern, an example of Asian maritime architecture that had survived intact for two thousand years since the Han Dynasty.

The third junk, meanwhile, was following closely behind the second junk, likely preparing to bear off the wind and stand by to cut off the brig's escape route and to lend support where needed. From the junk closing on *Boston Maid* from the east a sudden thunder of cannon fire rang out. A hundred yards to windward of the junk, a plume of seawater shot into the air. Those on the brig understood the implication. It was an international signal of hostile intent and a warning to the vessel being pursued to heave to.

"Sod off, ya bastards!" Walsh spat as he watched the plume settle back down in a wash of white foam. "Learn to shoot, why don't ya?"

At his position near the wheel, Edward Walsh surveyed the arena of battle. The junks, he knew, were following battle protocols nearly as old as their country. They were closing in from two directions in a giant pincer that would trap their prey between them before coming off the wind and cutting off any chance of escape. Walsh took the wheel from the mate and brought the brig as tight to the southeasterly breeze as she could lie. As he suspected, this feint of flight forced the two junks farther apart. Lacking jibs, the junks followed *Boston Maid* as best they could.

One of the junks to the north had moved broadside to the wind and opened fire on the brig with three cannon shots. Whether the shots were meant to frighten or to destroy, they plunged harmlessly into the sea far off their mark. That junk lay temporarily in irons as the other two junks followed an oblique line of pursuit.

It was time.

"Ready about!" Walsh shouted through a speaking trumpet. He spun the wheel hard to windward. "Stand by to loose sails!"

Gradually, steadily, the brig's bowsprit came through the wind until it was pointing north by east. With her sheets eased, she was now on a broad reach, her fastest point of sail, her bowsprit aimed like a harpoon at the heart of the junk to the east.

Walsh returned the trumpet to its becket and raised his right arm. He caught Stokes's eye and waited, waited, until the distance between the two vessels had narrowed to the width of a mighty river.

"Tear off the canvas and make ready the starboard guns!" he cried. Two teams of three men ripped away the canvas covers and hauled on the breeching ropes of the two 12-pounder guns. Iron wheels squeaked in protest on the wooden deck until the heads of the gun carriages bumped against the brig's bulwark and the guns' muzzles protruded eight inches out from the brig's weather deck.

Stokes cupped his hands at his mouth. "Ready!" he called aft.

The junk, apparently sensing that such bravado meant that not all was as it should be, swung her bow to port to present her own starboard battery. Sailing on the opposite tack, *Boston Maid* shadowed the junk's move. Taking full advantage of her two jibs and foresail, she executed the maneuver far more adroitly than her foe.

The captain's arm sliced downward. "As your guns bear, Ben!" he cried out. "On the downroll!"

Stokes knelt behind the forward gun. Seconds elapsed. *Boston Maid* was on the crest of a large cresting wave and was coming down from it when he stood up and stepped to one side.

"*Firing!*" he bellowed and yanked hard on the gun's lanyard. A twelve-pound iron fist exploded from the muzzle in a flash of white ash and orange flame. The ball, traveling at the rate of two thousand feet per second, punched into the junk amidships, stoving in the hull and sending deadly shards into the air that tore into flesh and wood, until it struck and overturned an enemy gun with a mighty *clang!* Men speared through by shards of splintered wood or with a leg or arm blown off, their lifeblood flowing out, screamed in terror and moaned in pain.

The din became raw panic when the brig's aft gun unleashed a volley of grapeshot into the melee, a mammoth blast of iron pellets and shrapnel that tore through everything in their path, leaving streaks of blood and gore and mangled body parts to mark their passage.

As *Boston Maid* swept past the stricken junk, Walsh, with an air of apparent indifference, consulted the weather and sea conditions and the brig's compass bearing as if he were collecting data to include in the day's log entry. Only then did he search the waters for a potential second victim.

There was none. The other two junks had seen enough.

Satisfied, Walsh handed the helm back to his second mate. "Set her on a course due west by a quarter south, Russ," he instructed. "I'm going below."

"Due west by a quarter south, aye, Captain," Russell Crain acknowledged deferentially.

CHAPTER 5

HINGHAM, MASSACHUSETTS
November 1846

Melinda Cutler opened the heavy front door of her home on South Street and gasped. Her legs buckled and her heart began to race. Quickly Richard stepped inside to steady her. But rather than fainting she pulled him close and burst into tears. When he gently tried to loosen her grip to allow him to take a step back, she gripped him all the harder.

"Richard! Oh, my sweet Lord, I have waited so long for this day. I feared it would never come." He had not seen his usually composed mother so overcome with emotion since the day his father died. "I can scarcely believe my eyes! Please tell me I am not hallucinating!"

"No, Mother, you are not hallucinating," Richard laughed, giving her a quick squeeze. He kept his arm around her waist as he closed the front door against the November chill. "Your prodigal son has returned." He drew a handkerchief from a side pocket of his dark blue uniform overcoat and dabbed at her tears. "And I suspect I will be here for a spell."

"Here? In Hingham?" She stepped away and looked at him cautiously, fearing to hope. "For how long? How long is a spell?"

"I can't say for certain yet," he hedged. "But at least a few days. On this trip," he added hastily when she looked away in disappointment. "I am planning to return to Hingham soon," he assured her, "and I will have Anne and Jamie with me then."

Her eyes went wide.

"And when we return, we will have Jamie's little brother or sister with us. Yes, Mother," he added in response to Mindy's questioning look.

43

"Anne is with child. We'll need to find a suitable place to live, of course. We can't expect you to put us up here in your home. At least not for too long. I'm hoping to find a house on this trip." He smiled at her.

"What are you telling me, Richard?" she half-whispered.

"What you just heard," he laughed. "I am telling you that Anne is expecting and that we are moving to Hingham, whether or not the family still wants me to take over Cutler & Sons. I have been away too long. It's time to come home."

Melinda covered her mouth with both hands. "This is far more than I dared hope for. How do Anne and Jamie feel about living here?"

"Excited."

She threw her arms around him "Another baby, Richard! So there will be *two* grandchildren for me to spoil!"

Richard hugged her back. "That's right. The baby is due in a month, which is why Anne could not accompany me on this trip and why I must return to Alexandria on Saturday. We need to make arrangements for the house there and see to a hundred other things. There is much to do. We'll get it done in short order, though. You and the family have my promise on that, Grandmama!"

"Darling boy, you and Anne and my dear grandchildren are welcome to stay here with me for as long as you wish. The longer the better, though I already have a house in mind for you to consider. It's on Lafayette Avenue, not far from here. It's available, and whenever I walk past it, I've imagined you—" she paused. "What about the Navy, Richard? Are you planning to resign your commission?

"I don't have to, Mother. Not yet, in any event. Secretary Bancroft has granted me an extended leave, with full pay."

Melinda laughed through her tears. "My oh my oh my! This is all too much for an old lady to digest! Come, Richard, doff that coat of yours and join me in the parlor. I have kept you standing out here in this drafty hallway for too long. We shall enjoy a nice cup of hot tea by the fire. Oh my, oh my, what plans we have to make!"

Richard shrugged off his heavy woolen coat. "You are hardly old, Mother," he said as he hung his coat on the familiar peg by the door. "Rumors have reached me as far away as Alexandria that you are the belle of every social event in town and that disreputable gentlemen of all stripes try to gain your favor." He gave her a pointed look.

Her high spirits fell a notch and her mouth twisted in a moue. "Yes, I suppose we do have to discuss Harlan. But please, not today. Today is a day for celebration!" Gripping his arm lest he suddenly disappear, she led him into the parlor.

* * *

During the next two days, Richard made the rounds of Cutler relatives and close friends living in or near Hingham. Word of his arrival spread quickly, and invitations to luncheons, dinners, and afternoon teas came rolling in. Although he appreciated the kind attention, when it became too much, he sought refuge, as he had since childhood, along the carriage paths, the gently rolling hills, and the rocky shoreline of World's End, a 250-acre peninsula jutting out into Hingham Bay. The land had been preserved in trust by Hingham's forefathers nearly two centuries earlier for the enjoyment of future generations. Even at this time of year, when decaying leaves covered the paths and the skeletal trees stood starkly against the backdrop of a pewter gray sky, he found a separate peace at World's End. Here as well he found inspiration for the life that was to come and the plans he had to make.

Early on Wednesday morning, three days before his departure for Alexandria, Richard and his mother sat down in the formal dining room of her home to take breakfast together. Although it was not yet eight o'clock, Melinda Conner was perfectly put together. Her hair, white now rather than ash blonde, was dressed in a simple style in keeping with her age. Her elegant blue woolen morning dress was accentuated by a lacy white shawl draped across her shoulders. Other than her hair, the only indications of worry and advancing age were tiny crows' feet at the outer edges of her eyes and thin wrinkles elsewhere on her once smooth face.

"It is wonderful to see you looking so well, Mother," Richard said as he stood behind her chair waiting to seat her. "I thought of you often while I was trapped in the bottom of the world in New Zealand, you know. There were times when thoughts of returning home were all that kept me going."

"Thank you, Richard," his mother returned. "That is kind of you to say, and I shall never tire of hearing you say it!"

Once his mother was seated, Richard took the place set for him on her right.

An older woman smiled warmly as she emerged from the kitchen bearing two plates of eggs and mutton chops. As a young girl newly arrived in America, Lala Morath had come highly recommended to serve as nursemaid to Richard Cutler shortly after he was born. Warming at once to her responsibilities, she had found a home in Alexandria and then in Hingham, and had stayed on as Richard grew older, returning to Wales but once to visit her ailing mother. Today, the prospect of having not one but two little ones in her care filled her with eager anticipation.

"*Bore da*, my lady," she said to Melinda in her traditional morning greeting. "And a very good morning to you as well, Master Richard," she said, addressing him by his boyhood title, a habit she either could not or would not break. Bustling over to Richard, who stood to greet her, she carefully deposited the breakfast dishes on the table before giving him a kiss on the cheek.

"It's always lovely to see you, Lala!"

"I'll be back shortly with the coffee and toasted cheese," she said, adding in familiar fashion, "*Mwynhewch!*"

Richard and his mother watched her go, then turned their attention to the plates before them. Richard cut a small slice of mutton and combined it with a piece of egg white on his fork. He chewed contemplatively for a moment, then swallowed and remarked to Lala when she returned, "I had forgotten how delicious your cooking is, Lala. I have never had better anywhere in the world."

"That pleases me greatly to hear, Master Richard." She put a single platter of toasted cheese between Richard and Melinda, poured out two cups of fragrant black coffee, and was halfway through the kitchen door when she remembered something. She returned to the table, produced a letter from the wide front pocket of her apron, and handed it to Richard.

"This was hand-delivered late yesterday afternoon. You were upstairs, my lady, taking your bath, and Master Richard, you were out. I put the letter on the hall table, but apparently you did not see it. I am sorry."

"No harm done, I am sure," Richard said as he took the envelope and examined the thick paper sealed at the fold with a circle of melted red wax embossed with the letters **LB** in black.

"Something of interest?" his mother inquired.

"We'll see after breakfast. It's from Boston."

"Long Wharf?"

"No, I don't believe so."

"My goodness. I wonder who could have sent it," she said expectantly.

"I have a hunch. Whatever it is can keep for a bit. We have other things to discuss." He put the letter aside and took a bite of toast and a sip of coffee. His mother did the same. "We have been avoiding an important subject, my dear." When she didn't comment he continued, "Forgive me for prying into your personal affairs, but I want to know what happened to that fellow Harlan Sturgis. I thought about him often—too often—while I was away. When last I saw him, he was pressing his suit rather vigorously, and you seemed disinclined to resist him."

Melinda nodded slowly, avoiding his gaze. "You have every right to ask, Richard," she said softly. "Other members of the family have asked me the same thing, and far less diplomatically. Your Aunt Diana is one."

Richard laughed. "Yes, she is unusually forthright for a woman. What did you tell her?"

Their eyes met and held. "I told her the truth. I told her I don't know what possessed me to take up with a man like Harlan. A woman's folly, I suppose, to believe words of love and loyalty when your heart warns you that those words are most likely a lie.

"Mind you, there were times when I truly did enjoy his company and when I did feel rather close to him, especially in the early days of our acquaintance. He was witty and wise and fun back then. I was flattered by his attentions and by his, shall we say, over-eagerness to help me with the house and with running the family business. After all, I believed him to have been a close friend and business confidant of your father.

"Yes, I see the look you are giving me—and I remember the looks you gave me back then. And as it turns out, you were right. My only excuse is that his interest in me and his credentials in business seemed genuine. I kept asking myself if, after all these years, I could find love again. I so wanted to. It's what *every*one wants, isn't it? I pray you can understand that." She stared down at the half-eaten food on her plate.

He reached out and took her hand. "Of course I understand, Mother. We all do. I don't blame you. Nobody believes you did anything wrong. I am happy Sturgis is gone, though," he added, "and good riddance to him."

"Good riddance, indeed," she said.

Richard waited a moment. Then: "What changed your mind? About Sturgis, I mean."

Melinda shrugged. "A gradual decay of confidence, more than anything else. His definition of 'helping' was to ask questions about our merchant ships and our trade routes and ports in the Orient. At first, I found nothing amiss. After all, he was once a merchant trader himself. Before selling out, he owned several vessels and was heavily invested in overseas trade. So, I marked down his questions to professional interest. As time went by, however, his questions began to make me a little suspicious."

"So, what did you do?"

"I confided in your uncle William."

"What was his reaction?"

"As you would expect. He didn't like Harlan to begin with, and he didn't trust him. He believed that he had a hidden agenda of some sort, that he was too inquisitive and gathering too much information about Cutler & Sons. He asked me straight out to end the relationship."

"What did Uncle William think Sturgis was up to?"

"He had no better idea than I had. Or if he did, he wasn't saying."

"Other family members?"

"They all felt the same about him. I understood, but still I was hurt. Until I started paying closer attention and until . . . that day."

"What day?"

Melinda hesitated. "The day I happened across an incident that gave me serious pause. It unsettled me greatly, but to this day I'm not sure why."

"Tell me about it."

"One moment, please, Richard." Melinda picked up a small bell from the dining table and gave it a jingle. When Lala appeared from the kitchen, Melinda asked for a glass of water.

"Right away, my lady," Lala said. "Master Richard, may I bring you anything?"

He shook his head. After Lala had reappeared with the water and had closed the door to the dining room behind her, he said again, "Tell me about it, Mother. Please."

Melinda drank from the glass and dabbed at her lips with a cloth napkin. "On the day in question, it was in June, Lala and I had gone out shopping for fabric and some other household items. We intended to be out for most of the day, but we finished early and returned in the early afternoon. When we arrived, Harlan was sitting on the back veranda with another man. They had not heard us come in the front door."

"Who was the other man?"

"I don't know. I had never seen him before, and I have not seen him since."

"You didn't go out to say hello?"

"No. Something held me back. I stood there in the hallway, listening. They didn't know I was there, and for a reason I didn't understand, I wanted to keep it that way. I sent Lala upstairs. Neither of us made a sound."

"What were the two men talking about?"

"It was difficult to make out. They were speaking in hushed tones. I'm fairly sure they were not discussing the weather," she added dryly.

"That's all? Two men speaking softly to each other on a veranda? Why did you find that unsettling? It seems innocuous enough."

"I agree. And I admit that I could be wrong, that my doubts about Harlan were misplaced. I would like to believe that. But I do not. There were some words I was able to hear quite distinctly, and there was something sinister about the way they snickered whenever they mentioned Turkey."

"*Turkey?*"

"Yes." She laughed. "The country, darling, not the bird. I distinctly heard them repeat that word, and I found their . . . *salaciousness* offensive. I don't know how else to put it. What could be sinister about Turkey? What can a merchant hope to acquire from there except rugs? And coffee. Exquisite rugs and coffee, to be sure, but rugs and coffee, nonetheless. It just doesn't add up."

"No, it does not," Richard agreed.

"In fact, too many things didn't add up, and that is why I decided to discontinue my association with him. He made me uneasy."

Although many questions remained, and Richard heard warning bells, he decided to let the matter rest there. For the moment.

Whether on business or for pleasure, the voyage across Quincy Bay was one that members of the Cutler family had enjoyed for generations. Depending on wind and sea conditions, the trip took between one and two hours. The route followed was one taken countless times since the Cutlers' earliest days in Massachusetts, increasing in frequency after Cutler & Sons moved its headquarters from Crow Point in Hingham to Long Wharf in Boston to better serve expanding markets in North America and abroad.

The wind blew from the southeast, putting the sloop on a comfortable broad reach. Although the skies were clear, the air carried the tang of impending winter. Unless conditions changed during the day, which was unlikely, the voyage back to Hingham would be less pleasant. At the moment, however, Richard was content to sit on the cabin top with his back to the mast and let the chilly ocean air caress his senses.

As the sloop glided placidly past the stark shapes and drab colors that defined Massachusetts in late autumn, his thoughts drifted back to yesterday morning's breakfast conversation with his mother and the enigma that was Harlan Sturgis. Her mention of Turkey had triggered three memories in quick succession: something that Governor Fitzroy had said to him in Auckland more than a year earlier, an insight Reginald Brathwaite had shared with him later in Sydney, and a remark by Secretary Bancroft during their recent meeting in Washington. As though following an overgrown and poorly marked path with no destination in mind, he tried to find the connection between the four seemingly disconnected comments spoken in four corners of the world. What did they have in common, if anything, and what did they point to, if anything? As implausible as it seemed, there *had* to be a link. It was all too coincidental to be accidental.

At Long Wharf, the vessel's young mate secured the packet boat fore and aft to bollards on the wharf. With the initial bump of hull against dock, Richard buttoned the top brass clasps of his Navy officer's coat and grabbed his leather satchel. "Thank you, Douglas," he said to the boat's master. "And I thank your son for his good help. I apologize to you both for being such poor company."

"Quite understandable, Captain," Douglas returned. "No doubt you have much on your mind."

"Too much," Richard said with a rueful smile. "See you at eight bells." He waved goodbye and stepped off the boat onto the short ladder leading up to Long Wharf proper.

"Shall I remind Mr. Henley of your appointment?" Douglas called up. Charles Henley, the long-time administrator of the Boston offices of Cutler & Sons, was second on the list of Richard's visits this day.

"Please do," Richard said looking down at the boat. "I don't think he'll need much reminding, however. We're having lunch at his favorite haunt at Faneuil Hall. Remind him that it's at one o'clock. Don't confuse him with naval time. Hell's bells, he calls it."

Douglas laughed and fashioned a mock salute.

Richard turned toward the landward end of the half-mile-long wharf. Built in the early 1700s, the dock had become a hub of international commerce. At the base of State Street he saw, as expected, a cluster of carriages for hire, each with a single horse in harness. Richard approached the closest one, and at the coachman's invitation climbed aboard. He settled back into the comfortable seat cushion on the single bench facing forward.

"Where to, yer honor?" the coachman called down.

"Eighteen Marlborough Street," Richard called up.

"Very good, yer honor."

Richard knew the route well, and this morning he relaxed as best he could as the coach rattled and jounced up State Street past the imposing red-brick facade of the former City Hall featuring the two golden lions that were among the last vestiges of royal authority in America. From there the carriage wound its way to Tremont Street, where it met, first, the historic Boston Common, the nation's first public park, created in 1634, and then the Boston Public Garden, created two hundred years later as America's first public botanical garden. Although the colorful blossoms of spring and summer were long gone, the views through the carriage's glass window were nonetheless pleasing to the eye.

Minutes later, as the carriage crossed Arlington Street and took a sharp right onto Newberry Street, Richard withdrew a large gold coin from his pocket. When the carriage took another sharp right onto Marlborough Street and juddered to a halt, he stepped out and flipped the coin up to the coachman.

"No change required," he said.

"Bless ye, sir," the surprised coachman said as he examined a payment worth more than twice what the ride had cost. "Would ye like me to be here to take ye back to the wharf?" he asked, tipping his hat. "Or somewhere else, perhaps? There'd be no charge for that one."

"No, thank you. I'm planning to walk."

"You sure? It's a mite cool out today."

"I'll walk, but thank you," Richard said and waved the coachman off.

He walked up to the front door of Eighteen Marlborough Street, opened it, and stepped into a marble-tiled hallway of black-and-white diamonds. At the far end was a sweeping staircase that disappeared upstairs to the left, where presumably the publishing offices were located. To the left of the front doorway, Richard noted a large reception area containing a slightly frayed Oriental rug, two camelback sofas, two high-back chairs, and two side tables. Appropriately, there was also a sizable bookcase hosting a collection of clothbound books. Toward the entrance to the room was a mahogany desk on which were displayed neat piles of papers, several books, and a selection of quill pens.

The well-dressed young man seated behind the desk quickly rose when he noticed Richard standing in the hallway and walked over. "Welcome to Little, Brown & Company," he said cordially. "How can I help you?"

"I am Richard Cutler, come to see Mr. Richard McDonough," Richard answered. "I believe he is expecting me."

"Indeed he is, Captain Cutler. If you will please follow me."

The young man led the way down the hall past what appeared to be a conference room, judging by the long, dark polished table and Chippendale chairs arranged around it. Across the hall from it was a small, snugly furnished alcove. Like everything Richard had seen thus far in this building, the alcove bespoke the company's style more than its financial success. Richard smiled inwardly. A company profile of understated elegance free of pretentions and false claims was a concept endorsed by his family since the age of his great-grandfather, Thomas Cutler. Substance over style was a cornerstone of Cutler & Sons' corporate philosophy, and the similarity with what he saw at Little, Brown was not lost on him.

The young man showed him into the alcove. "Please do take a seat, Captain. Mr. McDonough will be right with you," the young clerk said deferentially.

"Thank you," Richard returned.

Only a few moments later, an older man appeared in the doorway. He was dressed in business attire, although his plain brown suit and white dress shirt seemed slightly oversized, as though the man had recently lost weight or his tailor had not done a proper job fitting it to him. But his attire was unimportant. It was the gentle gray eyes behind wire-rimmed spectacles that immediately defined him. Richard sensed a sharp intellect and a highly educated mind behind them.

Richard stood. "Mr. McDonough, I presume?

"Captain Cutler, I presume," McDonough said in reply. The two men shook hands warmly, each taking the measure of the other. "Please, sit down. May I send for coffee or tea?"

"No, thank you." Richard felt an unanticipated awkwardness, and sensed he was showing it.

"A pleasant voyage from Hingham?" McDonough asked kindly, as though accustomed to the anxieties of would-be authors in the presence of a publisher.

Richard smiled. "It is always pleasant for me, whatever the weather, whatever the season."

"Spoken like a true sailor. You are indeed fortunate. If you will have nothing now, may I take you to lunch after our tête-à-tête? I should enjoy that very much."

"I am sorry. I should have enjoyed it as well, but I must again decline your kind offer. I have already a luncheon engagement."

"Ah, well, my loss. Perhaps next time. Shall we turn to business, then? I want to thank you for your letter and for the promise of what is to come. I assume you have it there in your satchel?"

"I do." Richard reached into the satchel and produced a stack of handwritten papers. "This is not all of it, of course. But I believe it's a good representation."

"I'll be the judge of that," McDonough said as he accepted the papers from Richard. He placed them carefully on his lap and without another word started reading, his interest confirmed by an occasional "hmm" or "uh-huh" or "oh my." He skipped a few pages and resumed reading. "I hope you don't think me rude," he remarked at one stage, without looking up or interrupting his reading.

"Not at all. It's why I'm here."

"Yes, quite." McDonough skipped more material, and after reading a few more pages asked, "Did you write this?"

"Some of it. Most of what you see there was written by my wife."

"Anne."

"Yes."

McDonough removed his wire-rimmed spectacles, held them up to the light of a small window, and then withdrew a kerchief from a side pocket. As he cleaned the lenses, he seemed preoccupied by something other than the job at hand. Minutes passed in silence.

To Richard, those minutes seemed interminable. "Are you . . . Do you like what you have read so far?" he asked tentatively.

The question snapped McDonough's attention back to the room. "It needs work," he ruled forthrightly. "Quite a bit of work, actually. I would change the opening, and I see a number of other opportunities for improvement. But that is to be expected. From what I have read, I believe the book is going to be a gem. Did all this really happen? I must admit, I had my doubts when I read the synopsis in your letter."

"It happened," Richard said bluntly. "If anything, Anne and I have understated the facts."

McDonough shook his head. "No, no!" he said emphatically. "We can't have that. Never understate the facts in a book like this. If this book is to achieve its full sales potential, we need raw emotions and a flirt with disaster around every corner. If we achieve that, I believe this book is destined for glory." He looked Richard squarely in the eye. "Tell me true: Are you and Anne prepared to put in the hard work to make that happen? And do you realize that she most likely will not be able to put her name to it? As you may know, women authors don't usually publish their works under their own name."

"Anne certainly is aware of that, and she is determined to see this through. It has become her life apart from her family. I will do what I can when my business obligations allow."

"That's what I wanted to hear. And remember, I'll be there right beside you."

"Do I take it, then, that we have an agreement?"

"We do. Unless, of course, you have other publishers on the hook."

Richard could not suppress a smile. "This may be a poor confession to make at a time like this, but we have no other publisher in mind. Mr. Bancroft insisted we give you the first look."

"A good man, George Bancroft. And a good writer, if a bit wordy. I am greatly indebted to him for sending you to us. And I appreciate your candor." McDonough stood up. "You won't change your mind about lunch? I would have enjoyed chatting more with you. However, be assured that we shall have many such occasions in the weeks and months ahead. In the meantime, please tell your wife, for me, that she is a fine writer. And please tell her, too, that Little, Brown is very pleased to be her publisher."

Richard stood. "I shall tell her that word for word, Mr. McDonough. She will be thrilled, I assure you." The two men shook hands. "What now? I assume we sign something?"

For the first time that morning, McDonough's face broke into a broad smile. "Heavens no, Captain Cutler. There is no need for such formalities at this stage. You may rely on me to have the details of our understanding confirmed to your satisfaction when you and Anne return from Virginia, just as I will rely on you to deliver the full manuscript to me in a timely manner. Trust is at the heart of any publishing agreement. After all, we are two gentlemen from Boston, are we not?"

CHAPTER 6

Christmas Day was past, and a few days into the new year the last vestiges of the holiday celebration in the Cutler household had mostly disappeared. What lingered were the memories shared with family and friends. Chief among those memories was dinner at noon on Christmas Day with George Brathwaite, Anne's younger brother, who served as Great Britain's ambassador to the United States, and his wife, Cassandra, a woman of note in the city's society pages. On Christmas morning, little Jamie had basked in the glow of special attention, good food, and the small army of toy soldiers and the squadron of model ships he found arrayed on the floor of the parlor. As he eagerly fell into the dual responsibilities of field marshal and commodore under the watchful eye of Rachel Brown, the adults had retired to the parlor to christen a bottle of Cadiz sherry, a gift from the Brathwaites.

"A Christmas toast," Richard exclaimed, lifting his glass.

"A Christmas toast," the others concurred.

"Exquisite," Cassandra judged the sherry after taking a sip, "even if I do say so myself. I must admit, there were times during the past two years when I feared we would never again enjoy such an occasion together."

For a few moments, the only sound in the room was the snapping and popping of the fire on the hearth. The silence was broken when George Brathwaite said with a contented sigh, "From those heavenly aromas, I take it that Abigail is once again performing her magic in the kitchen.

She is a wonderful cook, worthy of a royal assignment. You are fortunate to have had such a loyal and gifted servant in your employ for so long."

"Abigail is more a member of the family than a servant," Anne corrected her brother.

"I am quite aware of that," Brathwaite said, "and I apologize if I misspoke. Nonetheless, I shall greatly miss her culinary wizardry after you leave Alexandria. If either of you thinks for one moment that Cassandra and I braved the icy Potomac this morning just to enjoy your company on Christmas, you are sadly mistaken. Alas, Boston is too far away to pop in for a meal. I assume you will be taking Abigail with you?"

"Actually, I think not," Anne replied. "Her family has lived in these parts since before the Revolution. Plus, I understand there is a suitor involved. A local man, a gentleman tobacco farmer. She seems quite smitten."

"Lucky fellow," George chuckled. "If the adage is true that the way to a man's heart is through his stomach, Abigail can have all the male attention she desires."

"George, really!" Cassandra admonished. "Mind your tongue! That was inappropriate!"

As George and Richard exchanged a grin, Anne put in, "Our thinking is that Abigail will remain in Alexandria on full wages. She will be at your disposal if and when you wish her service. She will be living here, in this house, as she did whilst Richard and I were . . . away. We shall not be selling our home, after all. Not just yet, at least."

"Holding on as a hedge?" George asked her.

Anne looked at her husband, who said, "Not a hedge as much as an investment of sorts. Until we do decide to sell, our home will be open to you and your family and guests. And to us when we can no longer do without Abigail's cooking. Next week I will inform Secretary Bancroft that our home is also at the disposal of the Navy Department to accommodate traveling dignitaries—after clearing it with you first, of course."

"I say, that is most generous of you," George Brathwaite said. "Most generous indeed."

"Your generosity to us speaks for itself," Richard replied, "and the Navy is being most accommodating to me and my family. It's the least Anne and I can do to show our appreciation."

A call from the kitchen announced that Christmas dinner was soon to be served. A moment later, they watched Rachel gathering up Jamie and guiding the protesting youth toward the kitchen.

"Have a nice dinner with Rachel, darling," his mother called out to him. "This evening, your father and I will have Christmas supper with you. Just the three of us."

When quiet had been restored, Richard drained his glass and stood. "Shall we?" he asked.

"Yes, my dear brother, let us," George Brathwaite responded. He stood as well and offered his hand to his sister. Anne, now in her third trimester, took the hand and was brought gently to her feet. Once she had her balance, he offered her his arm. Richard offered his to Cassandra, and together the two couples walked slowly through the parlor toward the Christmas feast awaiting them in the dining room.

"Oh look! Richard! Come quick! It's snowing!"

Richard put down the papers he was reading in his study and hurried to Anne's side. He found her standing by the grand piano in the parlor, staring out into the dusk at the snow swirling around the homes on the waterfront. Although the snow had barely begun to accumulate, it was falling steadily in small flakes, a good indication it would continue for quite a while before it ended. They could barely see the dim oil lamps within neighboring homes and the sputtering street lights that stood at regular intervals along the river walkway.

"Now *that's* something we haven't seen much of in recent years," Richard exclaimed, his own boyhood memories triggered. He put his arm around Anne's shoulders. "Pity the snow didn't make it for Christmas."

Unexpectedly, fervent words spoken two years earlier in a very different setting surged up to savage his conscience. *"I will take you there,"* he had promised her as he held her close and dried her eyes. *"I will take you to see the mountains, and I will take you to see the snow, however far away that island may be and however long it takes to get there. I pledge*

59

this to you on my sacred honor. I love you, Ataahua." As the mental image ebbed, he tamped down the memory, but not before Anne had noted the transformation.

"Are you all right, my dear?" she asked with concern. "For a moment you looked quite out of sorts."

He smiled and shook his head. "I'm fine, Anne. Just a thought. It was nothing important." The duplicity of his words racked him with guilt.

She leaned into Richard's shoulder. "Should we wake Jamie? No," she decided, "best not. We would never get him back to sleep. He will be beyond excited when he wakes up tomorrow morning and looks out his window!"

"He'll be excited all right," Richard laughed, "especially if this snow keeps up all night. At this rate we should have five or six inches by dawn."

"We shall invite some of his friends over to build a snowman," Anne decided. "And then we shall have hot chocolate. After that we can—" Suddenly she tensed. He looked at her.

"What is it, darling? What's wrong?"

"Just a small stab is all," she assured him. "Nothing wrong." She placed a hand over her stomach, rubbed it in small circles, then drew Richard's hand to the spot, covering his hand with hers. "Do you feel it?" she whispered.

"Feel what? . . . No . . . wait . . . yes! By God, is that a kick?"

She laughed with delight. "That's our son, Richard. Or our daughter." She continued to cradle her belly, her hand over his. "Either way, that's our precious little Sydney!"

She called out to him in the night. He was awake in an instant.

"Who is it?" he challenged the dark. "Who's there?"

"Ko ahau, Richard," a gentle voice replied. "Do not be alarmed. It's me, your Ataahua. Aroha ana ahau ki a koe. I love you."

"Ataahua? It can't be. You're . . . you're dead."

"No, Richard. Not dead. There is no death. I told you that many times. I come in love, and I come with our son. I have named him Hu. It means 'God rescues.' E whakaae ana koe?"

Two forms emerged soundlessly from the shadows. Ataahua was smiling. The boy was very young, younger than Jamie. She was as beautiful as he remembered her, dressed in a traditional piupiu skirt of woven flax.

"Do I approve?" he asked incredulously. "Is that what you asked me?"

"Ae."

"Sweet Jesus, Ataahua. This cannot be happening." He shook his head vigorously, as if to drive away demons. "No! This is not happening!"

She came closer to him, holding the boy's hand. "Ae, dear Richard. It is happening. Do you not love me still?" Her voice went flat. "Please tell me you do. You promised always to love me. Do you not remember? I was bleeding in my hut. You picked me up in your arms and held me to you. You were weeping. You said—"

"I cannot love you, Ataahua," he interrupted, beseeching her to understand. "Not in that way. Not anymore. Anne is alive! She survived the wreck. She is here beside me. See?" His eyes swung to where Anne should have been but was not.

"Anne!" he wailed. "Where are you, Anne? Anne!"

Warm arms embraced him in the darkness, and he clung to the reassuring presence.

"Wake up, Richard! Wake up! You are dreaming!" She held him, speaking softly as though to a child, stroking his back as though comforting that child. "Wake up!"

Slowly he emerged from the abyss of a trancelike state. He looked around the candlelit room, blinking, at the bed, at the two dressers, at the candle in its gilded sconce on the desk holding their manuscript, at the damask curtain drawn across the big bay window. Everything was as it had been. As it should be. He was home. He was safe. Ataahua wasn't here. She had never been here.

He swiped at his eyes with the heel of his palm. "It was a nightmare, Anne, not a dream," he said, still fighting to emerge from its hold, regretting his cruelty, even in a dream, to a woman he had once loved. "I am so sorry I woke you."

"I'll be right back."

"Where are you going?" he asked anxiously.

"To make you a cup of tea. It will help settle you. Will you be all right here for a moment?"

He nodded sheepishly. "Of course."

When she returned from the kitchen, she found him sitting up in bed, staring down at his lap. She sat on the edge of the bed next to him and handed him the steaming mug. He took a sip and inhaled deeply once, twice.

She gave him several moments, then said: "Richard?"

He met her gaze unwillingly. "Yes?"

"It's high time you told me about Ataahua." Her tone was sympathetic yet firm.

"Who?" he asked innocently.

"Do not play the jape with me, Richard. Tonight is not the first time you have cried out her name in your sleep. We need to have this conversation. We need to clear the air and put this matter to rest."

He dropped his gaze and sat in silence. When all he could manage was, "I don't know where to start," she said: "I suggest you start at the beginning. First question: Who is Ataahua? Obviously, she is someone of consequence. I'm waiting," she added when he remained silent. "As your wife and as the mother of your children I deserve to know the truth."

He took a deep, steadying breath. "Yes, you do," he said quietly.

"Very well, then. I repeat my question. Who is Ataahua?"

He blew out a breath. When he spoke, she had to strain to hear him. "A Maori woman . . ."

"Yes, I gathered that."

" . . . of the Ngapuhi tribe. She was a skilled and compassionate healer, revered by her chief and by the other members of her *iwi*, her tribe."

Anne fought back tears, determined to hear the tale. "Go on. Where did you meet her?"

"On the march north from the peninsula with the survivors of the wreck. A band of Maori warriors was observing us from the bush, although we didn't see them. Ataahua was with them. A week or so out, there was . . . an incident with the Maori. You have read about it in my journal . . ."

"Yes, but go on. Assume I know nothing."

"The incident was our fault. Private Plummer, one of the Marines, spotted the Maori in the woods, panicked, and fired blindly. The Maori returned fire, killing or wounding a number of my men. Ataahua tended to them all, right there on the beach, and later in her village after we were taken there."

"The *pa*, you called it. The tribe's fortress."

"Yes."

She swallowed hard. "That's where you fell in love with her." It was not a question.

He exhaled a quivering breath, reaching out to take her hand. She didn't withdraw it. "Not at first. At first, she wanted nothing to do with me. She regarded me as just another worthless *pakeha*, white man. But over time we began to have . . . feelings for each other. She was a great comfort to me, Anne, and she was a great comfort to my men. She saved the lives of several of them." His eyes beseeched her understanding, if not her acceptance. "I didn't plan it. I certainly wasn't looking for anything like it. Please believe me. I thought you were dead. I had to give you up. I had to let you go. Ataahua provided spiritual comfort as well as . . ."

She dashed away a tear. "Physical comfort."

"Yes. She healed me in mind and body in ways that would be difficult to describe to white men."

She flinched. "Please God, spare me the details. I have one important question to ask, and you must answer it honestly. Are you still in love with her?"

He nodded reluctantly. "I did love her, and in some ways I suppose I always will. To deny that would be to deny her, and that I cannot do. But that does *not* mean I ever stopped loving you. I never did. I never will, even if you cannot forgive me. Not only did she understand my love for you, she appreciated it. She told me it defines who I am as a man. Were she here, she would tell you these things herself."

"When you speak of Ataahua, you speak of her in the past tense. Is she dead?"

"Yes. She died in an assault on her *pa*. I was on my way there with the military supplies and British soldiers I had promised Chief Nene I would bring. By then, I had already decided to leave New Zealand—and her—and sail to America with what was left of my crew. Jack and Jonty will verify that."

"I'm sure they would if I were to ask them," she said dryly. "The *pa* was destroyed, wasn't it? That's what you wrote."

"The attack on the *pa* was over by the time I got there. Ataahua had been mortally wounded by a blow to the head. I found her dying in her hut, and I stayed with her until the end. When she died, I buried her." He exhaled hard, his hand gripping Anne's arm tightly as he fought his emotions.

"I see," Anne said, her voice shaky. "Is there anything else?"

"No," he lied. "There is nothing else." There was one piece of information he would not, hw could not, divulge. Ataahua had not died alone.

Anne's lips were tightly pressed together, yet to his surprise she took his other hand in hers. "Then I suggest we leave it there, Richard. I am glad you told me. The explanation was long overdue. Mind you, I am not thrilled to learn that you bedded another woman so soon after my presumed demise. But those were challenging times for us both, and I think I can live with the consequences. It was a dark night of the soul after all, and under the circumstances we both faced on that island, to condemn you for accepting comfort where you could find it would be unfair. Not to mention hypocritical."

He pulled away slightly on hearing that word, but when he threw her a questioning glance, she said nothing more on the subject. What she did say was, "This may shock you, Richard, but what I feel for Ataahua at this moment is gratitude."

"Gratitude? In heaven's name, why?"

She rose awkwardly to her feet and looked down at him. "She saved your life, did she not? She saved you, and she sent you back to me. Are those not reasons enough?"

He drew her gently down beside him and pulled her head to his chest. For a long interval they remained entwined, gently massaging each other, offering mutual comfort and reassurance, drowsing and waking, until the new day and a snow-covered landscape brought cries of excitement from

Jamie's room down the hallway. Those cries were followed, moments later, by the hard stamp of bare feet running down the hallway.

* * *

Five mornings later, Richard appeared as scheduled at the twin oak doors of the Navy Department. He wore the blue-and-gold panoply of a ranking naval officer and carried his woolen uniform coat over his arm, unnecessary in a warm Virginia sun that had all but melted the last vestiges of the snow. Two Marine sentries saluted him and stamped musket butts on the stone landing. After Richard returned the salute, one sentry turned on his heel to open one of the doors and lead Richard inside.

When, a minute later, the Marine opened the door to the secretary's office at the far end of the corridor and ushered him inside, Richard expected to see George Bancroft or perhaps young Thomas bidding him welcome with an offer of tea or coffee. Seeing no one, he ambled over to the bookshelves behind the secretary's desk. There he found what he was looking for: a stack of books, each bound in leather with the same trim size. He picked up the book on top of the stack and opened it to the title page. Yes, there it was: *A History of the United States* prominently printed above the author's name and, in smaller type at the bottom, the publisher's imprint and address.

Succumbing to an irresistible urge, he ran his fingers over the thick calfskin binding, then lifted the book and breathed in the heady, leathery scent of a recently bound book. He thumbed quickly through the first few pages, wondering how he would feel when he saw his name on the title page of the book he and Anne had written, knowing that the pages to follow contained his story.

He had just returned the book to the stack when a booming voice exclaimed, "Well, if it isn't Richard Cutler! I have finally caught up with you!"

Smiling broadly, Richard turned toward the familiar voice to find a man of height, age, and physique similar to his own grinning at him. This was someone he knew well. Fast friends since the age of twelve, they had matriculated at Governor Dummer Academy and Harvard College before enlisting in the Navy together. As junior officers, they had fought in numerous campaigns in southern Florida against the Seminoles on the mainland and pirates in the mangrove islets that dotted the southwestern coast. Each man owed his life to the other.

"Do my eyes deceive me?" Richard retorted with equal glee. "Is it the legendary Jack Brengle I see standing before me? *Dei laudentur!*"

Brengle shook his head sadly. "You never were much good at Latin. You've likely been practicing those two words since First Form, and you still haven't got it right."

"I hear you, my friend." Richard Cutler and Jack Brengle shook hands firmly, then threw protocol to the wind and embraced and slapped each other on the back.

"Look at you," Richard chuckled moments later as he held his former executive officer at arm's length. "Somehow, no doubt by trickery and deceit, you have managed to come up in the world!" His gaze swept over an officer's uniform similar to his own. A yellow stripe ran down each trouser leg, and two rows of gold buttons ran down the front of his dark blue uniform coat. Brengle's curly black hair, once long and disorderly, was clipped short and proper, and his gray eyes smiled in affection. "Has the Navy finally taken leave of its senses? That's a captain's uniform you are wearing!"

"A commander's uniform, unfortunately. Too many captains, too few ships."

Richard nodded knowingly at this common lament. "Do you have your own command?"

"Ironically, I do. She's the brig *Somers*."

Richard's eyebrows shot up. "*Somers*? Isn't she . . . ?"

"Yes," Brengle said, anticipating the ubiquitous question asked in nautical circles. "She is indeed the vessel where a bloody mutiny occurred and the perpetrators were hanged at the yardarm. Three years ago in the Indies. And yes, she is the only U.S. Navy vessel to be so disgraced. Which is clearly the reason the Navy gave command of her to me. I can't make things worse, can I?"

"A black mark on a proud vessel named for a true American naval hero." He clapped Brengle on the shoulder. "If any man can restore the soul of an illustrious ship and make things right, that man is you, Jack. Where are you bound?"

"With you, to a fine eatery I happened upon nearby. It's only a few minutes' walk from here. Yes, I know you have an appointment with Mr. Bancroft. He is looking forward to seeing you, but I am afraid that your meeting has been put off until later in the day. The secretary has been summoned to the White House for an impromptu cabinet meeting."

"Something in the wind?"

"I reckon so. President Polk is determined to have his war with Mexico, come hell or high water. Secretary Bancroft and Secretary Buchanan may have their doubts, but they'll keep their thoughts to themselves. War is coming, mark my words."

"And you are being called to duty."

Brengle grinned, unable to hide his excitement. "I am. *Somers* is currently undergoing what is being called routine maintenance at the Portsmouth Navy Yard. In fact, she is being provisioned for a long stint in the Gulf."

"Blockade duty?"

"Just so. Her shallow draft, speed, and ten 32-pounder carronades make her ideal for the job."

"What other ships are preparing to sail to the Gulf?"

"The usual suspects: *Constitution, Constellation, Congress,* and *United States.*"

"Is Jonty Montgomery on any of those ships?"

"Jonty? No. He is the newly minted third lieutenant—at age sixteen, mind you!—in *Columbia*, Captain Terence Neale."

"Terence? I'll be damned. I had dinner with him in Batavia on the voyage to New South Wales. A fine fellow, though a bit too tentative and by-the-book for my taste. Is he still attached to the East India Squadron?"

"He is. So is Commodore Strong. And now, so is Jonty."

Richard snorted. "Which heartless bastard assigned the poor lad to that squadron? After all he went through in New Zealand."

"As I understand it, Jonty put in for it himself. And I imagine the heartless bastard who inspired him to volunteer for that service is you. You were his hero. Goes to show how bamboozled a young man can be, whatever his intelligence and courage." Brengle gathered up his coat and blue-visored hat. "Come, Richard. I'm famished. We can talk more over lunch. I want to hear about Anne and Jamie and all that is going on in your life." He opened the office door and motioned to Richard to lead the way out. "I warn you, though, I am particularly keen to discuss the position your family is prepared to offer me at Cutler & Sons when I retire from the Navy. The salary provisions you are bandying about are really quite persuasive!"

CHAPTER 7

ALEXANDRIA, VIRGINIA, AND BOSTON, MASSACHUSETTS
February 1847

Harlan Sturgis folded his arms across his chest and stared out through the mullioned window at a wintry scene of snow, dazzling sunlight, and immense privilege. On the opposite side of the iron gate that enclosed the park that separated the two matching rows of Greek Revival townhouses were other dwellings inhabited by the city's elite. He smiled smugly. That townhouse over there, a short way in from Beacon Street and lying within the shadow of Phillips Grammar School, had once been occupied by John Hancock himself, the man whose bold signature on the Great Declaration helped to pave the way for rebellion against the Crown. Each home within the opulent Beacon Hill alcove bespoke wealth. Whether that wealth was inherited or earned did not matter. It was wealth either way.

"My kind of city, my kind of people," Sturgis mused aloud. "And this is the perfect setting to mark who I am, where I am, and what I am." He chortled at his own wit. "No one will ever think to question a gentleman living in such splendor. Why, it would be downright ungentlemanly!"

He hooked his thumbs into the thin side pockets of his old-fashioned satin waistcoat. It had taken some doing and a considerable dip into capital to secure this place and the place on Jeffries Point. But the combined costs would be a trifle in comparison to what he would bring in if everything went according to plan. And by God, it would go according to plan! His strategy was sound, and his investments would add valuable assets to his portfolio and cash to his accounts, more than enough to impress any snooty Brahmin. "And those pompous snobs will likely be my first and best customers!" He barked a laugh.

Three hard raps on the front door followed by two softer raps summoned him through the sparsely furnished parlor to the front of the townhome. He opened the door and allowed entry to two scruffy men who appeared ill-at-ease in this grand neighborhood. They gazed around the hallway and parlor, mouths agape, as they stomped the snow from their boots onto a mat.

"Did anyone see you come here?" Sturgis demanded roughly. Their threadbare overcoats, which likely saw double duty as blankets, clearly marked them as undesirables.

"Nay, yer 'onor," the taller of the two men replied. "Not a soul, I assure ye." Despite his unkempt appearance, his dark eyes were sharp and highly focused.

"You're quite sure of that, Gus?"

"Quite sure, sir. Upon me soul."

"And you, Simon?"

"The same."

"Very well. Keep it that way. As you have surely realized, you two don't exactly fit in here. Your presence could arouse suspicion. Until we have things under way, we need to steer clear of people minding our business. You should come here only when you absolutely must, and even then, only at night."

"We understand, sir, indeed we do. But Simon and I reckoned, well, sir, we reckon you would want to know."

"Know what, pray?"

"We have the girl . . . in custody."

Sturgis nodded. "Good. Is she . . . compliant? Did she resist your efforts to bring her?"

Simon answered. "At first she did. But Toby 'n Gus convinced her to come with them. They told 'er what you told 'em to say, and they treated her like a lady. She even brought along a book to read while she waits for you. I've never seen the like of that. Who does that sort of thing?"

"Someone with better breeding than yours," Sturgis answered him. "Is Toby keeping an eye on her? Is he seeing to her needs?"

"I reckon," Simon snickered. "Ain't hard duty, if you catch me drift. She's a beauty, that one." He gave Sturgis a nearly toothless grin.

A dark cloud passed over Sturgis's face. "I pray to God I don't catch your drift, Simon. Listen to me and listen well. No harm is to come to that young woman. No harm whatsoever. Her last name may be Seymour, but she is a Cutler, and don't ever forget it. What's more, she is a lynchpin of our plan. While she is under our . . . protection, she will be accorded the respect she deserves. I am holding you personally responsible for her well-being. Cross me, and you will regret it. Do *you* catch *my* drift?"

"Loud and clear, boss," Simon replied sullenly.

"Right, then. You and Gus can go. I'll be down later this afternoon to check on things."

"Very good, yer 'onor," Gus said obsequiously. He bobbed his head and turned to open the front door.

Simon turned with him. "See you then, Harlan," he said.

"That's Mr. Sturgis to you, Simon," Sturgis snapped. "Don't you ever forget it!"

* * *

"Richard, darling, I fear something may be wrong."

Richard looked up from the letter he was writing to his mother. "What is it, Anne?"

Anne placed both her hands on her belly. I haven't felt the baby kick for a while. I'm not feeling anything in there at all."

"For how long?"

"Several days." Her voice was shaky. "Should we consult our physician?"

Richard replaced his quill pen in its inkwell and studied his wife's face, where lines of worry were very much in evidence. "Have you spoken to Rachel? She has considerable experience as a midwife. She helped deliver Jamie, after all."

"Most of what she knows she learned from Te Whina and other Maori women. I trust her judgment, but she is no physician."

"And we have Abigail," Richard reminded her. "She too knows a thing or two about childbirth."

"I agree, she does."

"I think you have just answered your own question. What is Rachel telling you?"

"That the baby is likely turning in the womb. Getting ready to make his grand entrance. She doubts we have anything to worry about. She said I should continue to get plenty of rest. It shouldn't be long now. But I still worry, and I'm getting tired of resting!"

Richard got up and took her in his arms. "I may not know much about childbirth, but that sounds like excellent advice to me. If Rachel had serious concerns, she would tell you, don't you agree?"

Anne nodded slowly. "I suppose I do. So, you think I am stewing over nothing?"

He tilted up her chin and gazed into her eyes. "No. I do not think that." He led her to his chair, sat down, and patted his thigh. "Come, my love. Why don't you and our little Sydney sit with me for a spell."

"God's bones, Richard," she laughed. "If I do that, we will break the chair and most likely your back!"

"I'll take that chance. Come, Mrs. Cutler. Sit with me and try not to worry. All will be well."

* * *

Jeffries Point on Noddle Island had seemed the ideal location for his business operations, just as Louisburg Square had seemed the perfect location for his residence. Having made that decision, Harlan Sturgis had purchased a clapboard house from a local sea captain seeking to retire inland. The Point, as it was called, was only two miles from Boston's Chinese district. Too, it was within easy reach of the town of Winthrop to the east and, to the south, the Charlestown Navy Yard and the formidable sight of USS *Constitution* and her sister ships riding at anchor in the cold harbor waters. Despite its convenient location, Noddle Island was a world separate from the mainstream, its small population of immigrants sprinkled with local folk seeking privacy and anonymity. These were the sort of people Sturgis was seeking out—people who minded their own business and who kept other people's affairs at arm's length.

He was convinced that these clusters of small islands noted for their modest homes and their ten well-constructed stone wharves would one day be a preferred area of Boston, and he wanted in. Now that William Sumner and his two partners had begun developing the land into tidy grids of streets and building plots, and buttressing the waterfront with additional wharves, warehouses, and breakwaters, it was just a matter of time before land values soared. They were stagnant at the moment, but his business instincts told him that would soon change. And he was seldom wrong. Which was why he was looking to scoop up additional tracts of land on Noddle and Apple Islands, and why he was planning to invest heavily in the East Boston Company. That was where the real money was going to be made: in developing the land and selling it parcel by parcel. Before he could do that, of course, he had to be invited in. The East Boston Company was in many respects a private club. To get access, you had to "belong." To belong in a city like Boston, you had to have money, of course, but you also had to have the right bloodlines and the right connections. Money he had, and he would soon have a great deal more. Bloodlines he also had. His grandfather had fought with Colonel Prescott at Bunker Hill, and his father with General Jackson in New Orleans. As for connections, he would get those too now that he possessed the hallmark of polite society: a fashionable residence on Louisburg Square.

And once he was accepted by Boston society, there would be no limit to his investments in land in Boston and in the stock market in New York. And in his newest endeavor. There would be no stemming the flow of cash into his coffers. Rumor had it that Tom Perkins—a Boston Brahmin who defined the term—had amassed a million dollars in one year from the smuggling of opium from Turkey into China and the United States. A million dollars! In one year!

"Ah, Mindy Cutler," he sighed as his hired coach rattled over the causeway connecting the town of Chelsea to Noddle Island. "Had you had the courage to believe in me and work with me, we could have grown old and rich together. Too bad that your uppity family had to interfere with your destiny."

The twin wheels of the coach jounced in and out of potholes on the narrow, ice-gutted road leading to the southern tip of Jeffries Point. When it neared the two-story clapboard house, Sturgis banged on the roof of the coach and pointed out the window at his destination. The coachman pulled gently on the reins and the coach came to a stop.

Sturgis opened the door and stepped out into air rendered frigid by strong gusts of wind off the Atlantic. He pulled his scarf tight around his neck and shouted up to the coachman, "Be back here in an hour and a half. It will be dark soon after that, and we'll need to get back to Boston while there is still light. In the meanwhile, find an alehouse to warm yourself. Drinks are on me. Don't overdo it." He handed the coachman a gold Double Eagle.

"Why thank you kindly, good sir," the coachman said, taking a moment to examine the coin's intricate design. He thought to further express his gratitude, but Sturgis had already disappeared inside the house.

* * *

When he gently shook her shoulder, Rachel opened her eyes and quickly sat up.

"What, Captain Cutler?" she asked anxiously. "Is it Lady Anne? I'm so sorry. I fell asleep!"

"As well you should have. Yes, it is Lady Anne," Richard said worriedly. "I think it's her time."

Rachel swung off the bed in the chamber she shared with Jamie and gathered her night robe off a nearby chair. "It will go fine, Captain," she said reassuringly. "Just fine. Trust me."

"I do trust you, Rachel. So does Anne. May God go with you both!"

She gripped his shoulder, then flew from the room, careful to close the door softly behind her so as not to wake Jamie.

For several moments, Richard sat on the edge of the bed in darkness save for a shard of moonlight filtering in through a narrow slit where the two thick window curtains did not quite join. He listened intently for any sound from down the hallway. To his relief, he heard nothing beyond the gentle, rhythmic breathing of his son. *Thank Christ he stayed asleep. That's one less worry.*

He bowed his head and, though not an overly religious man, clasped his hands in prayer. "Dear God," he murmured, "watch over Anne in her hour of need. Do not let her die. Heavenly Father, I beseech you, do not take Anne from me again!"

The sound of someone running down the hall brought him fully alert. It was too soon. Much too soon. He held his breath and felt a sickening void in the pit of his gut. To his relief, the running stopped halfway down the hall, presumably at the linen closet where extra towels and linens were stored. Moments later, the closet door banged shut and footsteps retreated hastily back up the hall to the master bedroom.

Seeking a distraction and needing to do something useful, he decided to go downstairs to stoke the fires and add to the supply of hot water in case it was needed. On his way out of the bedroom, he pulled the coverlet over his son's shoulders and gently touched his hair.

In the hallway, illuminated by the dimmed light of oil lamps placed on small tables set ten feet apart, he turned left to take the back steps leading down to the kitchen. A quick check showed the hearths in the parlor and dining room still gently burning and throwing off heat; nonetheless, he piled on more logs from the ample supply on hand in the rack by the back door. For a moment, he thought to bring up additional logs to the master bedroom but decided against it. There was already a sufficient stock in there, and he had strict orders not to enter unless summoned. Rachel and Abigail would see to what needed to be done.

With the fires now blazing in both hearths he set to work removing ashes from the big cast iron stove in the kitchen. After scraping them out, he replaced the open space with small logs, sticks of kindling, and old pages of newspaper twisted tightly together. A strike on a tinderbox had the fire going and warmth spreading throughout the room. He filled the kettle and placed it on top of the stove. Before the water reached a boil, he ladled out several cups full and poured them over coffee grounds already placed in the upper chamber of a small two-tiered copper kettle.

Once the hot water had dripped through a cloth filter into a lower chamber, the coffee was ready. Although the process took a while, the result was worth the wait. Plus, its preparation gave him something to do.

With a comforting mug of hot coffee before him, Richard sat at the kitchen table, listening intently, hearing nothing beyond the ticking of the mantle clock in the parlor. Whether the silence indicated something good or bad he could not determine, though he feared the latter. Childbirth was a difficult business. He jumped to his feet when an agonized shriek pierced the silence. It was muted by the townhome's thick walls and flooring, and by the distance between where he was sitting and Anne was lying—but that piteous wail had been heart-rending. He stood, fists clenched, fearing he would hear more and fearing he would not. But he heard nothing further. The house was silent.

He collapsed back into his chair. As minutes passed with frustrating slowness, Richard's thoughts drifted, not away from Anne but toward her. What it must be like for her now upstairs, giving birth for the second time? The first time, he knew, had been fearsome, without her husband there to support and encourage her, without even knowing if her husband was alive. How cruel and lonely that must have been for her.

He could not have been there for Anne, but he could and should have been there for Ataahua. He thought of her lying so dreadfully injured in her hut, her head bashed in, her left arm broken, her torso and legs smeared with blood from her wounds and from the small clump of tissue expelled from her body—its features, its sex, unformed and unidentifiable. Ataahua and their child, dead. And now Anne upstairs, suffering horribly. *Dear God*, he thought with a start, *what kind of sinner am I? What kind of man thinks of another woman while his wife is in agony only a few feet away?*

He lifted his eyes toward the ceiling, willing his love to reach through the wall to where she lay struggling, to comfort her, reassure her, save her. *Not again*, he vowed. *God, I beseech you, not again!* He put his face in his hands.

A touch on his shoulder brought him back. He looked up through bloodshot eyes to see Abigail standing before him, her smooth brown face aglow.

"You have a daughter, Captain," she said. "A beautiful, healthy daughter. Mother and baby are doing just fine. Did you hear me, Master Richard?"

It took a moment to register. When it did, he shot to his feet and, for the first time since knowing her, he took Abigail in his arms and hugged her. "Can I see them now?" he begged.

"Of course you can," she laughed. "You're the father!"

Richard kissed her forehead. "Thank you, my dear Abigail," he choked. "Thank you very, very much!" He bolted out of the kitchen and into the front hallway, and raced up the front stairway, taking the steps two at a time.

* * *

Sturgis found her in the parlor, a woman in her late twenties sitting on the only armchair in the room, her legs propped up on the matching ottoman as she read from a book she held on her lap. Her heavy woolen dress was simple but appropriate for a New England winter, and her thick, brownish-blond hair was coiled neatly around her ears. Her slender, graceful shoulders led down to the gentle swell of her breasts. Behind her, through a window spotted with crystals of frost that seemed impervious to the sun's feeble warmth, stretched the white-capped blue expanse of the frigid Atlantic.

"Good afternoon, Lucy," Sturgis said as he removed his overcoat and hung it from a peg. He picked up one of the two Shaker-style chairs in the room and brought it over. "It has been a while since I last saw you. How are you?"

She had been watching him from the moment he entered the room, her wary expression a blend of curiosity and suspicion.

"You do remember who I am, don't you?" Sturgis said, noting her hesitancy.

She nodded. "You are Mr. Harlan Sturgis. You are a friend of my aunt Melinda. Or you *were* her friend for a time."

Sturgis smiled. "I like to think of myself as a friend of your entire family."

"That is not my understanding, Mr. Sturgis," she countered calmly. "Am I your prisoner here?"

"My prisoner? Good heavens no, my dear young lady!" Sturgis chortled. "How could you think such a thing? You are my honored guest."

"Am I indeed? In that case, I am free to leave?"

"Of course. I have a coach returning within the hour, and it will take you anywhere you wish to go, at my expense."

"To Cambridge?"

"I was assuming you would want to go to Long Wharf. Regis House."

He was referring to a fashionable residence across from Faneuil Hall where unmarried women of means were welcomed but not closely supervised, an arrangement that suited Lucy perfectly.

"So you know where I live."

"It wasn't hard to determine. Simple detective work."

Lucy eyed him. "And why would you go to that trouble?"

"Mere curiosity, my dear. I suspected you'd be living in one of the nicer enclaves of the city. I was curious as to which one."

Lucy closed her book and folded her hands demurely, striving to hide her misgivings. "You have a rather odd way of inviting guests to what I assume is your home. Why was I brought here by those two dirty thugs? It is certainly not a place I would choose to visit. Not that I was given any choice. And if I am your guest, why am I being kept under guard?"

"So many questions," Sturgis said lightheartedly. "I will explain everything in due course, if only you will let me. And I believe I will do so to your entire satisfaction. Before I do that, however, I want to ensure that you have been treated well today by my associates and that they have afforded you every courtesy."

"I find your flowery language insincere, Mr. Sturgis. I have no real complaints beyond what I just told you, but I had other plans for the day. If you have matters to discuss with me, simply make arrangements to meet me in town."

"Understood. As to your charge about being held under guard, nothing could be further from the truth. As I indicated, you are free to leave whenever you wish."

"Very well. I will leave now." She started to rise.

"Before you go," Sturgis said, his voice rising, "please hear me out. I went through considerable trouble arranging this meeting, one that I believe will greatly interest you because it involves significant benefits for you. My coach will be here within the hour, as I said. I am not asking for much of your time."

She paused for a moment, then sat back down, clearly curious about his intentions.

He pointed to her book. "Are you enjoying that?"

"I am."

"What is its title, if I may ask?"

"*Sybil.*"

"Ah, yes. Benjamin Disraeli. A poet and a statesman espousing the conservative cause and support of the downtrodden." He smiled at her obvious surprise. "I believe the book provides an appropriate basis for our preliminary discussion this afternoon."

"*Preliminary* discussion?"

"Yes. This meeting will be short. But I trust there will be others to follow."

Lucy flapped her hand at him impatiently. "Kindly get to the point, Mr. Sturgis. What is it you wish to discuss with me?"

"Opium."

Lucy's eyes widened. "I'm sorry, I don't think I heard you properly. What did you say?"

Sturgis smiled. "You heard me. Opium. Elixir of the rich and famous, and elixir of the poor and downtrodden. Disraeli would approve. That is to say, Sybil would approve."

"Mr. Sturgis, I—"

Sturgis held up his hand. "A moment, Miss Seymour, if you please. Allow me to state my case."

She nodded. "Very well."

"Thank you." He got up and moved his chair closer to hers, then sat back down and crossed his legs. "Please understand that I am putting myself at risk by telling you what I am about to tell you. Not from the law. From members of your family and others who think as they do. If they were to get wind of what I am about, it could become troublesome for me."

"Why? This is all a mystery to me, Mr. Sturgis. Exactly what are you talking about?" She seemed more at ease now, more confident.

He looked her in the eye. "Do you know what an opium den is?"

Her gaze did not waver. "I do."

"Ever been in one?"

"No, certainly not!"

"Would you like to?"

She shrugged. "I suppose I would, actually. I have friends who have tried opium. They rather liked it. I imagine I would, too."

"Your answer does not surprise me. I have always thought of you as an inquisitive and highly intelligent young woman who knows her own mind, and whose vision is not clouded by blind obedience to outdated social conventions. You are a free-thinker, as am I."

Their eyes held for a moment before Lucy said, "Opium dens are found mostly in China, are they not?"

"China is where they originated, but they are becoming increasingly popular in the United States. In cities such as San Francisco, Chicago, and New York, they have become part of the landscape. And now, Boston."

"Boston?"

"Yes. Today there are two opium dens in the Chinese district of Boston. Tomorrow there will be three."

She considered him. "Yours, I assume?"

"Just so."

"Where does the opium come from? Do you import it from China?"

Sturgis nodded. "You ask good questions. The answer is not a simple one. Suffice it to say for the moment that much of it comes from India, through China. The rest comes from Turkey, either through China to the United States or directly from Turkey in a ship similar to that brig you see tied to the wharf out there." He pointed at a two-masted vessel barely visible through the window, her sails furled, secured to the closest wharf on Jeffries Point. During the past hour the sky had clouded over and a gentle snow had begun to fall, obscuring the view.

Lucy followed his direction. "Your ship?"

"Not mine. She belongs to a business associate of mine. That brig sailed here from Istanbul with a cargo worth a king's ransom. Turkish opium is of a higher quality than opium from India, which is why my establishment will offer opium only from Turkey." He grinned. "People will demand my opium because of its quality. My competition will serve the dregs of society while I serve the upper class in a very tasteful setting. A compelling business model, do you not agree?" His grin broadened.

Her expression remained inscrutable. "The use of opium for anything other than medicinal purposes is illegal, is it not?"

"A natural question to ask, Lucy, but you are misinformed. The use of opium is illegal in China but not in the United States. To the contrary, it may surprise you to know that much of the infrastructure of Boston—its hospitals, schools, and libraries, for example—being built today is financed by tax levies exacted from the importation and sale of opium. I am paying my fair share of those levies, I can assure you. And that is just the tip of the iceberg, as they say. I am not overstating the facts when I say that the prosperity of Boston, and of Massachusetts in general, is dependent on the importation of opium. The same holds true in the other cities I mentioned."

Lucy had been listening intently to what Sturgis was saying. When he finished, she said, "I confess my surprise. I had no idea."

"Not many people do. It is not something that the mayor of Boston or the governor of Massachusetts or the president of the United States wants publicized. Your father was a prominent barrister in Boston, wasn't he, before taking over Cutler & Sons? And your grandfather was a prominent physician?"

Lucy nodded.

"Then surely through your excellent family connections you know a number of prominent barristers currently practicing in Boston."

Again Lucy nodded.

"You could ask any one of them and they would verify every word of what I just told you. But I ask you not to do that. Not just yet."

"Why not?"

"Because that would implicate me."

Lucy looked puzzled. "I don't understand. Why should that bother you? If the importation and use of opium is legal . . ."

Sturgis waved that away. "Public perception, my dear. Public perception. The fact that opium is *legal* does not *ipso facto* make it morally *acceptable* to polite society, which views it as *déclassé*, as the French would say, something dirty and beneath their social stratum. Any money earned from it is likewise considered corrupt and dirty." He shrugged. "People like your parents and other relatives are entitled to that opinion, of course, as I am entitled to mine."

"Even though polite society will be among those first in line to purchase your opium."

Sturgis looked at Lucy Cutler Seymour with genuine admiration. "Yes, hypocritical of them, isn't it. Once again you are right, Lucy. You do understand. I was quite sure you would."

"Perhaps. But I still don't understand why you are telling me all this. What do you want from me? You're not asking me to manage your little operation, are you?"

Sturgis laughed, shook his head. "No, I am in the process of hiring Chinese staff to do that. But there is a key role for you to play in all this if you are interested, and if you are willing to keep your participation a secret from your family, at least for a while. The rewards could be substantial."

Moments elapsed. "I'm listening," Lucy said finally. The muted clop of hooves and the low rumble of carriage wheels on rough cobblestones signaled the arrival of the coach.

"I will tell you more on our way to Long Wharf," Sturgis promised her. "Soon you will understand that my 'little operation' is not so little, and your participation could be very lucrative for you, my dear. You will be able to afford the finest luxuries Boston has to offer."

CHAPTER 8

BATAVIA, DUTCH EAST INDIES
April 1847

As Lieutenant Jonathan Montgomery approached the gates of the ten-foot-high wall that had once protected the old colonial Dutch capital, he wondered that tiny Holland had managed to maintain an iron grip on the 17,500 Spice Islands for two centuries. The Dutch had grown rich satisfying the inexhaustible demand in Europe and North America for the cloves, nutmegs, peppers, and other exotic spices that grew in these tropical islands. But their monopoly had proved unsustainable when the Dutch East India Company declared bankruptcy in the early nineteenth century. Competitors from many nations rushed in to capitalize on this propitious turn of events. One such competitor, Cutler & Sons, established its Far East headquarters in Batavia and from there conducted a far-reaching and lucrative commercial enterprise.

Once through the tall wrought-iron gates and inside the wall, Montgomery turned to gaze back at the harbor. *Columbia* was there, of course, anchored close in with her sails furled to their yards in Bristol fashion and her gun ports closed. High up at the peak of her ensign halyard the Stars and Stripes fluttered in the awakening midmorning breeze. Anchored not far from *Columbia*, in addition to merchant ships of assorted nations, were two other American steam frigates of the East India Squadron keeping company with three Royal Navy warships of Britain's Western Pacific Squadron. In the distance, he could see the string of small islands that protected the northern approaches to Batavia Bay. Montgomery searched those approaches for the telltale smoke that would indicate that three additional British warships were arriving on schedule. But the skies and waters were empty.

His gaze shifted to the man twice his age who had accompanied him and was standing deferentially at his side. In keeping with the stifling heat and humidity the man was, like Montgomery, dressed casually in buff trousers and a light, white cotton shirt with sleeves rolled up to his elbows. Like Montgomery's, the man's weathered face had been burnished to a copper bronze by months at sea under a tropical sun. Nothing about the man suggested he was a noncommissioned officer in the United States Marine Corps save for his uniform hat, the sea-service musket slung over his left shoulder, and his rigid attention to every detail involving a superior officer. When their eyes met, the Marine saluted smartly.

"Thank you, Sergeant," Montgomery said, returning the salute. "You needn't accompany me further. I believe I know the way from here. That church steeple yonder," he pointed to a towering church steeple of Dutch architecture in the distance, "is a dead giveaway. And aside from that one, I am well versed on the landmarks I need to look out for."

The Marine tensed. "Aye, sir. But begging your pardon, sir, I have orders from Captain Neale to see you to the Klen . . . um . . . "

"The Koningsplein," Montgomery said. "Very well then. No point in arguing with the captain. It's not far, a mile or so. And who knows what vagabonds and vipers we might meet along the way?"

The Marine showed a ghost of a smile. "Aye, sir. And I shall be here if we do."

The route into the city proper was not difficult to identify. It followed the east bank of the Jakarta River, a substantial waterway that bisected the city and carried goods and people to destinations throughout the town. Colorful local vendors noisily hawked their wares among the women doing their washing in the dirty water. Sidestepping them, Montgomery and his escort made way for carriages and riders on horseback, and dodged around teams of oxen pulling rafts laden with produce and people. The people guiding the oxen seemed mostly to be Asians dressed in short pants, simple black tunics, and yellowish conical hats. Few of them made eye contact with the two Americans, either because they were too engaged in what they were doing or because, Montgomery suspected, they had no reason to acknowledge them.

Everywhere were reminders of their former colonial masters. The tidily laid-out streets and gardens in which Europeans had once strolled in white finery beneath shady parasols and tall palm trees stood as testimony to Dutch taste and efficiency. Even today, forty years after Dutch rule had ended, many of the business executives and government officials in Batavia were of Dutch extraction and had lived most of their lives on these tropical islands.

"A question, sir, if I may," the Marine suddenly said.

Montgomery stopped and looked at him. "Of course, Sergeant. Fire away."

"Well, sir, I was just wondering . . ."

"Yes?"

"I was just wondering, sir, does this place remind you of where you were when you were shipwrecked?"

"Of New Zealand, you mean?"

"Yes, sir. 'Tis an island like these here, but that's about all I know of it. My mates and me have heard of your story," he explained, "and are keen to learn more."

"I am flattered by your interest, Sergeant," Montgomery said, walking on. A slender Javanese woman with high cheekbones and long, glossy black hair distracted him for a moment when she gave him an appreciative glance as she passed by. He returned her smile before continuing. "There are similarities," he said. "After all, New Zealand is not such a long distance away from here. Java is much lusher, though, with thicker vegetation. And it's hotter here than there. And a good deal more humid."

"Are there different seasons in New Zealand, like at home?"

Montgomery grinned. "Not as we know them in New England, at least not in the northern island where we were."

"What about the people? Do they look like the people here?"

"The white people—the *pakeha* as they are called in New Zealand—look much the same. Which is to be expected, isn't it? They are all originally from Europe." When the Marine did not respond, Montgomery went on. "The New Zealand natives, or Maori, are Polynesians. They are a fierce, warlike people, but they are also proud and dignified, and they share a strong sense of God and family—more so than many *pakeha*—and a strong sense of community. In that way they are much like the Indians in our West. The tribe we thought had captured and imprisoned us ended up saving our lives on multiple occasions. My shipmates and I tried to return the favor by fighting their enemies with them. Call it mutual respect."

"Most of your ship's crew died, we heard."

"Yes," Montgomery said sadly. "I was the only midshipman out of eight to survive the wreck and a year in the bush, and one of only twelve members of the crew to survive from a ship's complement of more than two hundred men."

The Marine whistled softly. "Was it luck, do you think, or the will of the Lord?"

"The latter, I'm sure. With a lot of help from Captain Cutler and his executive officer, Jack Brengle."

"That was quite an ordeal for a young lad, if you will forgive my saying so, sir."

"Of course, Sergeant. I was young, yes, but boys become men quickly in such circumstances."

"Aye, sir, they do," he said slowly, perhaps thinking of his own experience.

They came to a large city square bordered on all four sides by gray-stone and red-brick buildings of two or three stories. A few buildings—including the Stadhuis, or city hall—featured Greek-style columns at the doorway. Each building was separated from its neighbors by rows of teak, rattan, or pine trees. To the right of a European-style Protestant church was the red-brick and gray-stone building that marked the Far East headquarters of Cutler & Sons.

Montgomery stopped and turned to the Marine. "We have arrived, Sergeant. You are hereby dismissed. Please inform Captain Neale that I shall be returning to duty by the start of the first dogwatch as he requested." Less formally, he said, "Thank you for your company."

The Marine saluted. "My pleasure, Lieutenant. When time allows, I look forward to hearing more about your experiences in New Zealand." With that, he turned on his heel and departed.

Montgomery walked up the three steps to the landing and knocked on the heavy wooden door. To his surprise—and delight—the door was opened not by the servant he was expecting to see but by an attractive young woman of his own age. Her thin muslin dress and brightly embroidered slippers bespoke the warm, humid air of Java, and he couldn't help noticing that her neatly coiled hair had a reddish tinge that matched the scattered freckles on her pert nose. Her blue eyes flashed in welcome, and her wide smile revealed perfect teeth. The quality of her attire suggested that she was a young lady of status, and the impish twinkle in her eyes as she took his measure told him she might be rather fun to know.

Their eyes met and held. "Good morning," she said brightly. "May I be of help?"

Still bound by her eyes, he could not immediately respond; social propriety seemed to have abandoned him. He cleared his throat, apologized, and blurted out, "Who are you?" He turned beet red at his unforgivable rudeness.

She covered her mouth to hide her smile at his embarrassment. When she spoke, her voice revealed an unexpected self-confidence. "I could ask you the same question, young sir. But since you asked first, I will answer first. My name is Daisy Cutler. Now it is your turn."

Again he cleared his throat. "My name is Jonathan Montgomery. I am third lieutenant of the United States ship-of-war *Columbia*, currently anchored in the harbor. I have come to pay my respects to Mijnheer De Vries on behalf of Captain Richard Cutler."

"Oh my," Daisy exclaimed, making a show of fanning her face with her hand. "A naval officer! An *American* naval officer, no less. My heart, be still. By all means, Lieutenant, please do come in!"

Montgomery hesitated, then stepped into a pleasantly cool hallway with thick stone walls and a high vaulted ceiling that captured the cooler night air and held it for much of the following day. Colorful tropical flowers decorated the tops of tables standing against the walls, filling the air with their perfume and keeping at bay the rank odors of the city outside.

As they walked down the corridor, Montgomery admired the oil paintings adorning the walls of the hallway and the nicely furnished rooms they passed by.

"This is a very impressive home, Miss Cutler," he remarked as they neared the end of the hallway.

"Do you find it so? May I take it that your home is somewhat smaller?"

"Indeed. My home is a humble little house in the state of Connecticut. That's a state in New England."

"I know perfectly well where Connecticut is, Third Lieutenant Montgomery," she snapped. "I have been educated in geography as well as the arts."

He grinned. "My sincere apologies, Miss Cutler." He made a sweeping gesture with his right arm. "Do you live here?"

She nodded, her tone turning more serious. "My father and I live on the second floor. This floor is used for business mostly. Mr. De Vries lives nearby, in his own home, and of course we have servants to look after us. We entertain many guests, as you can imagine. And there are several guest rooms upstairs for those who wish to stay with us." She flashed an impish grin. "You are most welcome to do so as well, should circumstances warrant it." She dropped her eyes and added regretfully, "although I doubt you will find cause to."

"Perhaps not. Nonetheless, I will keep that kind offer in mind. Your father is Ben Cutler, I believe. Is your mother not with you as well?"

"My mother died some years ago in Barbados, when I was quite young. I don't remember much about her."

"I'm sorry."

"It's kind of you to say that, but there's no need to be sorry. As I said, I never really knew her."

"So you are here with just your father, then?"

"Just so. Ben Cutler has been the deputy director of Cutler & Sons here for only a few weeks. We are of the English strain of Cutlers, or, as we like to say, the West Indian Cutlers."

Montgomery nodded his understanding. Conversations at sea and in New Zealand with Richard Cutler had taught him a little of the Cutler family history. In the mid-1700s, Thomas Cutler had sailed with his wife, Elizabeth, to Boston to seek new business opportunities for his extended family. Together with his brother William, who had remained in England, they came to own two sugar plantations, one on the island of Barbados and the other on the island of Tobago. With the produce of these two plantations, and with ready markets in America and Europe, the Cutler family joined the triangular trade route that was enriching many New England shipping families, including Cutler & Sons.

"Where is your father now?" he asked as they reached the end of the hallway.

"Upstairs. You are about to meet him." She opened the door to the back stairway and, to Montgomery's surprise, cupped a hand at her mouth and gave an unladylike shout, "Father, we have a visitor!"

A door opened above, and a deep voice inquired, "Who is it?"

"A young American sea officer come to pay his respects. He has a fine cut to his jib and he's giving me the once-over. Please come quickly. Who knows what might become of me if you dally!"

She laughed at Montgomery's shocked expression. "Don't worry. My father knows I am teasing. He quite despairs of me ever becoming a proper lady."

Ben Cutler hastened down the back stairs muttering to himself. When he reached the foot of the stairs he walked into the hallway and up to his visitor, offering his right hand. "I am pleased to meet you, Mister . . . ?"

Daisy spoke up before Montgomery could answer. "He is Lieutenant Jonathan Montgomery. *Third Lieutenant* Montgomery. Of the American ship-of-war *Columbia*. Yes, he *is* quite young to hold the rank of a commissioned officer. But his superiors must see something promising in him."

"Please forgive my daughter's impertinence," Ben Cutler said. "Her antics amuse her and seem harmless, though I fear they will one day be her undoing. In any event, I am pleased to meet you."

Montgomery glanced at Daisy, who was keeping her eyes modestly downcast. "No harm done, Mr. Cutler. Indeed, I am flattered by your daughter's attention to me. I would say that you are a most fortunate father." Out of the corner of his eye he saw a tiny smile and the beginnings of a blush on her face.

"Well, I am pleased to hear you say that." His daughter's attention to the young man had not gone unnoticed, and Ben Cutler took a moment to study the tall, slender American standing before him. There did seem to be something compelling about the youth. "My nephew Richard Cutler had very good things to say about you in a letter I received from him not long ago. That is, if you are the chap known as 'Jonty.'"

"Jonty!" Daisy giggled. "How sweet! You look just as I would expect a Jonty to look."

Montgomery blushed. He dared not look at Daisy. "'Jonty' was my nickname as a child," he confessed to her father. "Unfortunately, the name carried over to my service as a midshipman in Captain Cutler's ship."

"I see," Ben Cutler said. "Well, we will not subject you to a name you don't like, although I must say I agree with Daisy. The name suits you."

When Montgomery offered no comment, Cutler added, "On that note, let us have some light refreshments in the garden while you cool yourself from your walk. And you will stay to luncheon with us, of course."

"I would be honored," Montgomery said. "I have been granted leave from my ship until the start of the first dogwatch."

"That's four o'clock, Father," Daisy interjected.

"Thank you, Daisy," Cutler said, adding with a touch of sarcasm, "as the scion of a shipping family I *have* managed to pick up a bit of naval terminology. "This way, Lieutenant," he said, gesturing toward the doorway opening into a lush garden. "Please be seated, and then tell us what brings you and your ship to Batavia. We are most keen to know the details, aren't we, Daisy?"

A servant girl appeared immediately carrying a tray with a pot of tea and a dish of assorted honey cakes. As she was silently distributing the tea and cakes, Montgomery said, "As I told your daughter, sir, I came here to pay my respects to Mr. De Vries, with Captain Cutler's compliments, as I promised Captain Cutler I would do. And of course, to pay my respects to you . . . and your daughter," he added hastily. He smiled, blushing again. "Though I must confess that I did not know you were in residence."

"Ah, that is why you are here *today*," Ben said, "and both Daisy and I appreciate your candor. But what I mean to ask is, why has your ship put in to Batavia Bay? Perhaps it is to join forces with a Royal Navy squadron?"

When Montgomery merely smiled, Cutler pressed, "Does it have anything to do with the Chinese smugglers that infest these waters? If so, you are here with my blessing. The pirates are growing bolder and more ruthless by the day. Cutler & Sons has lost two ships and valuable cargoes in recent weeks. Word has it that good men were slaughtered and thrown to the sharks. I'm a bit dubious about that. Captured sailors bring high ransoms. But whatever the truth, we must have it out with them once and for all. Those bastards are a bane to our business and a threat to our very existence. Do excuse my language, please," he added to Montgomery. Daisy seemed unmoved by the profanity.

"We will do our best, sir, I promise."

"Of *that* I have no doubt," Ben Cutler said. "You'll be sailing immediately, then?"

"And then you'll return here, to us," Daisy ordered, clearly expecting no argument. "In the meanwhile, Mr. Third Lieutenant Jonathan Montgomery, you are to take good care of yourself!"

Montgomery could only nod, overcome by a sudden rush of emotion. Was it possible to fall in love instantly and irrevocably? He thought it might be.

CHAPTER 9

BATAVIA, DUTCH EAST INDIES
April 1847

Try as he might, Jonathan Montgomery could not erase thoughts of Daisy Cutler from his mind—longing thoughts that were both delightful and unsettling. Here he was, in the harbor aboard *Columbia*, and there she was, ashore at her home, the seat of her family's business in the Orient. As the gull flew, the distance separating them could not have been more than a mile. But to him it seemed far greater.

From the soaring height of the mainmast trestle trees he could see, with the aid of a long glass, beyond the top of the wall into the city proper to the Koningsplein. He fantasized on more than one occasion that he could see Daisy moving about outside the now familiar structure next to her home.

On one occasion he actually *did* see her, he was sure of it. He was on *Columbia*'s weather deck watching a gun crew clean and polish the twin cannonades on the foredeck. A chance glance ashore revealed a young woman walking alone outside the wall by the wharves with a basket over her arm, her head turned toward *Columbia*. Although her large, broad-brimmed hat prevented him from seeing most of her face, he was convinced it was Daisy.

His heart raced as he wondered if she was looking for him. He dared not believe it. Yet he lost no time beckoning a midshipman patrolling the deck nearby. "Pass me your glass, if you please, Mr. Sears."

"Aye, sir."

Montgomery adjusted the lens to bring the young woman into sharp focus. She was looking straight at him. She recognized him. Quickly he dismissed the thought. She might know his ship, but she could not possibly make him out at such a distance with the naked eye. And it was presumptuous, to say the least, to think that she was looking for him at all. A spirited young woman of high social position had surely attracted the interest of many men of good standing. The suitors would be swarming around her like bees to honey pot. And he had just met her. He hardly knew her. She barely knew him.

Fool! he chided himself, pulling himself back to duty. "You, there!" he snapped at one of the sailors tending a carronade. "There's rust on that gun!" He pointed at a reddish smudge on the gun's black muzzle. "I want it off!"

"Aye, aye, sir." Although the sailor was perhaps three times Montgomery's age and the area in question was insignificant, the sailor nodded and set dutifully to work.

As a motion to his left caught his eye, Montgomery swung his glass and saw his ship's cutter being rowed by six men, presumably from the city wharves, out to *Columbia*'s anchorage. On closer inspection he saw the ship's captain sitting in the cutter's stern sheets. Nothing in his deportment or expression suggested what his business ashore might have been. *Odd*, Montgomery mused. It was rare for the captain not to inform his officers that he was leaving the ship. One thing he knew for certain: the captain had not informed his lowly third lieutenant.

At six bells in the afternoon watch, *Columbia*'s officers gathered, as ordered, in the frigate's spacious after cabin. In addition to Montgomery and Neale, there were the ship's two other commissioned officers: First Lieutenant William Bowen and Second Lieutenant Charles Chadwick. Also present were Lieutenant Jason Albright, the square-jawed, red-haired captain of Marines, and two warrant officers: the affable and highly capable sailing master Lyall Dean, and David Marston, the officious senior midshipman who, if circumstances demanded, would step into Montgomery's spot as acting third lieutenant. Despite the searing heat and nearly unbearable humidity, the six officers were clad in full undress uniform of buff, dark blue, and gold in deference to a visitor in their midst.

Captain Neale introduced the man as Sir Edmund Evans-Peale of Her Britannic Majesty's sloop-of-war *Rattlesnake*. The blood-red sash running diagonally across the impeccably dressed British naval officer's chest identified him as a commodore in the Royal Navy. The eight men stood around the substantial rectangular wooden table used by Captain Neale either to conduct the ship's business or to entertain guests when the smaller table in his dining cuddy was deemed too small. Attached to the walls and bulkheads were paintings of seascapes and specially designed shelves holding books, charts, navigation implements, and other essentials of life at sea. All six of the cabin's windows were hinged open to allow in sultry harbor breeze, although it did little to temper the heat. When Neale bade his officers sit, they complied in almost perfect synchrony.

"Gentlemen," Neale said when the cabin was quiet, "I am sure you already know why we are here—both in this cabin and in Batavia as a whole. Chinese pirates and, increasingly, pirates from Japan are preying upon our merchantmen and those of Great Britain and other European nations. Their aggression is in direct violation of international law and in defiance of the orders of the Chinese emperor. These pirates, who refuse to accept our authority, are seizing our vessels and bringing them to their lairs along the northern coast of the South China Sea, especially in and around Hong Kong, despite the British naval base there. They are holding cargoes and crews for ransom and warning that if ransoms are not forthcoming in a timely manner, our captured sailors will be killed.

"British intelligence confirms that selected crew members have been beaten and slaughtered to set an example. Thus far, our combined efforts to bring them to justice, one way or another, have been unsuccessful. As many of you are aware, the armed merchant brig *Boston Maid*, owned by Cutler & Sons and commanded by Captain Edward Walsh, engaged and destroyed a war junk off Hong Kong several months ago. Our hats go off to Captain Walsh and his crew. Unfortunately, however, it seems his success served only to enrage the pirates, and to embolden them. *Boston Maid* subsequently disappeared. We have good reason to believe that she was attacked and captured, but the authorities have not been informed of the names of any sailors taken prisoner. The Chinese Intelligence service has offered to assist us, but so far they too have come up empty.

"It is time to increase the stakes. We must put a stop to this piracy once and for all. We must strike hard, and then we must strike hard again. We must send these scoundrels a message of shot and grape that says in no uncertain terms that there is a price to be paid for any harm done to our sailors and ships, now or in the future. It is a gamble, I admit, but I believe it is a gamble worth taking. The pirates may kill their captives as revenge, but I don't think so. The prospect of ransoms will keep those Americans alive as long as the pirates believe there is a chance they will be paid. We are here with Sir Edmund to plan our battle strategy. Ours will be a joint operation between the American and British navies, with the support, such as it is, of the Chinese emperor. China's navy is much diminished after the war with England, so it can do little to help us. Sir Edmund is the commodore of our combined Anglo-American squadrons, and we are all under his command, myself included. What we are about is well within the parameters of the recently signed Sydney Accords."

Neale unrolled a chart on the table and secured its four corners with granite paperweights. The chart revealed the northern regions of the South China Sea, highlighting the island group of Hong Kong, including Macau and Guangzhou, and the eighteen-mile-wide estuary of the Pearl River winding northward to the ancient port of Canton. It was a chart familiar to these sea officers. Prepared in 1810 for the British East India Company, its demarcations, delineations, and soundings were drawn in large part from ancient sailing charts created by Zheng He in 1425. Despite their age, the charts had repeatedly proven accurate and reliable.

"Gather in close, gentlemen, and give Sir Edmund and this chart your full attention, and you will learn what Her Majesty's Navy has in mind."

* * *

When Sir Edmund had finished his directives and excused himself to return to *Rattlesnake*, Captain Neale sat back and addressed his officers. "There you have it, gentlemen. We have our sailing orders, and we have our marching orders. We weigh in three days. Make your preparations. Shore leave for all crew members is hereby canceled without proper authorization—which means my permission. My responsibility now is to coordinate everything with the other ships in our squadron. The winds finally are freshening. May the Almighty do us the courtesy of maintaining that wind for the next week. You are excused, gentlemen. Good afternoon."

The officers rose, saluted, and began filing out of the cabin. Montgomery was the last to leave, but Neale raised a hand to stop him. "Mr. Montgomery, a word, if you please."

"Aye, Captain."

Montgomery returned to the table and stood rigidly before his captain.

"Be at your ease, Lieutenant," Neale said. "What I have to say is not official business, although I believe it will be of considerable interest to you."

Montgomery clasped his hands behind him but otherwise remained as he was. "Sir?"

Neale reached to the side of the desk and picked up a letter whose seal had previously been broken. He unfolded the paper and appeared to reread it before saying nonchalantly, "I received an interesting invitation whilst ashore this morning. On rather short notice, I must say."

"An invitation, sir?" Montgomery said politely.

"Just so. It is a dinner invitation extended by Pieter De Vries. I met him briefly yesterday when I went to pay my respects to him. It seems that Mr. Ben Cutler and Miss Daisy Cutler will also be attending this dinner. All very proper, you understand." He looked up to meet Montgomery's startled gaze. "The affair is to be held at Cutler & Sons' headquarters this very evening. Most intriguing. Most intriguing, indeed. And, rather unusually, the invitation includes an offer to pass the night in a guest room provided by the Cutler family."

"I see," Montgomery mumbled, biting his cheek to hide his dismay.

"Apparently," Neale went on in the same airy tone, "they don't wish to be responsible for a drunken American naval officer falling overboard on his way back to his ship. Not a very high opinion of our Navy, is it?"

"No, sir." Montgomery shook his head then looked quickly away. Rumors belowdecks said that Neale was very popular in social settings, particularly with the ladies. He understood why. Terence Neale was tall, debonair, and witty, with a disarming smile. Daisy would find him enchanting. "Why are you telling me this, sir?" he ventured.

"Why? Because I value your opinion. Should this invitation be accepted? Yes or no."

"I really can't say, sir," Montgomery replied stolidly. "Your life ashore isn't my business."

"Well, I believe it should be accepted," Neale said, "even though we are on a war footing. It would be the height of rudeness and folly to decline an invitation like this, especially with the lovely Miss Daisy Cutler in attendance as the *de facto* hostess. The fact is, I have already accepted it. So our discussion is really quite moot."

Montgomery bit his lower lip. "Then why seek my opinion, sir?"

"I was curious as to your reaction."

Montgomery swallowed hard. "Yes, sir. I agree with you," he said firmly. "I wholeheartedly agree with you. The invitation should be accepted."

Neale nodded. "Then that settles the matter. Thank you, Lieutenant. That is all."

"Aye, aye, sir." Montgomery snapped a salute and turned on his heel.

"Oh. There is one more thing, Lieutenant."

Montgomery turned around. "Sir?"

Neale glanced up from a stack of papers he had picked up to read. "I expect you back aboard ship no later than eight bells tomorrow afternoon. I have asked Mr. Marston to stand in for you in your absence."

Montgomery's jaw dropped. "Sir . . . ?"

"Be off with you, Lieutenant. Enjoy yourself. I shall *not* expect a full report from you upon your return."

His knock on the front door of Cutler & Sons headquarters was answered by a slender *booi* dressed in the traditional silk dress of Qing Dynasty household servants. Her ebony hair was held in place atop her head by a pair of what looked like knitting needles. She bowed politely before stepping back and opening the door wider.

"Welcome, sir," she said in a soft, musical voice. "You are expected." She motioned toward a drawing room located a short distance down the grand hallway. "If you will please follow me."

The elegant room proclaimed Cutler & Sons' prosperity and refinement. Montgomery's attention was immediately drawn to the two men who rose to their feet when he entered the room. One man he recognized. "Good evening, Mr. Cutler," he said. "I am happy to see you again."

"And I, you, Lieutenant Montgomery," Ben Cutler responded. He came over to shake hands. "May I have the pleasure and honor of introducing you to Pieter De Vries, the managing director of Cutler & Sons in the Far East."

"My honor, Mr. De Vries," Montgomery said politely, shaking the director's hand in turn. "I have heard much about you from Captain Richard Cutler," he said as he looked into the barrel-chested Dutchman's hooded gray eyes. De Vries, Montgomery knew, was a protégé of Jan Vanderheyden, the legendary first director of Cutler & Sons' Far East operations. It was Vanderheyden's recommendation shortly before his death that had elevated De Vries from middle management to the lofty position he now held.

De Vries smiled. "Thank you, my young friend," he said in a slightly guttural accent. He gestured with his hands as he spoke, as though conducting an unseen orchestra. "I was sorry to miss you on your previous visit, but I had business in Singapore. I have heard your praises sung since my return, however, most of them from our young hostess for the evening." He looked past Montgomery. "Good evening, my dear."

Montgomery turned around, and there she was.

"Hello, Mr. Third Lieutenant Jonathan Montgomery," she greeted him warmly.

"Miss Daisy." His pulse quickened as he took in her silk evening gown, which exposed the smooth, unblemished skin of her shoulders and upper arms. Her thick golden hair was dressed in shiny ringlets, and a gold pendant hanging from a thin ribbon around her neck drew his attention, inevitably, to the swell of her breasts. "You are beautiful this evening, Miss Cutler, if I may be so bold."

"Oh, you may," she said.

On an irrepressible impulse he walked over to her, bowed in formal French court fashion, took her right hand in his, and pressed his lips against her silken flesh, allowing the kiss to linger as he raised his eyes to meet hers. Her skin had a faint yet pleasing flowery scent he did not recognize.

"*Charmant!*" De Vries exclaimed. "Bravo, Lieutenant Montgomery!"

Daisy's eyes twinkled, but she greeted his gallantry sweetly, with none of the arch teasing of their earlier encounter.

"Shall we?" Ben Cutler suggested into the ensuing silence, motioning down the hall.

The dining room, located next to the kitchen, was an equally attractive space. The long, rectangular table and twelve chairs were Chippendale, and the rug that covered nearly the entire floor was of Turkish design and manufacture. A large porcelain vase in the center of the table held colorful local flowers that perfumed the air. At one end of the table, where four place settings had been arranged, the flames of four candles in a silver candelabrum fluttered in the light breeze wafting in through two open windows.

Conversation was lively, and as the light supper of fish, local vegetables, and a delicate white Bordeaux was coming to an end, Montgomery fixed his eyes on Daisy, directly across the table from him and smiled. She returned his smile and nodded approvingly when her father, seated next to Montgomery, rose to his feet and raised his glass.

"To our guest," he exclaimed, looking down at Montgomery, "and to the United States Navy he represents and its efforts to eliminate piracy in these waters."

"Here, here!" Pieter De Vries bellowed. "Vell articulated, Mr. Cutler! Vell articulated! Let us now enjoy our dessert, my friends!"

At the close of the meal, Montgomery stood. "This has been a special evening for me," he declared. "The food was delicious and the wines superb. I thank you all for your kind hospitality. I am only sorry to see the food and the evening consumed."

He looked across the table at Daisy, then looked at her father. "Sir," he said, "might I request the honor of your daughter's company for a short stroll in the garden?"

Ben Cutler nodded knowingly. "Of course, Lieutenant. By all means, take my daughter outside and enjoy the fresh air with her. It will soon be dark and hard to see, so mind your step."

Montgomery did not miss the double meaning in Cutler's advice. "I shall, sir." He and Daisy excused themselves from the table. Montgomery gathered a lace shawl from a hall table and placed it around Daisy's bare shoulders before they walked outside through the rear entrance of the three-story building. The air had cooled with the sun's descent and carried the thick scents of night-blooming tropical flora. As they strolled on the wide path leading past a glade of stunted trees and flowering shrubs, Montgomery said, "I like your father, Daisy. Very much. I like Mr. De Vries too, but there is something special about your father."

"I quite agree," Daisy said. "He is a most unusual and gifted man. By the way, he feels the same about you, Jonty, and such praise does not come easily from him, especially when it concerns a young man who has shown an interest in me."

"You think I am interested in you?" he teased.

She kept her gaze straight ahead as they walked on. "I hope you are," she answered quietly.

He said nothing for a while, although his heart was racing. "Well, my lovely lady," he finally said, "I am indeed interested in you, I suspect more than you might imagine."

She nodded but still did not meet his gaze. "I can imagine quite a lot, Jonty. And my imagination has gone a bit wild since meeting you. I have imagined seeing you again and walking alone with you in the dusk." She finally lifted her eyes to his. "I realize that a well-bred young lady should not say such a thing to a young gentleman, but it happens to be the truth."

Jonty offered her his arm and said, "Daisy, may I ask you something? Something personal?"

"Of course. You may ask me anything."

"This evening has been utterly pleasurable in every way, but I must know: how exactly did my invitation to your home this evening come about?"

"What an odd question! What do you mean?"

"I mean just that." The hazel of his eyes met the blue of hers. He inhaled deeply. "You have met my captain, Terence Neale?"

"Yes, I have. He came here to pay his respects to my father after hearing about your visit to our home. A ship's captain looks after his young lieutenants, especially those he holds in high esteem."

"Me? In high esteem?"

"Yes, you. Does that surprise you?"

"A little. He has never said anything to me in that regard."

"Well, he wouldn't, would he? He is your superior officer."

"And he teased me with the invitation, implying that it was for him."

"Hmph. That was rather unkind. But the invitation was always to you, Jonty. I met Captain Neale when he was here. He is a charming man, and I was delighted to make his acquaintance. But most of all I was thrilled to hear him speak so highly of you. *I* was not surprised. Nor was my father."

"I am honored. Truly."

"As well you should be!" she teased. She nudged him with her shoulder.

They had reached the stone wall that marked the extent of private ownership. White lilies grew abundantly there at the end of the path, their aroma almost unbearably thick. "I don't mean to sound ungrateful," Montgomery said as they turned around to go back, "but just so I understand, why was the invitation originally sent to Captain Neale?"

Daisy looked down. Even in the deepening shadows of dusk, Montgomery could see she was blushing. "It was my idea," she said finally.

"*Your* idea? But why?"

"I thought if I sent the invitation with your captain, there would be a better chance that you would be allowed to accept it than if I sent it to you directly."

When Montgomery said nothing, Daisy's eyes widened. "What? You really thought that the invitation was meant for *him*? For Captain Neale?"

"Well, yes. That was what he implied, anyway," Montgomery confessed in embarrassment.

Daisy gave an unladylike snort. "Were you jealous?"

A pause, then: "Yes. I was."

She did not laugh or tease him as he had expected her to do. Instead, she said softly, "Thank you for admitting that, Jonty. I doubt many men would have."

As they approached the back verandah and the need to rejoin the others, Montgomery struggled to find the right words to say to her before surrendering their time alone together.

She turned to face him, her heart beating fast. "I care about you, Jonty," she said boldly, her words coming quickly. "I hope you understand that. Again, I may be too bold, but I don't care. I hardly know you, and yet I feel that I have known you for a very long time. Don't ask me to explain. I can't. What's more, I have come to believe in *you*. Above all, I don't want this—what I think we have found together—to end tonight." Her voice quavered as she spoke the last words.

He exhaled sharply. "Nor do I, Daisy! Dear God, nor do I!"

She closed her eyes as he drew her to him. Their embrace was gentle, their kiss tender but promising. As he pulled away to look at her, her hand touched his cheek in a caress so exquisite it caused him to tremble. Their next kiss was more urgent, but denying their mounting need, they reluctantly pulled apart as if by mutual accord and turned from the growing darkness to go inside.

CHAPTER 10

HINGHAM, MASSACHUSETTS
August 1847

The distance from Melinda Conner's home on South Street to Thomas Cutler's residence on Main Street was less than half a mile. The route took Richard Cutler toward the town center, where colonial-era buildings along South Street and parallel North Street offered local citizens a variety of shops and alehouses. There was as well the famous Anchor Inn, where, during the closing stages of the Revolutionary War, General Lafayette had met with Hingham resident Benjamin Lincoln, George Washington's second-in-command at Yorktown. At the intersection of South Street and Main Street, he took a sharp right onto Main. The Cutler family seat once occupied by Richard's great-grandparents was a hundred yards up on the left, not far beyond Old Ship's Church, a Puritan meetinghouse built in 1681 that was today the oldest house of worship in America.

"Good morning, Uncle," Richard hailed Thomas Cutler. Thomas was technically Richard's first cousin one generation removed, but they had long since settled on "uncle" as a more practical form of address, although the two men were only a decade apart in age.

Thomas had been working in his front yard garden but at the moment was leaning against the handle of his hoe. A confirmed bachelor, he was dressed casually in old-fashioned trousers tied below the knee and a loose-fitting cotton tunic; a wide-brimmed straw hat protected his head from the bright August sun. To Richard, he looked every bit the country squire from Concord, with no concerns beyond the proper tending of his vegetables and fruits.

Looks could be deceiving, however, as Richard was well aware. If he had declined the offer to assume control of Cutler & Sons, the honor would have passed to Thomas Edward Cutler. Had that been the case, the company would have remained in capable hands. Thomas was not a man of the sea, and he was by nature softspoken and laconic, but when he did speak, his words held substance. Of greater import, his business acumen and hard work and dedication to duty had served the family in good stead for many years.

Richard walked up to shake hands with him. "Gathering vegetables for the noontime meal?"

"Just fighting the weeds, my boy, or I'll have none to harvest." Thomas pulled off his hat and drew a faded handkerchief from his trouser pocket to mop his brow to its receding hairline. "Hot," he commented.

"A bit, yes. It's summer, after all. Will hasn't arrived yet?" Richard asked, referring to the third member of the Cutler & Sons brain trust.

"Not yet."

Richard consulted his pocket watch. "Eight-fifty-one. He still has nine minutes. He'll be here, right on time."

"I reckon he will."

"How is he doing? I haven't been able to spend much time with him for a while."

Thomas, again mopping his brow, said, "I reckon he's doing all right. A bit in despair about our younger generation."

"Why so?"

"You know why, Richard," Thomas said, tucking his kerchief in his pants pocket. "Or at least you've heard something about it. Since the recent family meeting he's heard a heap of dissent from young 'uns reluctant to speak out publicly. Not all of 'em, certainly, but enough to make a united front."

"You're referring to his ban on opium transport."

"I am. The company is losing a good deal of money by refusing to carry it. I appreciate how difficult it can be to part company with money, but I have plenty to live on and make me happy. All the family members do—for the moment, at least. But in the future? After you and I and those of our generation are dead and gone? That's what the young 'uns want to know. They want assurances that our sacrificing profits today won't doom them to poverty in the future."

Richard shook his head. "There can be no such assurances. It's not a matter of revenues and profits. It's a matter of how we as a family and we as individuals choose to conduct our lives and our business."

Thomas nodded thoughtfully. "That's how Will sees it. It's how I see it, too. As for the others, well, we'll have to wait and see. We all choose the principles in life we wish to live by."

Richard was about to comment further when a glance down Main Street revealed the aging family patriarch making his way up Main Street toward them.

"Good day, William," Thomas greeted the older man when William had joined him and Richard. "You're a minute late. But pay no mind, we forgive you. Do come and refresh yourself. I suggest we sit under the elm trees out yonder in the shade. It's too damn hot inside, and a breeze is kicking in. I'll ask Ibby to bring out beverages. What's your pleasure, Will?"

"Anything that's not warmed over flames."

"I'm with you on that. Richard?"

"The same, thank you."

"Right. I'll make it three."

As Thomas went in the front door to find his housekeeper, William and Richard walked around the house to the spacious backyard set off from its neighbors by a six-foot-high wooden fence that protected it from curious gawkers and unruly neighborhood dogs. The six stately elms spaced six feet apart in two rows provided welcome shade. William gestured toward four high-back, wide-elbowed wooden chairs that his father, Caleb, had constructed long ago, a source of pride now for Caleb's only child, Thomas.

"I saw Anne in town yesterday," William said to Richard after they were settled. "She had Jamie and Sydney in tow, and Rachel, of course. I can't believe how much those two young 'uns have grown. Soon enough

Sydney will be riding a horse and shooing off the young lads chasing after her."

Richard grinned. "They are indeed growing up fast," he agreed. "Too fast. I took Jamie out for another sailing lesson yesterday. He is learning the ropes far quicker than I did at his age. He's a born sailor, to the point of raising a ruckus when it's time to come about and head for shore. I swear the lad would rather sail than eat."

"Just like his grandfather and father. Adventuring is in our blood, I'm afraid."

"I suppose so, though I think my adventuring days are about over. After this next trip to Batavia I plan to stay closer to home."

Thomas emerged through the back door carrying a small tray with three tall glasses of lemon water. He set the tray on a sawn-off tree trunk that served as a table and handed around the glasses.

"Right, then," Thomas said firmly. "To the business at hand. I want you both to know that I have been invited by Mayor Quincy to serve on a special committee." The other two men nodded. Josiah Quincy Jr., a Whig politician from a prominent local family, had represented Massachusetts in the state legislature, served as secretary of state for Massachusetts, and was currently serving as the twelfth mayor of Boston.

"What sort of committee?"

"A committee to stop the importation and use of opium, Richard. The *Boston Medical and Surgical Journal's* recent report on the ravages of opium on the human body and the body politic says all you need to know. The mayor wants to obliterate the stuff and keep it from crossing our borders. If we succeed, other states may follow our example. And maybe then the federal government will be persuaded to take a stand. Much fruit can be grown from a small kernel."

"Who else is serving on the committee?"

"There will be ten in total, Thomas. Most of them will be influential citizens who live in the greater Boston area. Two have already answered the call. One is John Hudson," referring to the headmaster of Derby Academy. "So far, he is the only other Hingham representative on the committee. In addition, we have the Reverend John Jacobs," referring to the celebrated rector of St. Paul's Episcopal Church in Boston. "I understand that Jared Sparks, president of Harvard College, has expressed a strong interest, as has a member of the Crowninshield family in Salem. Charles Devens, our current senator, has also expressed an interest. Governor Quincy will announce the final slate in another month or so."

"A distinguished lot," William agreed. "Good men, all."

"And a worthy cause," Richard put in. "My congratulations on being invited, Uncle. It's a singular honor."

Thomas gave him a wry smile. "It's results I want, Richard, not accolades. You have two young children. I know you appreciate the importance of what we're about."

Richard nodded as William asked, "How do you intend to achieve those results?"

"That is for the full committee to determine once it's seated. I'm giving you fair warning that I will be calling on you both to assist when and where needed. I fear that if we do not act soon, Massachusetts and much of our country will go the way of China. The Qing emperor may be a ruthless bastard when it comes to keeping his people in check, but when it comes to opium and other drugs, we should follow his lead and make the stuff illegal. You know the issues involved, so there's no point in me repeating them. It is absolutely appalling that a twelve-year-old boy in Boston can walk into any apothecary today and walk out with as much opium as he has money to purchase, no questions asked."

"You can count on the family to support you in any way we can, Thomas. Better than anyone else, you know my position on the dangers of the opium trade. As I have said on numerous occasions, I want no part of it."

"Nor do I, William. Nor does Mayor Quincy. But it is not simply a matter of passing a law. There are ramifications. Boston receives considerable tax revenues from the importation of opium, and we earmark a share of that money for public projects that benefit our people. The money will have to come from other sources. Meanwhile, our so-called leaders do nothing to address the issue. They spew nonsense and line their pockets while people are dying. It's an abomination, I tell you! Respectable citizens of Boston are turning into worthless sots right before our very eyes! Surely we can find other sources of funding for these projects that do

not compel us to witness the slow decay of our society and way of life."
Thomas sat back and mopped his brow.

William and Richard exchanged amused glances. Thomas had his
dander up to a level rarely seen.

"Sorry for the rant, gentlemen, but this is a subject of some importance to me, as I know it is to you and to all God-fearing men." He lifted
his glass and sipped the cool water to soothe his throat, then said, "Other
topics for discussion?"

When neither William nor Richard spoke, Thomas continued, "In
that case, if Richard is amenable, I'll ask him to summarize for us his
impressions of Cutler & Sons after his first three months in office and
thoughts he might have for going forward. Just a summary, if you please.
You will have ample opportunity to expand on your findings and recommendations at the next family conference in October."

"Of course, Uncle," Richard replied. After a fifteen-minute overview
of the company's finances he concluded with, "So, as you can see, thus far
I have concentrated on becoming more familiar with our current policies
and procedures in America and the West Indies. In a word, what we have
in place today should continue to sustain us for many years to come. But
there is always room for improvement. We must avoid complacency. I will
delay making any significant recommendations concerning our Far East
operations until I have made the trip to Batavia and conferred with Pieter
De Vries and Ben Cutler. For better or worse, we should recognize that
change is coming. Before I can offer suggestions for how to capitalize on
that change, and to gain a better perspective on our opportunities, I need
to study what the competition is doing. And I need to spend time in the
Orient, where nearly half our revenues are currently being generated."

"Glad to hear you say that, Richard," William asserted. "I of course
agree with you. I have had my tours of duty there. So has Thomas. So
have you, of course, though in a different context. When do you sail?"

"By year's end, likely. I assume you and Thomas will stand in for me
while I am gone?"

"Of course," William assured him, "if the family will have us. I regret
that your voyage will take you away from your wife and children for much
of next year, but it can't be helped. I wish that we had a steam-powered

vessel in our merchant fleet to speed your trip. We are eagerly awaiting your suggestions on that, by the way."

"I agree that steam power is the future, but even a partial conversion to steam will entail a considerable investment," Richard pointed out. "We don't need to rush into it. Wind power will be with us for a long time to come. Today, steam power is for the Navy." He added with a smile, "I will be able to give you a firsthand report on steamships when I return, because I will be making the voyage to Batavia on a naval steam frigate."

"Do say! Which one?"

"I'm not yet sure. But whichever ship she is, she will be commanded by my friend and former executive officer Jack Brengle."

Thomas arched his eyebrows. "Brengle? Is he not stationed in the Gulf of Mexico?"

"He was. On blockade duty. But there is nothing left to blockade. The United States Navy and the Texas Navy have seen to that. According to a letter I received from Jack last week, Commodore Perry captured Villahermosa, the last port city in enemy hands along the Mexican Gulf Coast. Jack played a key role in that battle, and I look forward to hearing the details. He also said that General Taylor and General Scott are on the march toward Mexico City, the federal capital. The Mexican army and marines have so far offered only token resistance. When the fortress at Chapultepec falls, Mexico City will fall, and the war will be over."

Thomas held up a fist. "That is excellent news," he said. "But Mexico to the Far East is a big change. How did Brengle manage to get command of a steam vessel going to the Far East? That's a very big change of station."

"Jack saw the writing on the wall months ago and put in for a transfer to the East India Squadron. Apparently, he was bitten by the same bug that bit Jonty Montgomery, and he wants to get back there. It was his idea that we sail together in his new command, assuming I had reason to sail to Batavia. It will be his last assignment in the Navy before he resigns his commission and joins Cutler & Sons."

"He will be a very welcome addition to the company," William said. "But will the Navy approve his request to resign? And what about your own request? You still hold the rank of captain, do you not?" Richard nodded. "Then you will need the Navy to release you, as well."

"It's a formality only. I will get it, and so will Jack. Secretary Bancroft has already assured me of that."

"Well then, that appears to settle the matter," Thomas said with a smile. "And it settles our business here."

William raised his hand. "It does, except for one more item. Has either of you heard recently from Lucy?"

"Our Lucy, Anne Seymour's granddaughter?" Thomas asked.

"Yes," William said. "My sister is worried about her. She seems to be avoiding contact with the family."

Thomas frowned. "Well, she has always been a high-spirited girl who flaunts her unconventional thinking. Almost thirty years old and still not married! Her grandmother is often worried about her, and always for no reason. What has the lass been up to this time?"

"To my knowledge, nothing," William responded tersely. "Although she has not been home in a while, and messages sent to Regis House have apparently been returned unopened. Her grandmother may be needlessly concerned, I grant you, but given Lucy's sometimes odd behavior, we are in no position to take chances. What do you think, Richard?"

Richard nodded. "I am sailing to Boston on Friday to meet with Charles Henley. I'll drop by Regis House and see what I can find out."

Chapter 11

Boston, Massachusetts
August 1847

The sunlight filtering through the low gray clouds added an eerie, luminous quality to the mists hovering over the calm harbor. Scattered rain during the night had added to the clammy humidity. Another dank, dreary day was in store for Boston. Even the tops of the tallest trees were lifeless.

None of this was lost on Lucy Cutler Seymour as she made her way along Commercial Street. Though she certainly would not call herself a sailor—no women of breeding did—she prided herself on her knowledge of weather and nautical protocols. Not long ago, she had even considered making the sea her life as an active member of Cutler & Sons. When on board a ship and under way, Lucy's mood lifted as a sail to the wind and her confidence soared. Notwithstanding the superstitions most sailors harbored about having a woman onboard a ship at sea, Lucy was allowed to participate in appropriate ways within the Cutler family of seafaring men. Her presence lightened the mood on any vessel, and her navigational skills were welcome on any bridge. She thought she might have found her niche, however odd that niche would be for a woman.

That all changed during a cruise to Stonington, Connecticut, to deliver a load of lumber for a client. While she fought to block the memory from her consciousness, it still came back to her when she was helpless in dreams. She was belowdecks making an inventory. A sudden movement behind her, then she was pushed against the bulkhead. A dirty hand clapped over her mouth. The man tearing at her dress. An older man, newly mustered, with shifty eyes. She had disliked him on sight. "I'll just take a minute of your time, pretty miss." Breath smelling of whiskey and rotten teeth. Fighting, fighting. Then: "Here, now. What's going on here? Hold, you bastard." Free to move, she pushed past the two men and raced above decks. She locked herself in the owner's cabin and remained there for the remainder of the voyage, refusing to speak, refusing all food and water.

Lucy steadfastly refused to say anything about the attack or press charges, perhaps not wishing to besmirch her own character, but the change in her was clear and immediate. Although he was not formally charged, Cates, the newly mustered sailor, mysteriously appeared with a swollen eye and cut upper lip he claimed to have received when he fell headfirst down a companionway. Without Lucy coming forward there was little the Cutler family could do beyond expelling Cates from Cutler & Sons with a stern warning never again to set foot on a Cutler vessel. Not since that fateful cruise had Lucy stepped aboard another merchant vessel. She became quiet and withdrawn, trusting no one and avoiding male company.

At the intersection with State Street she paused to watch the activity on Long Wharf, such as it was on a Sunday morning. Ship stores and counting houses were closed; save for a few men on-loading or off-loading cargo from ships tied up at dockside, it was as quiet there as in the city proper. Out to sea, beyond the ninety-foot-tall lighthouse on Little Brewster Island, she recognized a jaunty three-masted schooner under full sail. *Sea Miss*, captained by an old family friend, Luke Fenwick, was making her slow turn to port to shape a course Down East. Judging by the frequent luff of her sails, the breeze out there was not much stronger than the breeze in the harbor. On an impulse, Lucy waved to sailors on board who likely knew her but could not possibly have seen her. Releasing a heavy sigh, she resumed her walk as church bells throughout Boston started ringing out a call to worship.

* * *

Twenty-five Beach Street was a nondescript address in a nondescript part of the city. Located down Washington Street a short distance from the Boston Common, the building sat on land reclaimed from tidal flats, as was most of neighboring and more affluent Back Bay. Originally settled by Anglo-Bostonians, it had been resettled in turn by Irish, Jewish, Italian, and, recently, Chinese immigrants who liked what the area had to offer: a well-defined cultural enclave situated near Beacon Hill and other fashionable neighborhoods whose residents possessed the wherewithal to support entrepreneurial ventures.

When Harlan Sturgis saw Lucy approaching the modest dwelling that housed his local operations, he swung open the door and called out to her. "Top of the morning, Lucy. You are right on time, as always."

"Good morning, Mr. Sturgis," Lucy returned when she reached the door. She jerked away when he placed a hand on her shoulder.

"Now, Lucy," he bantered unctuously, "I thought we agreed that you would call me Harlan. You make me feel old and useless when you call me Mr. Sturgis, and I am neither of those things. I wager my vitality and stamina would both please and impress you given the opportunity."

She stiffened and met his gaze squarely. "My answer to you today is the same as it was yesterday. I will continue to call you Mr. Sturgis. Ours is a business relationship and will never be anything more."

She held his eyes until he blinked and looked aside. "Very well, have it your way," he groused. "Come inside. We have business to discuss downstairs. No need to doff your coat. I shan't keep you long. It's Sunday after all, a day of rest." He barked a laugh.

The building she entered belonged to a Chinese couple from Shanghai known as the Chens. Chen was not their Christian name, but like their first names it was too difficult for most Westerners to pronounce. To their clients they were simply Kimball and Sarah Chen.

The man Lucy knew as Simon was seated in the shadows near the stairway leading downstairs. Sturgis had explained to her early on that either Simon, Gus, or Toby was stationed there at all hours to ensure security and propriety. Lucy had doubted that explanation but said nothing to challenge it.

Lucy ignored Simon's deferential nod as she followed Sturgis downstairs and into a well-appointed room that was furnished with cushioned sofas, each with an oblong teak table next to it. On each table was a tray of paraphernalia related to opium use: long-stemmed ivory and silver pipes; separate pipe bowls made of blue and white porcelain or jade, most of them inlaid with intricate designs; and a brass or silver oil lamp.

Though she did not use opium herself, Lucy knew the drill, having witnessed it on several prior occasions. After an opium "pill" was placed in a bowl and set atop the funnel of the oil lamp—a funnel designed to channel the required amount of heat under the bowl—the opium inside the bowl began to vaporize. The smoker, reclining on a sofa, would then attach the bowl to a pipe stem and inhale the vapors. After a short while he—or she—would be transported into a "pipe dream." The method was simple yet highly effective. And highly addictive. Repeat customers were the bread and butter of an opium den first-timers.

Sturgis had taken great pains and spared no expense to ensure that his customers returned. No bamboo pipes for them, he explained to Lucy. Far too common. His opium was of the highest grade and came from Turkey routed through China. The paraphernalia to work the opium came straight from China, as did the couches, rugs, wall hangings with Chinese characters, and decorative porcelain vases. Even the staff of silk-robed female attendants came from China via the port of San Francisco.

"The decor and equipment that define the heart of an opium establishment must reflect the financial means of the clientele you are seeking to attract," Sturgis had lectured. It was his mantra, and as far as Lucy could tell he was growing rich from it.

It being Sunday morning, there was no one else in the chamber save for two attendants doing last-minute touch-ups before the door opened for business at one o'clock. Sturgis crossed the room, fished in his pocket for a small ring of keys, selected one, inserted it in a keyhole, and opened the door into the small, spartan chamber that served as his private office. Slumping onto a wide-elbowed chair that squeaked when he put his weight on it, he reached for the small desk and opened its center drawer. Because there was no other chair in the room, Lucy stood.

"This is for you," Sturgis said curtly as he dropped a thick leather pouch on the desk.

Lucy eyed the pouch skeptically. "What's in it?"

"Your compensation."

"How much?"

"Fifty dollars."

Although she quickly recovered from her astonishment, her tone reflected her surprise. "*Fifty dollars?* To what do I owe this windfall?"

"Why, for your services, my dear. I told you at the outset that I would reward you handsomely if you brought in the patrons who bring in the money. That you have done, and you have done it discreetly. How you have managed to do that without arousing suspicion I do not know. Nor do I wish to know. I am asking no questions and I expect no answers." He pointed at the pouch on the table. "Keep doing what you are doing, keep talking up the den to your friends and acquaintances, and I shall soon double that amount. It will be much more than that should you ever change your mind and agree to procure . . . additional services for my customers. You know what I am referring to."

"Of course I know what you are referring to. You are wasting your breath. My answer is no and will always be no."

Sturgis shrugged. "Suit yourself." He pushed the pouch across the desk toward her. "Take the money. It's yours. Well earned."

"Thank you." She lifted the pouch, which contained an amount equal to an annual salary for many people.

"Count it if you like," he said offhandedly. "I shan't be offended."

Lucy pocketed the pouch. "That won't be necessary,"

"Well, thank you for that, at least," Sturgis said. He rose to his feet and drew a breath. "You are doing a fine job, Lucy. I mean that sincerely. In just a few short months your efforts have allowed me to recoup my entire investment. Do you know what that means? It means that from this day forward it's all gravy, save for paying normal day-to-day expenses. Unlike your aunt who refused to put her faith in me, you could have your fair share of that gravy, if only—"

"Yes," Lucy interrupted, making to leave. "If only. Good day to you, Mr. Sturgis."

* * *

"How do you find the accounts, Captain Cutler?" Charles Henley asked. "Are you pleased? Have you any questions?"

Richard rubbed his eyes with his thumb and index finger, then glanced up from the heavy leatherbound book he had been perusing for the past three hours. The thick book was filled with carefully crafted figures relating to Cutler & Sons' global business activity and performance. Reviewing and interpreting these figures was not necessarily a pleasant task, but Richard knew that it was a necessary one.

"Entirely, Charles," Richard said to the Boston director of Cutler & Sons. "It's a lot to take in, but I am making progress thanks to your tireless explanations and your saintlike patience with a dullard like me. Cutler & Sons is clearly in good hands. I have learned a lot from you."

"Not at all," Henley said dismissively. "My job is to itemize and report what your family and crews produce, and to ensure that everyone is compensated fairly for their efforts. Could I offer you tea or some other beverage? You've been hard at it for two days, and it's Sunday, remember? You should rest."

Richard consulted his watch. "Nothing at the moment, thank you, Charles. I am planning to take afternoon tea with my cousin."

"Oh? Might I summon a conveyance for you?"

Richard shook his head. "No need. Regis House is a short walk from here. I'll be off as soon as I square this last row of numbers and then spruce up."

"Regis House? Ah, so it is Miss Lucy you are off to see. Please send her my kind regards. I hope you will have a quiet and relaxing afternoon."

Richard smiled ruefully. "Not much chance of that, I'm afraid. You know Lucy."

"I do know her, and I wish I had more opportunities to see her. A sprightly lass. She'll make quite a real catch for some fortunate young man. Were I fifty years younger, I'd give that fellow a run for his money."

* * *

When the Cutler packet boat had docked at Long Wharf two days earlier, the first thing Richard had done was to walk down Commercial Street, through Faneuil Hall, to the Federalist-style brick edifice of Regis House. Finding Lucy away, he left a note with the landlady, a woman of strict sensibilities named Miss MacAleer. The note informed Lucy that he would drop by for a visit on Sunday afternoon at three and wished to speak with her then. He hoped they might share a pot of tea at Murray's.

She was waiting for him in the front hallway when his footsteps rang on the front veranda at precisely three o'clock and she heard his muffled voice soothing Brutus, the guard dog stationed there to protect the young ladies inside. She got up from the settee to greet him as he opened the front door.

He looked solid and reliable, as always. He was dressed, as she was, in clothing of understated elegance. He was clean shaven, and his shoulder-length chestnut hair was neatly parted left to right. Nothing about him suggested he was a high-ranking naval officer, just as nothing about her suggested that she was a member of a wealthy Boston shipping family.

Richard removed his tricorne hat. "Hello, Lucy," he said. "I am happy to see someone I care about looking so well."

"And you, Cousin," she said pleasantly. "I am pleased to see you."

He glanced over her shoulder. "Good afternoon, Miss MacAleer," he said to the diminutive concierge who had emerged from her office two rooms down the hallway, apparently to find out who the caller might be. "I was hoping to have the pleasure of seeing you."

"Thank you, Captain Cutler," she replied stiffly. "A pleasure to see you as well." Without further comment, she turned on her heel and disappeared into her office, closing the door behind her.

"Talkative as always," Richard remarked conspiratorially when he and Lucy were alone on the veranda. "But she keeps a sharp eye on things around here, and for that I am grateful."

Lucy stifled a laugh that Richard had rarely heard from her in recent years. "What's funny?" he inquired.

"I'll let you in on a little secret," Lucy said. "I think Miss MacAleer is sweet on you. The poor woman just doesn't know how to express herself properly to a gentleman, so she runs and hides. Now, Brutus here knows how to greet you," she added, stroking the fur of the black-and-white bulldog tethered to a sturdy stake in the yard. "He barks at everyone else. But not at you. Look at him. He's slobbering all over you. You must have something other visitors do not."

"I do," Richard said. "I have my beloved cousin to accompany me to afternoon tea." He offered her his arm, and she slipped her hand through the crook of his elbow. Together they walked in silence toward Faneuil Hall.

Murray's had been a favorite haunt of the Cutler family since before the Revolution, when Thomas Cutler, the original family patriarch, had billed it "the finest eating establishment in Boston." The stone and timber building offered a sense of stability and perpetuity as well as good home cooking and spirits, and joviality to patrons of all classes and ages. The interior was cool and candle-lit even on sunny summer days such as this one, and the dining tables were communal, long, and often untidy, to no one's displeasure. That and the raucous behavior of the largely female serving staff were essential parts of the dining experience. Their friendly banter kept people coming back for more.

Because it was midafternoon, Richard and Lucy had no trouble finding an empty table that afforded a semblance of privacy at its far end. Once they were seated, a burly waitress with ample bosom and derrière came over to take their order. Lucy ordered a stein of Yuengling beer. Richard followed suit and asked for a plate of sandwiches.

Richard watched the waitress go, then turned and grinned across the table at Lucy. His smile faded. "What is it, Lucy?" he asked with real concern. "Something is troubling you. What is it?"

When she continued staring down at the table, he said, "You are not talking just to your cousin here, you know. You are also talking to a friend who cares about you and would do anything to help you."

She nodded, "I know you would. And I know why you have come to see me today."

"You do? Can I not just take my favorite cousin to tea?"

She shook her head. "You are worried about me. My family is worried about me."

"I can't deny that. Is there cause for worry?"

She hesitated. "I suppose the answer to that question depends on your perspective."

The beer and sandwiches arrived, placed before them without fanfare. When the waitress left, Richard asked, "Is there a man involved?"

Her eyebrows shot up. "No!"

"Sure about that?"

"Quite sure!"

"What, then?"

Again she looked down, toying with her stein. Moments passed. Across the room a waitress erupted in bawdy laughter, apparently at something a male patron had proposed to her.

"Would you like to go somewhere else? Someplace quieter?"

She shook her head. "No. I like this place. It's fine."

Another interlude of silence followed as each pretended to eat.

"Look, Lucy," Richard said, leaning forward when the silence became awkward. "I am not going to pry. I respect you too much to do that. But understand that nothing you might have done or might say to me today could possibly change how I feel about you. If you want to tell me something, please do so. If you don't want to, then I suggest we—"

"I have taken a position," Lucy blurted out.

Richard blinked. "A position? What sort of position?"

"A position that pays me fifty dollars a month."

Richard's jaw dropped. "Fifty dollars a month! That's more than we pay the master of a merchant vessel." Suddenly it struck him with a sickening blow. The professions that paid a young woman that kind of money were few. "Who is paying you this money?"

Lucy looked away. "I'm sorry, Richard. I can't tell you that."

"Why?"

"I gave my word that I would not."

"To whom?"

"Obviously I can't tell you that, either."

Richard studied her. "Are you being threatened?"

"No. Not as such."

"Lucy, you're not . . ." His face, flushed with embarrassment, finished the sentence for him.

"Richard! No!" she hissed. "Certainly not. I would never do that."

Richard exhaled slowly. Only one other possibility came to mind. "I believe you, Lucy. But may I assume that this position involves some other unsavory activity?"

She looked away but said nothing.

"Does it involve the opium trade?"

She swallowed hard but said nothing.

"Lucy, why? You don't need the money. Your share of the family business is a generous amount. And there are many opportunities for a woman of your capabilities if you wish to occupy your time profitably. Just this afternoon Charles Henley said to me that he wished *he* could hire you. He would, you know. If you want a job, we could find you a good one either at Cutler & Sons or at some other reputable establishment in Boston." He held up a hand to forestall her objection. "You wouldn't have to get on a ship. You could live exactly as you do now but without the fear and the risks and, I suspect, the emotional stress. You are so loved, my dear."

"I know," she whispered.

"So, why . . . opium, is it?"

Lucy had her answer ready. "Opium is not so bad, Richard. It's neither evil nor illegal. I'm told that even Queen Victoria uses it."

"It's said that she does, yes, but in moderation and only under certain circumstances. Opium is not yet illegal, true. But it most certainly *is* evil. I know people who use too much of it, and the result is always the same. They become addicted, and it becomes a vicious cycle. The more you use, the more you want to use. The more money you have, the more money you spend on it. Fathers are no longer able to feed and shelter their families. They spend everything they have on opium, not because they enjoy smoking it but because they can't live without it. Their families are put out on the street, penniless. Little children suddenly find themselves the objects of scorn and derision with no escape, nowhere to go. Many of them become thieves or prostitutes. Their health deteriorates. Do you want to have that on your conscience? Those poor children? Is all that suffering worth fifty dollars a month?" A horrific thought struck him. "You're not *taking* the damn stuff, are you?

"No, Richard, I am not," she replied emphatically.

"Well, that's a relief." He looked across the table at her. "Lucy, will you promise to think about what I just said? Will you do me that one favor? And will you trust me to always do and say what I believe is in your best interest?"

Her nod of assent, when it came, was so slight that it was almost imperceptible. Richard could do no more today, but the matter was far from settled in his mind.

CHAPTER 12

HONG KONG, SOUTH CHINA SEA
August 1847

The stamp of bare feet on the deck above his head woke him. He lay supine on his bunk listening. He heard no cry signaling the approach of land or an unidentified vessel. The familiar thrum of the steam engine belowdecks assured him that the repairs made in Batavia were holding. The slow cruise north had been delayed as a result of those repairs, but there had been no choice in the matter. Their progress was further slowed by the four boats they were towing behind them.

Lieutenant Jonathan Montgomery glanced at the Rotherham pocket watch laid out on the table beside him and noted the time: 4:34. Nearly five hours had passed since he had been relieved as senior watch officer, and a mere twenty-six minutes remained before the wardroom steward would rap on his door and the doors of the other commissioned officers.

Montgomery reached for the kerchief next to the watch and mopped beads of sweat from his face. "Bloody steam bath," he muttered under his breath. "What was I thinking to request a transfer to this godforsaken swamp?" He thought about getting up, shaving, and donning the light cotton undress uniform the officers were permitted to wear in these oppressive conditions. At least then he could go topside where the air was breathable. But a sudden shift in course coaxed a refreshing breeze into his cabin and he laid back on the cot, cupped his hands beneath his head, and stared up at the bulkhead, thoughts of his last evening with Daisy streaming through his mind.

"I realize your life is not your own in the Navy, Jonty, but please promise me that you will find some way to come back to me!"

Their final embrace in the garden, her scent filling his senses, had kindled passions that threatened to undo them both, until an inbred sense of propriety bid them reluctantly apart and inside to where Ben Cutler and Pieter De Vries were waiting for them. The nights since had been torture for him. He wondered if it was the same for her.

When they said goodbye at the docks of Batavia Harbor, he had sworn upon his sacred honor that he would come back—not just *to* her but *for* her. He would take her away and make a new life with her in America. Although they barely knew one another and had no reason to believe that Montgomery's duties *would* bring him back to Batavia, he had spoken with such conviction that she believed him absolutely, had clung to him as though her will alone could make it so. As the ship's boat had returned him to *Columbia* he forced himself to sit rigidly in the stern sheets, staring ahead and not back at her.

A light rap on his cabin door broke into the reverie.

"Come."

A young midshipman opened the door and stepped inside. "Two bells, sir," he said with a salute. "The captain's compliments, and he requests your presence at an officers' meeting at four bells, here in the wardroom. I thought you might want this in the meantime." He held out a mug of steaming black coffee. "Cook will have coffee and food on the table then, but I thought I'd jump the gun on him, knowing you were on watch duty earlier."

Montgomery gratefully took the cup and breathed in the heavenly aroma. "You are a saint, Bartlett," he said after sampling the rich brew. "Consider yourself promoted to admiral." He took another sip and nodded approvingly. "After this I can wait to eat, knowing that whatever our cook cooks, Cook sure can cook!"

Bartlett chuckled as expected at the stale joke. Jeremy Cook, the wardroom steward, was the son of an African American sailor and a Creole woman he met in Martinique. Wherever young Jeremy had learned his trade, he had learned it well, and regardless of his failings as a mariner, the quip "Cook sure can cook" in all its variations was a constant refrain in *Columbia's* wardroom. Captain Neale, whose rank required a personal steward, often remarked after being invited to the wardroom for supper that his officers had been dealt the better hand.

At 6:00, however, Captain Neale was all business. "Good morning, gentlemen," he said to his three commissioned officers, the red-haired captain of Marines, and four of the ship's complement of seven midshipmen who had gathered around the large wardroom table at which the commissioned and senior warrant officers ate their meals. Against the bulkhead behind them, in a U-shaped sequence, were the officers' cabins, the size and position of each cabin dependent upon rank. The midshipmen's spartan quarters were down on the orlop, the lowest of *Columbia's* four decks, a time-honored purgatory for all "young gentlemen."

"Please be seated," Neale said.

The eight officers sat down and scraped their chairs in toward the table. Neale remained standing.

"Please help yourselves to coffee. We shall leave the rest of Cook's delicacies until after our briefing. Let me begin by summarizing our situation. British and Chinese intelligence sources indicate that a pirate fleet of between thirty and forty war junks is somewhere ahead. Exactly where ahead we cannot be certain. The information is fairly old, and there are no semaphores anywhere nearby. The pirate fleet was last sighted south of Hong Kong. If it's still in these waters—and it may well be, given the number of coves and inlets the ships can duck into—we should spot them later this morning. If not, we'll go in search of them. It is no easy task to conceal thirty ships, whatever the circumstances. But whatever the circumstances might be, we'll be ready for them.

"At our present rate of speed—five knots, give or take, about the best we can safely manage with boars in tow—we should raise Hong Kong by the start of the forenoon watch. As we approach Hong Kong from the south, the British squadron will be approaching from the east. If neither squadron sights the pirates, we will combine forces and steam west from Guangzhou. We will find the pirates and the merchant vessels they have seized," he said with strong assurance. "When we do, we will attack.

"You know your assignments, and I have every confidence in your ability to carry them out. Nonetheless, we shall review your orders now.

CHAPTER 12

The only change since our last briefing is that Lieutenant Bowen and Lieutenant Montgomery are switching roles. Mr. Bowen is now in command of the gun deck here in *Columbia*, and Mr. Montgomery is in command of boat number six. You have all been trained to fill any role on this ship, so this shift should cause no difficulties. Now is the time to pour a second cup of coffee if you wish."

An hour later, Montgomery emerged on the quarterdeck along with the first and second officers. Though the air was thick and humid, a persistent southwesterly breeze provided a measure of relief after the stifling wardroom.

"Good morning, Mr. Dean," William Bowen greeted the sailing master, who was holding court at the wheel along with two midshipmen and a quartermaster's mate. "The captain will be on deck presently."

"Aye, aye, sir," Dean acknowledged.

"Our course and speed?"

"Course, due north. Speed, four knots."

"Any sign of the British squadron?"

Dean glanced up at the foremast crosstrees, where Ameus Hughes, an able seaman with keen eyesight, was keeping watch. When the British ships came into view, word of it would come first from him. "Nothing yet, sir."

"Very well. Steady as she goes, Mr. Dean."

"Steady as she goes aye, sir."

Montgomery glanced astern at the four wide-beamed open boats following *Columbia* like ducklings in a row. Each whaler-like boat was forty feet long, registered five tons, and featured a single sturdy platform amidships on which was mounted a howitzer. The cannon-like weapons were lighter than the ship's cannons, with narrower muzzles that could fire either on a level trajectory, like a cannon, or be elevated up to thirty degrees to lob shells at close range over a wall, earthworks, or a ship's transom. In reasonable seas, each boat could carry ten oarsmen, five to a side, and fifteen Marines. Each carried a mast as well, but those were dismantled and stowed beneath the thwarts. Number six boat, the second in line, was Montgomery's command. It wasn't much, but it was his first command, and he felt a surge of pride looking at it.

The battle plan called for boats five and six from the American squadron and boats one and two from the British squadron to lead the assault. The four other boats would hold position a short distance away and concentrate howitzer and rifle fire upon the enemy vessels until called upon either to reinforce the attack boats or to take personnel and prisoners off the junks. *Columbia* and HMS *Rattlesnake*, unable to steam far into the shallow bay, would stand by in deeper water with their greater firepower trained on the action. It was a battle plan devised by the British commodore based on his experience chasing down Chinese and Japanese pirates.

At two bells in the morning watch, the cry came down from above. "Deck there!"

Midshipman Samuel Hallowell, stationed at the base of the foremast, cupped his hands around his mouth. "Deck here! What do you see, Hughes?"

"Tai Mo Shan, sir," came the reply.

There was no possibility of error. Tai Mo Shan was the highest peak in the mountainous terrain of central Hong Kong, rising a mile and a half above sea level. From his perch on a ship's crosstrees, one hundred feet above the weather deck, Hughes could see its peak from sixty miles away.

"Very good, Hughes," Hallowell shouted back, "I shall inform Mr. Chadwick," referring to the second lieutenant currently serving as senior watch officer. Chadwick, in turn, informed the captain on the quarterdeck. No one on the deck could see the high peak, of course. Not yet. It would take several more hours of sailing for that to happen. There was a surprise in store for *Columbia* when it came.

"Sails ho!" the lookout suddenly cried out. He was standing with one hand wrapped around the upper mast, his other hand balancing a small long glass to his eye.

"Where away?" Hallowell called up.

Hughes pointed. "Dead ahead, sir! In the southern approaches," he said urgently.

"Junks?"

"Aye. All junks."

"How many?"

"A whole fleet of them, sir." Hughes paused to estimate the number of ominous-looking three-masted vessels. "I estimate between thirty and forty vessels! More are entering the bay from the east! And sir, I have the British squadron in sight, steaming west on a course of convergence!"

"Very well."

Hallowell quickstepped aft. Neale, on the quarterdeck, had already heard the exchange. In the distance ahead, the contours of Hong Kong and the islands in the large bay began to take form.

To a midshipman standing by, Neale said, "Pass word for the bo'sun!" A moment later, to the quartermaster at the wheel. "Keller!"

"Sir!"

"Aim for Lantau Island." The largest of the 230 islands making up the land mass of Hong Kong, Lantau Island dominated the western edge of the bay and Hong Kong Island on its eastern edge. The islands were shaped like two great crusher claws of a mammoth stone crab. "If these vessels are pirates, we must cut off their retreat to westward!"

"Aye, Captain!" Keller responded.

The boatswain appeared, a short, muscular man with a thick neck and arms to match. Around his neck hung a silver whistle, the sole indication of his rank apart from his black narrow-brimmed top hat. "Captain?" he said, saluting.

"Prepare to man the boats, Reeves. At my command!"

"Sir!"

As Reeves went forward to instruct his mates, Neale addressed his executive officer. "Mr. Bowen?"

Bowen stepped forward and touched the rim of his uniform hat. "Captain!"

"Assemble the gun crews and ensure that all is prepared. Make certain each gun captain understands that we will not fire until and unless we are first fired upon. It is the only way we can determine if those junks are friend or foe."

"Understood, sir," Bowen replied, adding, "Shall we beat to quarters?"

"Yes, by all means."

Bowen picked up a speaking trumpet and cried, "*Beat to quarters!*"

As young Marine drummers on the top two decks beat out a staccato tattoo sending gun crews to their battle stations, the two squadrons made for their rendezvous point under as much steam as circumstances permitted. As they approached the southern approaches to the bay, the lead war junks, many of them of substantial size, opened fire on them. Round shot streaked high over *Columbia* and slammed into the sea behind her.

"Bring her around!" the captain ordered Dean, who had replaced the quartermaster's mate at the wheel. As *Columbia*'s bow turned to starboard to present her port battery, Neale snatched up a speaking trumpet. "Mr. Bowen," he shouted through it, "fire as your guns bear!" Two midshipmen stationed on the quarterdeck quickstepped amidships to repeat the order down to the gun deck.

The force of five guns erupting in a near-simultaneous outpouring of shot and orange flame pushed *Columbia* sideways. Four 12-pound balls found their mark. One shot ripped into a junk's magazine and exploded. Within seconds, what had been the smooth teak frame of a substantial vessel was open water filled with floating debris. A second junk was holed at the waterline amidships, normally a fatal blow. She listed as she took on water but did not sink, her four watertight compartments keeping her afloat. Marines and sailors in the boats would have to finish her off.

The first salvo reduced the pirate fleet by almost half. Many of the smaller junks and one of six larger ones came about and fled into the temporary refuge of Hong Kong Strait, the wide channel separating Hong Kong Island to the south from the Kowloon Peninsula to the north. The remaining junks in the bay prepared to engage.

"Into the boats!" Neale commanded. The high-pitched squeals of boatswains' pipes sent men to their assigned places in the four boats that had been drawn up on the frigate's starboard side. Ten ropes were flung over the side, and Marines and sailors shinnied down them. The frigate's port guns continued to blaze at the junks in the bay, in concert with *Rattlesnake*'s guns. The guns went silent when the boats emerged from around the starboard side of both warships and began to make slow but steady progress toward the remnants of the pirate fleet.

Shot fired from enemy small arms peppered the water around and between the boats, sending up tiny plumes of water that increased in height and number as the boats neared the junks. The Americans and British answered with their howitzers. Although more accurate than the old-style cannon the pirates were using, the howitzers were fixed to their platforms and could be aimed only by pointing the boat's bow at the target, which entailed much back-and-forward stroking with the oars to bring them to bear. Despite the boats' slow progress, the pirate fleet was taking a pounding. Their own cannons, mounted high up, became less effective as the boats closed the distance. Even so, the pirates managed to blow a British boat apart, killing the sailors and Royal Marines on board.

Seated in the small bow thwart of boat number six, Lieutenant Montgomery alternated between keeping an eye on the goings-on ahead and keeping up the morale of the ten sailors straining at the oars and the fifteen Marines seated between them. "Steady, lads, steady," he called out encouragingly. "Not far to go now. Many of those sods have already shown us their heels, and the others are taking it on the jaw. Our job is to finish them off, and it's a job you'll enjoy doing, am I right, lads?"

"Yes, sir!" the boat crew shouted back.

"Good lads! Glory is ours today!"

A bullet whined past Montgomery's ear and thudded into a Marine sergeant seated close by on the second thwart. With hardly a sound, the Marine slumped forward. A private on the third thwart turned around and caught him. He felt for a pulse, then said to Montgomery, "He's alive, sir."

Montgomery nodded. "Stay with him, Private. Do what you can for him. Use this." He unwound his white cotton neck stock and handed it over. "It will help stem the flow."

An oarsman on boat five was hit. Montgomery watched as the Marine sitting next to the man cradled him down to the bottom of the boat before taking his place at the oars.

As they neared the lead junk, Montgomery could see that sizable chunks of its upper deck had been chewed up by howitzer fire, yet the deck was crowded by men shouting defiantly. He peered up at those peering down at him from over the junk's transom, their faces all but hidden behind it.

A pirate stood up and took aim at boat five with a flintlock pistol. Before he could fire, half his face was blown off by a fierce volley from two other boats.

Montgomery whipped his sea-service revolver from its holster and quickly checked its five chambers. All were loaded, as they had been when he last checked ten minutes earlier. A check of the extra shot he was carrying in a hard leather bag secured at his waist confirmed that nothing had changed there either. He reached under the thwart and pulled out a grappling hook secured to the end of a long stretch of hempen rope. The howitzer took one last point-blank shot at the junk. The shot stoved in the junk's hull and sent its crew flying.

Montgomery stood up and waved his arms, a signal to the flagship and to the other boats to commence covering fire. He swung his hook back and forth with increasing momentum, then flung it up with a mighty heave. To his satisfaction, the hook disappeared over the junk's transom amidships.

"To me, lads!" he cried. He waited a moment to make sure the hook was holding. Once assured it was, he planted the soles of his feet on the junk's tumblehome and step by step began walking up it. Behind him, Marines and sailors followed his lead, shouting encouragement to him and to themselves. Some of them carried breech-loading rifles slung over a shoulder, others a sword or cutlass or tomahawk or belaying pin. Above them, a cloud cover of bullets slammed into the junk's masts, sails, and superstructure, pinning the pirates down until the first wave of Marines was nearly up. Then it ceased abruptly.

Montgomery was first over the top and onto the junk's deck. He searched for a target, found one, and fired. A pirate who had been darting for cover behind a low-lying mainmast support lurched forward and fell face down. Another pirate raced forward toward the junk's bow. Montgomery shot him in the back. He fired two more rounds at the gun crew of a cannon as Marines and sailors stormed over the transom.

A motley mass of barefoot pirates wielding guns and cutlasses charged across the deck at them howling like banshees. Those in the lead fired their weapons. One Marine fell instantly. Another spun around in a full circle before collapsing onto the deck.

Under the harsh commands of Captain Jason Albright, the remaining Marines quickly formed two rows, one kneeling and the other standing behind them, and returned fire with devastating effect. The front ranks of the pirates fell backward, staggering into those behind them, but they regrouped and came on.

Montgomery's revolver was out of ammunition, all five chambers empty, and no time to reload. When a sword-wielding pirate raised his blade above a fallen Marine, Montgomery flung his pistol at him. The pirate ducked, and Montgomery drove his shoulder into the pirate's gut and his fist into the man's face, knocking him backward. Montgomery unsheathed the knife at his waist and in a single fluid motion yanked the pirate's long black hair, forced the man's head back, and slit his throat, then heaved the still-thrashing body overboard. He leaned down to offer the fallen Marine a hand up, then snatched his pistol off the deck and dropped to a knee to reload. Above him, a fierce, hand-to-hand battle raged, punctuated by grunts and screams, the curses of desperate men, and the stark clang of cold steel on steel. A malodorous stew of guts and gore and emptied bowels surged across the deck.

He was scrambling back to his feet in search of more targets when he slipped in the slurry of blood and gore and his feet slid out from under him. As he struggled to regain balance, a sudden searing pain assailed his left armpit. He tried to turn and face his assailant but could not. A moment later, he felt the blade being pulled out and then thrust back in. Falling onto the deck and gagging for air, his head spun and blackness enveloped him. A final volley of shots rang out. As his consciousness faded, another jolt of pain walloped him when the dead weight of a lifeless body collapsed on top of him. Then, blessedly, he felt nothing at all.

"Were you *trying* to get yourself killed, Lieutenant?" The voice came from far away, though he recognized the speaker. On two previous occasions—or was it three?—he had surfaced briefly before slipping back into darkness. This time he felt stronger. His eyes flickered open, and although his vision was blurred, he could make out the compact form of Captain Neale. And Captain Neale was standing next to . . . the ship's surgeon, who in turn was standing next to a young man of perhaps sixteen years.

As his eyes focused, he felt a surge of relief. *I'm alive!* Glory be! Back in his own tiny cabin in *Columbia*'s wardroom!

He exhaled slowly, then gave his captain a sheepish grin. "No, sir."

"Well, by all accounts that's exactly what you *were* doing. First, you volunteered for what you must have known was a suicide mission. Next, you were first up the side of that junk. And then you fought like a demon against great odds. It's the story of both fleets. You earned a heap of respect out there. Even Sir Edmund was impressed, and that, Lieutenant, is no mean feat." He turned to the man at his side. "Your thoughts, Dr. Hanrahan?"

"I have to agree with you, Captain," the surgeon replied matter-of-factly. "It seems the lieutenant has a death wish—and very nearly fulfilled it."

Montgomery looked from one man to the other, one clean-shaven, the other with a short-clipped black beard, the expressions on both faces noncommittal. When he tried to shift position, he found he was strapped in, immobilized. He could hardly move at all, though he instinctively fought to do so despite the pain it caused him.

"I wouldn't do that if I were you, Lieutenant," Hanrahan cautioned. "It won't get you anywhere. I knew you would try nonetheless, which is why I fashioned a figure-eight sling on you. We need to keep your shoulder immobilized if it's to heal."

Montgomery slumped back onto the pillows as a wave of nausea overcame him. "For how long?" he wheezed. "How long will I be like this?"

"For as long as it takes," the surgeon said firmly. "It could be only weeks or months. Or it could be a year or more. That blade cut through several tendons and struck your collarbone. The wounds are serious, I won't minimize them, but they will heal so long as you behave yourself. And you *will* keep your arm, though it will never again be what it once was."

Montgomery moaned softly. His bloodshot eyes swung in appeal to his captain, who shook his head. "You'll get no reprieve from me, I'm afraid," he said amicably. "You'll do what the doctor says. You are damn lucky to be alive, Jonty. For the foreseeable future, your place is on the beach."

Montgomery narrowed his eyes. "We'll see about that, Captain. But tell me: how fared the battle?"

"It was a resounding victory. Most of the junks that stayed to fight were destroyed. Some were sunk, others were burned. The pirates lost five hundred killed or wounded, and we rounded up another three hundred prisoners. They were a dogged lot, I give them that, but they were no match for us. No match for you, I should say. Much of the credit for our lopsided victory goes to you, Lieutenant. Your antics inspired the men to great heights. I heard them say later that they would follow you to Hell and back, if you commanded them. Both the United States and Great Britain are very much in your debt."

"The butcher's bill? On our side?"

"Six killed and eleven wounded, including you. British losses were higher, with the loss of boat number two."

"Jesus Christ! That should convince those sods of our resolve."

"Indeed. But bear in mind that their bases and hostages are on dry land. We may still be called upon to root them out of their lairs. We will rescue our sailors, whatever the cost. That has priority above all else. It's why we're here."

Montgomery looked at Hanrahan. "What now, Doctor?"

Hanrahan deferred to Captain Neale, who said, "*Now*, Lieutenant, you need rest, and plenty of it. And you need good food and good care." When Montgomery winced at a minor motion, Neale pointed a finger and said, "Be still, lad!"

"We'll be giving you some laudanum shortly," Hanrahan said. He nodded at the loblolly boy, who immediately left the room. "My assistant has gone to my cabinet to get you some. We'll be giving it to you from time to time in the days ahead, but only when necessary. Laudanum will take away the pain and ease your mind, but we must be careful with its use. Laudanum is an opiate, and opiates can become addictive if overused. Do you understand?"

Montgomery nodded. "I shall take very little, I promise you."

"Good. We don't want to see you compromised further in either mind or body. Now, arrangements are being made to ensure you get the best care possible ashore. At the earliest opportunity, you will be transferred to a place where you can recuperate in style."

Montgomery blinked. "Can I not stay here, sir? Where are you sending me?"

Neale smiled and reached down to gently pat his officer's good shoulder. "No, you cannot stay on board to recover. The movement of the ship would prevent your healing. But don't worry. I know just the place, Lieutenant. Leave everything to me."

CHAPTER 13

BATAVIA, DUTCH EAST INDIES
October 1847

The sound of voices woke him. The young woman's voice nearest to him was one he knew by heart. "What's happening, Daisy?" he murmured.

She removed the damp cloth from his brow and dipped it into the pewter basin of fresh water on the bedside table. Sitting on the edge of the bed, she squeezed out the excess water before dabbing the cloth at his cheeks, nose, eyes, and neck. New beads of sweat appeared immediately.

"What's happening, Jonty, is that you are being transferred. These men are hospital orderlies assigned to assist with the transfer."

Montgomery turned his head as best he could and saw four hefty East Asian men standing in the open doorway to his room. He shifted his gaze back to Daisy. "Where am I being transferred to? *Columbia*?"

"*Columbia*? Dream on, sailor. I should think you had your fill of her sick bay on the voyage here from Hong Kong. The seas were rough, do you not remember? Rough enough to hamper your recovery. Or so I was told. Lord only knows how long I will need to take care of you now," she said in mock disgust.

"You're not fooling me, Daisy Cutler," he chided her weakly. "You are thrilled by the prospect of nursing me."

"Pretty high on yourself, aren't you, Mr. Third Lieutenant?"

He took her hand and gave it a gentle squeeze. "No, I am high on you. I could not ask for a better or more beautiful nurse. I am grateful for your many kindnesses, and I look forward to more of them." He smiled suggestively.

She stood up. "Mind your manners, Jonty! There are people watching us, and you are supposed to be convalescing, remember?"

Daisy waved the four men into the room. He tried to sit up, but even that slight movement made him wince. His head fell back on the pillow. Although the figure-eight splint had been removed, he still felt weak and constricted. "Then I ask again: where am I being taken?"

"Why, home to Cutler & Sons, of course. We are putting you in the same room you occupied the night before you sailed. Whilst you have been in hospital we have converted it into a two-room suite, just for you. Do you remember staying there before?

He grinned. "How could I forget it? Among its other amenities it smelled delightfully of you. I pray it still does."

She shook her head. "You are hopeless, Jonty. Why I bother with you is a mystery to me."

"It's no mystery. You made me promise I would come back to you, and I have. I went through a lot of trouble to fulfill that promise. So, you owe me."

"Exactly what do I owe you?"

He dropped his eyes to her bosom. "A lot. But you can pay it in bits and pieces."

Daisy's brow creased. "Hush, Jonty," she whispered. "Behave yourself. You are embarrassing me!"

"I doubt that very much. You are not the sort of girl who is easily embarrassed."

She looked away, then back down at him. "Jonty, can you be serious for a moment? I want to ask you something."

"Of course."

She ran her tongue over her lower lip. "I know all about what you did in the battle. Everyone I have asked expressed admiration for your gallantry. It's quite a story." She touched his cheek. "But why? Why did you risk your life like that? Weren't you frightened?"

"No," he replied.

"Not at all?"

"No."

"Really?"

"Really. I wasn't frightened. I was terrified."

She tapped his hand. "Then why did you do it?"

"Duty, I suppose. My superiors were depending on me. So were my men." He smiled wryly. "And I wanted to impress you with my fearless bravery."

"Ridiculous! Don't you ever try to impress me again!"

As the orderlies prepared the heavy canvas stretcher on which they would convey Montgomery the quarter mile through the Koningsplein to the headquarters of Cutler & Sons, Daisy said, to change the subject, "You will find your room more comfortable than when you were last in it. We made all the modifications that Dr. Hanrahan suggested. We also consulted Sir Edmund's surgeon in *Rattlesnake*. Even the staff here at the naval hospital contributed advice, and will remain on standby to provide whatever assistance and resources you may require. I find it hard to believe," she added with her old archness, "but you are a hero."

Before Montgomery could respond, Daisy said to an orderly who had a decent command of the English language, "Take the Lieutenant away, Desai. Be careful with him. He may look healthy, but his wounds have yet to heal." She squeezed Montgomery's lower arm. "I'll check on you later, Jonty, when you're settled. Perhaps my father and I could join you for supper in your room this evening, if you feel up to receiving visitors."

"Depends on the visitors, my lady," he returned.

She walked off shaking her head.

* * *

Although he did his best to hide it, Montgomery's claims of recovery were more bravado than fact. The pirate's cutlass had caused considerable damage, particularly on the second thrust. In addition to severing two tendons, its tip had cracked a piece of bone off his clavicle. His prospects for returning to service looked bleak, according to the hospital surgeon. A week earlier, that same surgeon had taken Ben Cutler into his confidence.

"I fear the lieutenant will never again have full use of his left arm. It must be my sad duty to inform the American authorities that I have deemed Lieutenant Jonathan Montgomery unfit for military service."

Ben Cutler grimaced. "That could destroy him, I fear. The Navy has been his life since he was a boy."

"I am truly sorry, but it cannot be helped. Not only would he endanger himself, he would also endanger his shipmates."

Sadly, Ben Cutler nodded his understanding. "I ask only that you keep your diagnosis to yourself for the time being," he said dispiritedly. "Nothing is gained by telling Lieutenant Montgomery the truth now."

* * *

Supper that evening in Montgomery's suite was a casual affair, served upon a table to which he was gently assisted from his bed. The highly polished table was made of the same lustrous teak as the rest of the furniture in the house. Only the sofa, high-backed on one end and tapering to normal height on the other, was of European manufacture. When he first saw it, Montgomery likened it to a grand piano with its lid raised.

"You will appreciate its design," Ben Cutler had rejoined, "when you sit against the high end. You'll find it very comfortable, I promise."

"What is this?" Montgomery asked minutes later when a bowl of what seemed to be an elaborate soup was placed before him by a Javanese servant. "It looks and smells delicious."

"You'll find that it *is* delicious, Jonty," Daisy confirmed. "It's *soto ayam*, a chicken soup spiced with coriander to help restore your strength. The three little cakes in the center are rice cakes. Try one."

Jonathan picked up his white ceramic soup spoon, dipped it in the soup, and took a bite. "You're right," he announced. "It's quite nice."

Ben Cutler coughed discreetly before speaking. "I've been told that your squadron is returning to Batavia in several weeks' time," he said to Montgomery.

"Indeed? Do you know why?"

Cutler shook his head. "I am not privy to that sort of information, but I suspect it has something to do with resupplying the ships and giving the crews a taste of liberty ashore. Those men have been at sea for months. Of far greater significance to us, yet another Cutler & Sons vessel, *Boston Maid*, is missing."

"*Boston Maid?* Is she not the one that tangled with those three pirate junks off Hong Kong?"

"She is. She sent one junk to the bottom and scared off two others. Which is why I fear there may be treachery involved in her disappearance. Captain Walsh and his crew are among our most reliable men. We cannot afford to lose them, so we must find them and get them back, assuming they have been taken prisoner and are still alive."

"You have ruled out a storm at sea?"

"We have not ruled out anything," Cutler replied, "but we know of no storm in the South China Sea during the past few months strong enough to have claimed her. Not with an experienced master like Walsh in command. No, it is likely ransom money the pirates are after, which is why I believe Walsh and his crew are still alive. Dead men command poor ransoms. Both Sir Edmund and Captain Neale have pledged their help."

"Have you heard anything from the pirates? Anything at all to suggest they may be holding them hostage?"

"No. Nothing. And that, I must admit, *is* odd. We have never been contacted about *any* of our missing sailors. All we know comes from Chinese intelligence, which says that the pirates are holding an unidentified number of American and British sailors. I am assuming that they are contacting the relevant governments, but we've not been told about it."

"Do you know where the sailors are being held?"

"We're not sure, but the logical location is somewhere near the border of China and Vietnam, near the Gulf of Tonkin. It's an area rife with pirates and smugglers, and I believe many of them hail from there."

"Captain Neale won't expect Jonty to be up and about so soon, will he?" Daisy interjected. "He won't be taking him there?"

Her father patted her hand. "I am not Captain Neale, so I can't speak for him. But you need not worry yourself with such thoughts, my dear. I quite agree that it's much too soon. I suspect Captain Neale will pay us a visit nonetheless to check up on our patient here and apprise him of his squadron's business. Now please, finish your supper. You too, Jonathan. You both need to build your strength. There may be dark times ahead."

* * *

Jonathan and Daisy lived inside a bubble of quiet harmony for the next five weeks. Most days, the ongoing conflicts with Chinese pirates seemed far away. Reports from home were encouraging. The terms of the Treaty of Guadalupe Hidalgo that had ended the war with Mexico the previous February were just now filtering into the Dutch East Indies. Details remained vague, but it was clear that as a result of the treaty, America's claim to its manifest destiny was being realized at Mexico's expense. U.S. territory now stretched from sea to shining sea, and no country in the Western Hemisphere possessed the wherewithal to challenge America's ascendancy. Trade was flourishing. In 1846, Cutler & Sons had reported record earnings from its sugar and rum production in Barbados and its carrying trade in the Atlantic Ocean and, increasingly, in the Pacific. As a result of the Sydney Accords, new trade routes were being developed to Australia and New Zealand.

Yet there was bad news as well. The differences between the northern and southern states, as defined by the Mason-Dixon Line, were stirring a witches' brew of discontent. Thus far, however, only a handful of southern extremists expected the cauldron to boil over. Life was good, and by most accounts it was about to get even better for any American willing to put in a good day's labor for a good day's wage. Had not President Polk promised as much in his inaugural address?

Yet all the while Montgomery continued to improve. Sheer determination drove him through the pain-filled days and sleepless nights. His recovery was predictably slow, but each day he challenged himself to remain on his feet a little longer, to walk outside a little farther, and to lift increasingly heavy objects with his weak arm until the pain became too great and he was forced to stop. Slowly, ever so slowly, his strength returned, his appetite improved, and he began to contemplate the direction his life might take now that the constraints were easing. He still felt a sharp, debilitating pain in his left shoulder and arm, but he told no one about it, not even Daisy, with whom, he was increasingly certain, he was going to spend the rest of his life. By the time *Columbia* led three ships of a small American squadron into Batavia Bay, his hope of a return to duty was running high, tempered only by what that might mean for him.

"You are certainly looking more robust than when I last saw you, Lieutenant," Terence Neale remarked as he strode up to the wrought-iron table where Montgomery was sitting. "Something about this place obviously agrees with you." He shot a meaningful glance at Daisy sitting next to Montgomery. She dropped her gaze and blushed as the servant who had brought Neale to the garden bowed and left.

Although Neale motioned him to remain seated, Montgomery rose to his feet and saluted smartly. Neale returned the salute.

"How nice to see you, Captain," Daisy said. "Welcome back to Batavia. Will you have some tea? Or perhaps a glass of wine?"

Neale bowed politely. "Thank you, no, Daisy. This is not a social call. I dropped by this morning merely to inform my lieutenant that I have returned. If he feels up to it, he is invited to take luncheon tomorrow in *Columbia*'s wardroom with me and his fellow officers." His gaze lingered on Daisy. "Sadly, this will be a strictly male affair. The crew joins me in sending our regrets about that. We are all grateful for your care of our shipmate."

"You are most kind, Captain Neale, and welcome here whatever the circumstances. As for your third lieutenant, you are not intending to shanghai him, are you?"

Neale laughed. "Interesting term, that. It's quite in vogue these days. Sign of the times. To answer your question, no, we are not planning to shanghai the lieutenant, as tempting an idea as that is." He tipped his hat. "I must be off. Good day to you both. Daisy, my regards to your father and to Mr. De Vries."

* * *

Montgomery greeted his shipmates with a broad grin. It was like old times in the wardroom. They were all there, and all looked in good health: William Bowen, first officer; Charles Chadwick, second officer; Lyall Dean, sailing master, Jason Albright, captain of Marines; and Senior Midshipman James Marston, who had served as acting third lieutenant in Montgomery's absence. Most prominent, perhaps, was Jeremy

Cook, who smiled often and broadly at Montgomery as he served savory platters of food, beaming at the praise he received.

There was serious business to conduct. With the assistance of the Chinese government and its spies within the pirates' ranks, the whereabouts of *Boston Maid* and other captured merchantmen had been uncovered. As Ben Cutler had predicted, the vessels had been taken to Binh Giang in the Red River Delta region of Hai Duong Province near the Vietnam–China border. The disposition of the crews was unknown, but it seemed a safe bet that they were being held there, too. It was also a safe bet, according to Neale, that Binh Giang would be strongly defended. Any assault on it would therefore have to be an amphibious operation rather than a naval engagement. The conclusion that it would likely be a bloody and costly affair was left unsaid. All those present understood that.

Some months back, Neale told his officers, he had acted on a hunch and asked Navy Secretary Mason to send three additional warships to bolster the East India Squadron. Recent dispatches from Washington confirmed that his request had been approved and the three warships should be steaming to Batavia Bay in another month. In the meantime, Neale declared, *Columbia* and her sister ships, in league with the British, would continue to patrol the waters off Guangdong Province. Their mission was to keep the shipping lanes open while keeping pirates at bay until the allied squadrons could deliver the hammer blow and free the hostages.

"What is my role in this operation, Captain?" Montgomery asked bluntly when only Neale and Montgomery were left in the wardroom.

"Uncertain as yet, Lieutenant," replied the captain with equal bluntness.

"Uncertain? Why?"

"*Why?* Lieutenant, your left arm is of little use to you at the moment, and therefore of little use to me, this ship, and your shipmates. You could barely climb up the ladder from the cutter a while ago. I would have ordered a bosun's chair rigged to hoist you aboard did I not fear it would be too great an embarrassment to you."

Montgomery winced. "I appreciate that, sir. It would indeed have been a blow to my pride. As to my wounds, they continue to improve.

Progress is slow, I am the first to admit, and I have not always been forthright about the pain. But every day I am able to do a little more than the day before. In another three or four months, perhaps sooner, I will be completely recovered. I am ready for action now," he insisted. "I use my right arm to swing a sword and fire a revolver. And there is nothing wrong with my voice. I can still lead men who, to quote your own words, 'would follow me through the gates of Hell' if I ordered them to."

"I commend your courage, Lieutenant, and I do not doubt your resolve. I meant those words when I said them to you, and I will be the first to admit that your mere presence on deck in a tight situation would be an inspiration to our sailors and Marines. Under no circumstances, however, will I put you in harm's way simply to serve as a symbol." He heaved a sigh. "We'll see how you progress in the weeks ahead. Your surgeon at the naval hospital may not be optimistic, but I am. I know you. Ultimately, that surgeon will not be making that decision. I will make it, with input from Dr. Hanrahan. Starting tomorrow, you will see him twice a week for evaluation. Your fate is largely in his hands. Understood?"

"Aye, Captain!"

"Good. Now then, I have a piece of news to pass on to you. One of the three warships I mentioned that will soon be sailing here is *Chippewa*, recently off her stocks at the Philadelphia Naval Yard. Her captain is John Brengle. I believe you know him."

Montgomery's jaw dropped. "Jack? Jack Brengle is sailing to Batavia? As a captain?"

"As a commander, technically, but yes, as a captain," Neale informed him. "And that is not all. He is bringing with him another gentleman of your acquaintance."

"Who is that, pray?"

"Captain Richard Cutler."

"My *God!*"

"Well, actually he's not," Neale deadpanned, "though I understand you and some of his other men have elevated him to that high perch."

Montgomery looked thoroughly at sea. "Sir, that is wonderful news. I don't know what to say."

"There is nothing to say. You are dismissed. Go back to that Shangri La of yours. My regards to everyone, and especially to young Daisy. You do know she's in love with you."

"Do you really think so? Really?"

Neale narrowed his eyes. "You are a damn fine sea officer, Lieutenant, but when it comes to matters of the heart you apparently fall short. Based on my personal experience with women—which I am happy to report is quite extensive—that young lady is very much in love with you. And you clearly feel the same about her. Why you are so keen to leave her to return to battle is a mystery to me. Now, go. I have work to do. See Dr. Hanrahan before you leave and arrange to see him twice a week."

Montgomery hesitated by the wardroom door before turning around to face his captain. "Sir? The young lady? You are right. I am in love with Daisy, and I intend to marry her." He saluted, turned on his heel, and stepped out onto the berthing deck.

CHAPTER 14

Much had changed in Boston since Jack Brengle had first seen it twenty years ago. But much remained the same. As a student at Harvard College, he had been drawn to the colonial architecture and history of the city, from the home of Paul Revere in North Square built in 1680 to the genteel architecture of the early Federalist dwellings ringing Boston Common, the Public Gardens, and other conclaves of wealth for which the city had long been celebrated. Many deep-rooted Bostonians saw the subsequent waves of Irish, Italian, and Chinese immigrants as threatening to open the floodgates of change and transform a stronghold of Puritan and Congregational purity into a mishmash of undesirables who had little to offer God or man.

Brengle viewed such concerns and prejudices as both baseless and pointless. Boston remained a majestic city with its prosperity grounded in matters of the sea. The mansions of company owners and sea captains would always look down from the lofty heights of Beacon Hill upon the modest dwellings of the workers who fueled the engines of Boston's commerce. To his mind, no building better epitomized the spirit of Boston's past, present, and future than Custom House, a six-story, 300-foot-long brick building located at the far end of the city docks. Since the mid seventeenth century, Custom House had facilitated the inspection and registration of cargoes bound to and from ports near and far.

As he studied the mammoth Greek Revival building drawing nearer with each pull of oars, he was reminded of another custom house, the one in Salem where his boyhood friend and neighbor was working. Or had been working as an inspection officer when they had last seen each other. He wondered if Nathaniel Hawthorne was still employed there. Or had he finally nailed his colors to the mast to pursue his dreams in the literary community of Concord, Massachusetts? Brengle was determined to find out.

When the cutter nudged up against the massive stone-and-wood siding of Long Wharf, a dockhand high above reached out to grab hold of a bow line heaved up from below. When the dockhand called down to the cutter to confirm that the line had been secured, other sailors in the cutter steadied the craft as Brengle stepped onto the gunwale and gripped a slat of the ladder leading up.

"Await my signal, Mr. Hallowell," he said to the senior midshipman doubling as coxswain. "I don't know how long I will be ashore. It won't be more than a day or two."

"Aye, aye, Captain," Hallowell acknowledged. "We'll keep a sharp eye out. Good luck, sir." They exchanged salutes.

Brengle stepped from the gunwale onto the lowest of the sixteen rungs exposed at low tide. A blustery northwesterly breeze that carried the rank odors of rotting kelp and gutted fish billowed his cloak around him like a flapping sail as he began his climb. When his hand reached the top rung, he waved off an offer from the dockhand for a hand up and swung himself around the top of the ladder and onto the wharf. Facing the harbor and the frigate *Chippewa* anchored on its periphery, he lifted his arms up and down five times, indicating to his duty officer watching through a spyglass that he was safely ashore.

"Can I assist you, sir?" the young deckhand inquired deferentially. Clearly he was not accustomed to seeing a grand naval commander on this dock.

"Aye, my good lad, that you can," Brengle said. He removed his uniform hat and used his fingers to comb back his long dark hair before replacing the hat just so. "If you would, please direct me to the offices of Cutler & Sons."

"Certainly, sir. It's just over there." He pointed to a two-story wooden building with a polished stone base on the near side of a long row building that housed a ropemaker, judging from the copious amounts of hempen cord neatly coiled and stacked outside.

"If you step on rope, you've gone too far," the lad quipped good-naturedly. "You'll see the sign out front, in any event."

"Thank you," Brengle said. He produced a gold coin from a trouser pocket. "You have been most helpful," he added as he handed it over.

"Why, thank you, sir!" the lad gasped. "That is most generous of you. I didn't do nothin' but point out a building!" He nonetheless clutched the coin in his fist as though guarding a fortune. Which to him it was.

At the heavy oak door bearing a simple stone inlay announcing "Cutler & Sons" to visitors, he turned the handle and stepped into a warm space. A battery of eyes turned toward him as he took in the parallel rows of desks, each desk holding the tools used to measure and record accountability and profitability within a commercial empire. At the far end of the room, a substantial window framed the towering, white-tipped steeple of Old North Church.

Brengle removed his hat and bowed in silent greeting to the assembly of accountants, relieved when he saw a well-dressed man wearing spectacles making his way over to him. This was someone with authority.

"Welcome to Cutler & Sons, Captain," he said, offering his hand. "I am Charles Henley, the office administrator. To what do we owe this honor?"

"My name is Brengle, Jack Brengle. I am—"

"Of course!" Henley said enthusiastically. "I have heard your name mentioned many times. And always with respect and admiration. Just last week Captain Cutler reminded me of your pending arrival. I was not sure of the day. Welcome, sir! Welcome indeed!" He shook Brengle's hand vigorously.

"Thank you, Mr. Henley," Brengle returned. "I have often heard your name mentioned as well. Is Captain Cutler here?"

"Alas, no. He is in Hingham attending a family conference."

"How long will he be away?"

"I'm not certain. Might I suggest that we convey you to Hingham in one of our packet boats? We use them to ferry people back and forth. The winds are favorable at the moment, so it shouldn't take more than an hour or so. I have no doubt that Captain Cutler and all those in attendance there will be pleased to see you. Are you familiar with the Cutler residence in Hingham?"

"Only that there are several of them."

"Quite right," Henley chuckled. "Be at your ease. I will instruct the packet's master to escort you to the right one."

* * *

By the time the single-masted packet boat was secured to the dock at Crow Point the sun was on its downward arc, the western horizon glowing red and amber. The downpours of the previous day had left eastern Massachusetts a muddy morass. But the sky was a dazzling, clear blue dome now behind scudding white clouds. Brightly colored leaves still clung to tree branches and covered the wind-blown roadways and soggy grass. The late afternoon sun turned everything it touched to gold. As the packet's master walked with Brengle along the harbor's edge toward William Cutler's house, Brengle reflected on what Richard Cutler had often told him about the advantages of living in a seaside New England village like Hingham. From his first impression today, Brengle concluded that his shipmate had understated the facts.

Once welcomed into William Cutler's home, Jack Brengle was treated as one of the family. Richard Cutler threw propriety aside by openly embracing *Suwannee*'s former executive officer, and the rest of those present treated his arrival more as a homecoming than an introduction. Many of the South Shore Cutlers were there, called together to deal with a family emergency. William called a halt to the formal proceedings with a promise to present a firm plan of action the next day. News that Lucy Cutler Seymour had again gone missing called for action of some sort. Richard Cutler had promised that, if at all possible, he would delay sailing for the Orient until the matter was settled and Lucy was found safe.

After he and Richard had managed to slip away from the others to talk alone, Brengle said, "I realize that you and your family are facing an emergency of some sort, but I feel compelled to remind you that I have my sailing orders. That *we* have *our* sailing orders."

"I am aware of that, Jack, but we seem to have a family crisis here. My cousin Lucy—you have heard me speak of her—may be in trouble. No one has seen or heard from her in a while, and I haven't seen her since we had tea together on Long Wharf a while back."

"Does this sort of thing happen often?"

"With Lucy, yes, unfortunately."

Brengle pondered a moment. "Lucy. I do recall you mentioning her. Isn't she the black sheep of the family?"

"Some members of the family see her as that, though I sure as hell don't. I see her as a strong, independent-minded young woman who has had some difficult challenges to overcome. She does have odd ways, but when push comes to shove, she's a Cutler, always there for you. She has always been there for me, and if she needs my help now, by God she is going to get it, sailing orders be damned."

"How can I help?" Brengle asked without hesitating.

Richard shook his head. "It's good of you to offer, Jack. But you are under no obligation here. Perhaps it's best not to get involved."

"I am already involved, and I want to help," Brengle said firmly. "When I join your company, I will be joining your family, too. Before I do, I want everyone convinced of my loyalty and my abilities. There is surely some way I can help, Richard. So please let me."

"What about our sailing orders?"

"I'll deal with that. Besides, you said 'orders be damned,' and since you're the ranking officer in our little expedition, who am I to say nay?" He smiled. "If we leave Boston within the week, we'll stay on schedule. *Chippewa* is a fast ship."

Richard's jaw tightened. "Very well, Jack. And thank you. By the by, your loyalty and competence have never been called into question by anyone in my family. Excuse me for a moment, would you please? I'll be right back." He walked back into the room where the other family members were talking in small groups and quickly returned with a distinguished-looking woman past her middle years. She retained a youthful look, despite her years. Her chestnut hair remained thick and glossy, though streaked with silver. As a lifelong resident of Hingham, Diana Cutler Sprague understood family dynamics as well as anyone, and she knew by name or reputation almost everyone in the village.

"Jack, this is my aunt, Diana. Diana, you know this gentleman's reputation. His presence here today is most fortuitous."

She nodded, studying Brengle closely.

"Jack has offered to help with finding Lucy," Richard said. "I plan to incorporate him into our plans. I would entrust the lives of my wife and children to this man without hesitation."

Diana held out her right hand, which Brengle took in his own. "It is an honor to meet you at last, Commander," she said.

"The honor is mine, ma'am," Brengle replied before releasing his grip.

Richard motioned toward a sofa. "Have a seat, Auntie, and tell Jack what you told the family this morning. Something tells me it goes to the crux of the matter."

"Very well." Diana sat down and smoothed her dress. She looked at Brengle as she spoke. "I have long mistrusted a man called Harlan Sturgis. I believe he is somehow involved in Lucy's disappearance. For a time, Sturgis was courting Richard's mother. But I believe it was not matrimony or even friendship that he was seeking."

"What, then?"

"He was seeking information on the trade routes we use in the Mediterranean and the Orient."

"For the opium trade?" Brengle proposed. "That seems the likely reason."

"Yes. You are spot on. He was using the good name of Richard's mother and the good name of our family business to gather the information he needed and to advance his own interests. The fact that Richard holds a high rank in the Navy further served to legitimize his activities. When Richard departed for New South Wales and many of us were distracted by events in Mexico, the Indies, and Batavia, Sturgis saw his opportunity."

"To do what?"

"In short, to bribe the masters of Cutler merchantmen to smuggle opium into Boston."

"Begging your pardon, Diana, why smuggle it? As I understand the law, the importation of opium into the United States is not illegal. Was it just to avoid paying taxes?"

"In part, I suppose. The import tax deducts from his profits, which are exceedingly high. But it is also a matter of getting the opium from the Far East to Massachusetts. Sturgis has no ships of his own. Cutler & Sons has many ships, but it is strict company policy that none of them will ever carry opium. Thus his desire to bribe our employees to smuggle it in." She paused to look for a moment at Richard, then continued. "Regardless of how the United States government treats the importation of opium, we feel strongly about preventing it from entering our ports, especially on our ships. Once inside the country it leads to other problems besides the addiction of those it enslaves."

"What problems, for instance?"

"Prostitution, for instance. And the enslavement of troubled women, many of them well brought-up girls from good families—although their background doesn't matter. To enslave any woman is a crime."

"You have proof of this? And of Sturgis's involvement?"

"We are gathering the proof. None of these women has yet come forward. They are too intimidated, too ashamed. We need just one to speak up and point a finger of accusation. When that happens, we believe other women will find the courage to speak out."

Brengle looked confused. "Quite possibly. But I still do not see how smoking opium leads to prostitution. I'm at a bit of a loss because this scourge of opium is all new to me—and to most ordinary Americans, I should think."

"Opium leads to prostitution in one of two ways," Diana explained patiently. "If you are a woman, you may turn to prostitution to get money to support your addiction. Even women from wealthy families may lack cash. Men control the finances, you know. If you are a man such as Sturgis, you can introduce a woman to opium while pretending to be her friend, knowing it will make her vulnerable to his advances. Sale of opium itself provides good income, to be sure, but prostitution is where the gold is, and sadly there are many broken women out there who fell victim to the curse.

"Meanwhile, the government turns a blind eye. It does not want to know. It happily rakes in the levies while too many citizens who should know better are drifting in a haze of indifference and oblivion. Sorry. Jack, I do apologize. I am rambling."

"Not at all," Brengle protested. "You feel deeply about what you are telling me, and you have every right to ramble. You say you know several of these young women?"

"I do."

"Do you think Lucy knows these women?"

"Yes, and Sturgis knows she does. We fear that he may be forcing her to introduce women to opium with the idea of procuring them for his opium customers. They will become little more than women of the streets, then, harlots."

When Richard was certain Diana had finished speaking, he said, "What my aunt has just described, Jack, is essentially why the Chinese emperor banned the sale and use of opium in China. Would that we had a man like him in Boston."

"Better yet," Diana put in, "in Washington."

Brengle looked from Richard back to Diana. "To summarize, you believe this Sturgis fellow is already involved with prostitution, and he is now looking to get more involved with it."

"Yes, exactly that," Diana answered. "We are accumulating evidence to prove it."

"How so?"

"I had Sturgis followed by my cousin Zeke Crabtree. I have followed him as well. For five days straight one or the other of us followed him from his residence on Louisburg Square to the Common and to a building in what is fast becoming an enclave for Chinese immigrants. We've recruited others to watch at night. We are certain the building is an opium den."

Brengle raised his eyebrows. "How can you be sure of it?"

"The stench on the clothing of customers leaving the building is sufficient proof. Sturgis's morning routine is quite predictable. He arrives at about nine o'clock and stays until about one, then leaves, usually on foot, though occasionally he hires a coach. Where he goes, I do not know, although Zeke reported seeing him one afternoon at the Charlestown Navy Yard. A wherryman took him across the harbor to East Boston, and Zeke was unable to follow him further. There is something there, I am convinced, and I am convinced that Lucy is involved."

Richard remained silent, his promise to Lucy to say nothing about her involvement with the opium trade hanging heavy on his heart.

Brengle thought for a moment. "Going back to that house, Diana, are there guards there? Men paid to protect Sturgis and whoever else might be inside?"

Diana nodded. "We were discussing that very question when you arrived. Just one, I believe. One at a time, anyway."

"Are these men armed?"

"We assume they are. Several men who look like thugs rotate in and out. There are staff, too, young Chinese women. I suppose they clean the equipment and tidy up the place. They seem harmless, as near as we can tell. They do their work at night, then leave and reappear around ten-thirty the next day. Most days, the place opens for business at eleven."

"Have you given thought to going to the constabulary?"

"We're not going there, Jack," Richard broke in. "Not yet. As my aunt said, we don't have sufficient evidence of wrongdoing. Even though we know it's going on. Harlan is skilled at covering his tracks. Unfortunately, we don't have sufficient time to wait until we do have the evidence. Our sailing orders, remember? No, I see only one way to get satisfaction before we have to leave."

Brengle's lips curled into a wry, knowing smile. "What do you have in mind, Richard?"

"I suggest we act on what Diana has told us. I further suggest that we round up Zeke, and the three of us sail to Boston this evening. Tomorrow morning, we will pay Mr. Harlan Sturgis a visit. I'll find you a change of clothes. Bring your weapon."

* * *

As was Richard's custom when staying overnight in Boston, he took a cabin in one of the Cutler merchant vessels tied up at Long Wharf. Once he had had the option of staying at the Cabot townhome on Beacon Street at the base of Beacon Hill or the Endicott residence on nearby Belknap Street. But with the passing of Phoebe Cabot Cutler—Richard's great-uncle Caleb's wife—and, more recently, Richard's grandfather's longtime paramour, Anne-Marie Endicott, he found that a ship's berth at dockside served his purposes well enough. Plus, there was plenty of room on board to accommodate others.

Richard, Jack Brengle, and Zeke Crabtree were up early the next morning dressed in casual slop-chest garb of cotton trousers, shirt, and waistcoat. No one bothered to shave. Charles Henley had arranged for a quick breakfast of buttered bread and several pots of hot coffee to be delivered. He had not asked why the three men had passed the night on Long Wharf, and they offered no explanation. They ate quickly in grim silence, often consulting Richard's waistcoat pocket watch. Their window of opportunity was about to open.

At nine-fifteen, Richard got to his feet. Jack and Zeke followed. After a final check of personal inventory, they were on their way. The first port of call was Regis House, on the off chance that Lucy had returned during the previous day. She had not, so they continued.

It was a few minutes after ten o'clock when the three men reached their destination. All was quiet. The primarily residential neighborhood remained asleep late on a Sunday morning. They waited nearby and watched for another ten minutes but saw nobody going into or out of the building. When ten minutes were up, Richard led the way to the front door.

He turned the handle. To his surprise, it was unlocked. When the door creaked open, he gave it a gentle push.

"Who's there?" a gruff voice called out from inside. "We don't open until one o'clock."

Richard stepped inside, his eyes quickly adjusting to the dim light. To his right, at the end of a short hallway, was a closed door. Ahead of him was a flight of stairs leading down, he assumed to the opium den. To his left was another door, in front of which a burly, balding man was rising from a chair.

"What do you think you're doing?" he demanded. "Get out! I told you we don't open until one. Are you deaf?"

Richard pointed at the stairway. "Is Harlan Sturgis down there?"

"Who's asking?"

"I am."

The man stood blocking the door, arms akimbo. "And who the hell are you?"

"My name is Richard Cutler. Lucy Cutler Seymour is my cousin."

The man's firm expression wavered. He gawked at Richard and his two companions, his mouth working open and shut like the gills of a freshly caught flounder at the bottom of a skiff.

"Is Harlan Sturgis down there?" Richard challenged a second time.

The man nodded dumbly, his eyes locked on Richard.

"Tie the bastard up, Zeke," Richard snapped. "And gag him."

Just then, the door at the right end of the landing was flung open, and a middle-aged Asian man stormed out. He walked straight to Richard and glared up at his six-foot height. "Whoever you are," he snarled, "you have no business here. You have no right to do this." His aggression changed to fear when he felt cold steel at his temple and heard the double click of a pistol's hammer.

"I believe he does have the right," Brengle hissed.

"I'll summon a constable," the man responded without much conviction.

"Please do," Richard said. "It will save me the trouble. Now get back inside that room and shut the door. This establishment is closed for the day. My colleague over there tying up your goon will make sure your door stays closed. Got it?"

The Asian backpedaled to the open doorway, where a woman stood with a look of profound worry on her face.

"Call if you need us, Zeke," Richard called out as he and Brengle hastened down the stairs.

At the bottom they opened a door into what clearly was a place of business. There was no mistaking the nature of that business. A quick scan of the room revealed no sign of Harlan Sturgis or anyone else.

Brengle pointed toward a door at the far corner of the room. The two men strode to it and Richard knocked.

"Who is it?" a familiar nasal voice called out.

Richard Cutler signed Brengle to stay put and make certain no one interfered. He opened the door and went in alone.

Harlan Sturgis was sitting at his desk when he glanced up to see Richard in the doorway. Startled, he jumped up with arms outstretched, his expression one of surprised but fond greeting. "Well, I do declare," he said in his best mock Southern accent. "If it isn't my long-lost friend, Captain Richard Cutler!" He came around the desk to shake hands. "How have you been, Richard? Just the other day I—*oomph!*"

The fist that slammed into Sturgis's midriff made him double over and drop to a knee. Gasping for air, he managed to wheeze, "What the hell, Richard? Why . . . ?"

"Where is she, Harlan?" Richard growled.

"Where is who?" Sturgis gasped, barely able to speak. "Who are you talking about?"

"You know damn well who, you slimy bastard. My cousin Lucy. She has disappeared, and you know where she is."

Sturgis held out his arms to ward off another blow. "Richard, I swear, I don't know what you are talking about."

"Don't play games with me, Harlan!"

"I'm not playing games, I swear. I—"

Richard seized Sturgis under both arms, hauled him up to his feet, and strong-armed him back into the desk chair. "Where is she, you lying piece of shit!"

Holding Sturgis at bay with one hand, he yanked out desk drawers one by one and spilled the contents onto the floor. From one of the drawers fell a two-shot Derringer pistol. He picked it up and thrust it into his pocket.

"Dear God," Sturgis moaned, his hands massaging his belly.

"He's not going to save you now," Richard spat. "Where is she?"

Sturgis held out his hands in supplication, gagging as he fought for breath.

"*Where is she, God damn you!*" Richard shouted. "Either you tell me right now or I'll start breaking bones, your right arm first." He threw Sturgis onto the floor and rammed his knee into his groin. Grasping Sturgis's right arm in both of his, he started twisting the ball of the arm in its socket. "A little trick I learned from my Maori friends," he said, his anger boiling over. "It can work wonders!"

"No! Please! No more!" Sturgis screamed with the first searing pain. "God's mercy, Richard, please stop! Stop, I beg of you! No more!"

"Where is she?" Richard's voice was low, menacing.

Sturgis was moaning and breathing deeply, taking in tortured rasps of air. "She's safe. I swear it! She's here. In Boston. She has not been harmed. I was punishing her, that's all."

"You were punishing *my cousin*?"

Sturgis shook his head, said nothing.

"Take me to her."

"What? Now?"

"Yes, *now!* Get up, you miserable scum!"

* * *

Jack Brengle secured a coach and two on Boylston Street and shouted down to Richard that all was ready. Harlan Sturgis plodded up the stairs, his eyes cast down, his hands tied in front of him. Richard was close behind him, the Derringer nudging Sturgis in the ribs.

"Give us two hours, Zeke," Richard said at the top of the landing. "Two hours, then hightail it out of here!"

Crabtree pointed at the guard tied to a chair, his eyes bulging like marbles. "What about him?"

"Leave him. The law will be coming for him soon enough. Make sure no one comes in here. Get rid of any customers who show up. This place is closed."

Zeke nodded his understanding. "Good luck."

Richard muscled Sturgis into the coach next to Brengle. The two sat side by side facing aft. Richard sat across from them facing forward, the barrel of the Derringer barely visible in his right hand.

"God help you if Lucy is not at this address," Richard said icily.

Sturgis gave him a sullen look. "She's there," he said in a raw voice. "I told you. I haven't harmed her. Nor would I, ever. I am actually quite fond of Lucy. And I respect her. I was planning to release her tomorrow morning, no strings attached."

Richard ignored that. "You say you were punishing her. Punishing her for what?"

Sturgis shrugged. "We have a business agreement. I paid her a lot of money in advance to talk up my enterprise among her well-heeled friends. Then she quit on me. Gave me no reason, no explanation. Just up and walked away. With my money, mind you. She left me in the lurch. I was none too pleased, I can tell you. You wouldn't have been either. I found her and brought her back here for . . . further negotiations. When I assured her I would set her free and never bother her again if only she would return the money, she spat in my face. Not very ladylike for a rich brat, was it?"

Richard also ignored that. "What had you been paying her to do?"

"As I said, I paid her to promote my business to discerning customers among Boston's well-to-do."

"Which business are you referring to? Opium or prostitution?"

Sturgis appeared startled. "Lucy has never been involved in prostitution. Not on my account."

"Perhaps not. But I wager that many of your so-called discerning clients *have* been drawn into prostitution, as either buyers or sellers."

Sturgis had no answer for that. As the coach veered eastward at the Charlestown crossing, he looked briefly at Brengle beside him before addressing Richard plaintively. "Look, Richard, can we not work something out here? Can we not negotiate? I am a man of business and a man of means. I may have dabbled where perhaps I should not have, but I do have legitimate businesses, and like you, I do have principles. No one has been truly harmed by what I have done, and neither of us wants to drag our good name through the mud. I am willing to make generous concessions to you, to Mr. Brengle here, and to anyone else you name if only you would—"

"Save your breath, Harlan!" Richard snapped. "I am not for sale. Neither is Jack. A judge will decide your fate, not us. Kidnapping is a serious crime. The judge will be licking his chops."

Sturgis sighed audibly. He stared vacantly out the coach window, watching the scenery flash by, until the coach slowed and then jerked to a halt before a modest building typical of this struggling community whose biggest attraction seemed to be its proximity to the Charlestown Navy Yard.

Brengle pointed out the window. "Is this it?"

Sturgis nodded. "Yes."

Richard stepped out of the coach and looked up, shielding his eyes from the noontime sun reflecting off the sea. "Please wait here, driver," he said. "We shan't be long."

The driver touched the rim of his hat in acknowledgment.

At the front door Sturgis said, "Wait a moment." With his hands still bound together, he rapped on the door three times and then twice more.

"Is that you, Mr. Sturgis?" a voice inside inquired.

"It is, Todd. Open the door."

When the door opened a crack, Brengle threw his weight against it. The door flew open with a bang, and Richard shoved Sturgis inside.

"What the hell?" the man bellowed. From his trouser belt he pulled out a flintlock pistol.

"Drop it!" Brengle snarled, his sea-service revolver aimed between the man's eyes. "Drop it and raise your hands, or you are a dead man."

The pistol clattered to the floor, and the man held up his hands.

"Where is she?" Richard demanded. Todd glanced at Sturgis, then grudgingly motioned upstairs.

"Stay here, Jack. Cover them. Feel free to use that"—he indicated the revolver—"if either of them gives you trouble."

"There will be no trouble," Sturgis assured him.

Richard raced up the stairs. He opened the first door: nothing. He tried the second door: nothing. The third door was locked. He slammed his shoulder against it then kicked at it with the flat of his boot. When the thick oak door refused to budge, he returned to the top of the stairs.

"Jack!" he shouted down. "Get the key off Harlan and toss it up here. If he resists, shoot him."

Moments later, the key was tossed up. Richard inserted it into the keyhole and turned the knob to the right. The door clicked open.

Lucy was there, sitting by a window. She turned as Richard came in, then without a word got up and ran into his embrace. Tears came in a steady stream as she buried her face in his shoulder and her body convulsed in great heaving sobs. "'I'm sorry," she choked. "I'm so sorry! But I knew you would come for me. I *knew* you would."

He held her close until her shudders had eased. It's all right, Lucy," he said comfortingly. "You did nothing wrong. It's all right. It's over now. You're going home."

"Yes, home," she said quietly.

"Are you hurt?"

"No. Just scared."

As Richard loosened his grip on her, she asked anxiously, "Where is Harlan?"

"Don't worry about him. He'll get what's coming to him soon enough. At my request, *Constitution* has prepared temporary quarters for him, in her brig." He put his arm reassuringly across her shoulders. "Come, my dear, let's leave this hellhole, shall we? Jack is waiting for us downstairs."

"Jack?"

"Jack Brengle. He's someone you are going to like very much. I have asked him to escort you home."

"To Cambridge?"

"If that is where you want to go."

"It is."

"Good. I'm glad."

His hand moved to the small of her back as they walked together down the stairs.

CHAPTER 15

HINGHAM, MASSACHUSETTS
October 1847

Anne knocked softly on the door, then called out as she walked in. Richard was lying back in a bath of warm water that had been heated over a fire. He was nearly asleep, able to muster only a happy "mmm" at the sound of her voice. Boston seemed a long way away, although had he wished, he could have stood at the window and seen the rise of Beacon Hill in the distance to the northwest. He found it hard to believe he had been there only a few hours earlier.

"May I come in?"

"It would seem that you already are in."

"Aren't you the observant one," she quipped.

He grinned. "Are the children asleep?"

"Getting there. Rachel has them in bed." She knelt beside the tub, a portable shell of sheet copper made by a local tinsmith, dipped a washcloth into the soapy water, and wiped his shoulders. "Lean forward and I'll scrub your back." The bathwater swirled and gurgled as he complied. With smooth, gentle motions Anne started washing up and down, to and fro.

"Ahhh, that feels good," he sighed.

"What will happen to Harlan, Richard?" she asked abruptly. "I am worried about the safety of the children should he escape and seek revenge. He seems to have a way of weaseling out of punishment."

"Please don't worry, Anne, I've made damn sure he won't bother the Cutlers again. First there will be a trial. After that, if there is any justice in this world, a long jail sentence. For now, he is pondering his fate in *Constitution*'s brig, from which Captain Gwinn assures me there is no escape. Then he'll be transferred to a proper prison. He should be up for trial in a few weeks' time. Jack and I won't be here to bear witness, of course, but Diana and Zeke will be. And so will my mother. If we can convince one of his thugs to testify against him, and I wager we can—Thomas can be quite persuasive—Harlan will likely throw himself on the mercy of the court. Which will do him no good. We may not be able to get him on charges of smuggling opium, but there are other charges."

"Good. I'm glad. One thing still troubles me, though."

"And that is?"

Anne rose and pulled a chair over to the bathtub. "Why did Harlan approach Lucy in the first place? Yes, I know she has connections with Boston's elite, but surely Harlan must have surmised that sooner or later she would end up doing what she did: exposing him for the fraud that he is."

Richard shrugged. "I'm not so sure about that. To a man like Harlan, money and control are the crux of power, and power is everything. I expect he thought that Lucy would continue to do his bidding for as long as he kept the money flowing. Even when we had him firmly in our grasp, the bastard tried to bribe me and Jack to let him off the hook. And bear in mind that he was planning his misdeeds right under my mother's nose—and mine, for that matter. The notion that some people have principles and morals is anathema to men like Harlan. They turn a blind eye to law and logic, safe in the belief that punishment is meant to control *other* people."

"I can accept that," Anne said. "But tell me this: what convinced you that Harlan was involved in prostitution?"

"Aunt Diana, mostly. When I put it to Harlan, he confessed his guilt by not denying it."

"Fair enough. Do you know where his house of ill repute is located?"

"He did tell me that. For all the good it did. Turns out that Harlan was using a house on Charles Street at the base of Beacon Hill, not far from the Charles River. A fancy address for fancy harlots demanding a fancy price for their services. Apparently, the establishment was quite well known to those who had a need to know."

"Are you sure Lucy was not involved? In promoting the place, I mean."

"I have to believe what she told me, that she was never knowingly involved. The opium den's link to the house on Charles Street was not her doing and none of her affair. I do admit it's hard to swallow, but I believe her. Perhaps we'll never know the full story. The establishment is gone. The mother hen has flown the coop with her chicks in tow."

"Does anyone know where they went?"

"San Francisco, I expect, the new mecca for those with a lot of money and extravagant tastes. They say that gold is lying there on the ground in California for the taking. For anyone and everyone. If so, those 'ladies' are basking in sunshine either on the trail to California or on a ship bound for there."

Anne let out a genteel snort. "I wish them good fortune. Now stand up. I'll dry your back."

Richard stepped out of the bath. As Anne dried him, he said thoughtfully, "Whatever the truth may be, consider the pleasures and comforts those ladies will be offering to legions of lonely, homesick men."

"No, thank you." She handed him the towel. "Here, you finish the job. And while you're at it, consider that we have only two days before I become a very lonely woman. I suggest we make the most of them."

He tossed aside the towel. "I agree," he declared huskily.

* * *

Richard did his best to balance the needs of his family with the needs of his business before he sailed with Brengle. Jamie, now approaching four years of age, was old enough to understand that his father was leaving for an extended period, but not old enough to understand the ramifications. To him, these last two days were more like a holiday than a prelude to sorrow. He had his father's company for much of each day and did not think to ask for more.

On the morning of the second day, a glorious, late-autumn dream, Jamie sailed with his father to Long Wharf, where Richard, resplendent in the captain's undress uniform he had rarely worn in recent months, had a surprise in store. A ship's boat took father and son out to the naval frigate in which Richard and Jack Brengle were to set sail the next day. He sat contentedly on a stern thwart as six grunting sailors worked the oars, grinning at the little boy's wide-eyed fascination as they passed by merchant and fishing vessels of all sizes and rigs.

Ship's boats hurried back and forth between ship and shore like so many giant water beetles, tending to the needs of global enterprise. One of the six oarsmen, a straw-haired quartermaster's mate named Asa Eldritch, took every opportunity between strokes of his oar to explain to the boy the differences in sail plan of a brig compared to a barque, compared to a schooner. Jamie, seasoned commander of a fleet of wooden boats, listened gravely, even though he had heard it all from his father before.

"Toss oars!" the coxswain cried as the cutter approached *Chippewa*. Six oars rose sharply to the vertical and remained there as the cutter glided up to the anchored frigate.

As the ranking officer in the cutter, Richard Cutler should have been first off onto the makeshift platform at water level, and from there up the wide-rung steps to the port entry on the weather deck. Today, he deferred that honor to the ship's captain. After Jack Brengle was up and striding past a side party of midshipmen and boatswain's mates shrieking their whistles, Richard followed, holding Jamie's hand tightly until they were up on deck and the salutations started anew. Feeling very full of himself, accepting these honors as if they were intended for him alone, Jamie shook off his father's hand and with his chubby little fingers fashioned a salute to the quarterdeck, just as he had seen Captain Brengle and his father do.

Quartermaster's Mate Eldritch approached the two captains and saluted them both. "Begging your pardon, sirs," he said hesitantly.

"What is it, Eldritch?" Brengle inquired.

"Permission to show the lad about the ship, sir," he replied.

Brengle glanced at Richard, who nodded. "Permission granted," Brengle said. "Be sure to deliver him to the wardroom no later than thirty minutes from now, at"—he consulted his pocket watch—"eight bells. Understood?"

"Aye, aye, Captain!" Eldritch said. He held out a hand. "Come, Master James. If you're game, my shipmates and I will show you the workings of a United States Navy steam engine man-o'-war."

"I'm game, sir!" Jamie piped enthusiastically. In a quick response to his father's raised eyebrows, he added, "Thank you, sir! Thank you very much! Can I see the cannons first? Please? Can I?"

Eldritch gave him a mock frown. "That's Army jabber, matey. In the Navy we call them 'guns.' But yes, you can see them. They are our first port of call on the tour, and also our last."

Jamie squealed with delight. He gripped the sailor's horny hand, looked back once to flash his father a toothy grin, and turned his attention toward the main hatchway amidships. Richard and Brengle watched them go.

"This was all arranged, wasn't it, Jack?"

Brengle shook his head. "Not all of it. Eldritch's offer to show Jamie around was not in the script. He did that on his own. I hope you don't mind."

"Mind? To the contrary, I am grateful. Jamie is obviously thrilled, and this will be a new lesson for his education about ships and the sea. This is a day that neither he nor his father will soon forget."

Richard took a moment to look around him as he inhaled the fresh salt air and enjoyed the surprisingly warm autumn sun. He looked ashore at the mammoth golden dome above the Massachusetts State House, symbol of Boston's eminence in New England's affairs. The golden "sacred cod" weathervane atop the dome represented the importance of the fishing industry to the local economy. He glanced up at the sky. "Looks to be a fine day tomorrow, Jack. No sign of a change in the weather. Change will come, but I daresay it won't be by tomorrow."

Brengle, too, studied the sky. "I agree. We'll weigh in the morning midway through the forenoon watch, if that suits you."

"Suits *me*? Have you forgotten that you're the captain? I'm just a passenger."

"Perhaps. But I am keenly aware that you outrank me by seniority, and that in the not-too-distant future, assuming all goes according to plan, you will also be my employer."

"Let's agree to put all that aside on this cruise. You are the captain of this vessel, and I am a guest, nothing more. Not to change the subject, but have you anything to report about our friend Harlan?"

"No. But I may have some new information for you before we sail tomorrow," he added.

"Oh? Are you going ashore this evening?"

"Yes, as a matter of fact I am. I'm having supper with Lucy."

"With Lucy!" Richard pretended surprise. *Just as I planned*, he thought smugly. "Where are you taking her?"

"I was hoping you might suggest a place."

"Indeed I can. The Union Oyster House. It's on Union Street, a short walk from the wharf. The food is good and the atmosphere conducive to . . . quiet conversation. Which I assume is what you are after?"

Brengle nodded.

Richard lifted his eyebrows suggestively. "Must have been a meaningful drive to Cambridge."

"It was," Brengle said firmly. "And I stayed there the rest of the day. Lucy's grandmother insisted. She was delighted to have Lucy back. And Lucy was delighted to be there after all she went through."

"I can imagine. Well, I believe I can safely say that my family greatly prefers you to Harlan Sturgis."

"Thanks," he said sarcastically. "That's quite an endorsement. But don't go drawing conclusions," he said seriously. "I like Lucy. I like her a lot, and I feel sorry for her. But for now, it's important for her to know that she now has a friend she can depend on. That's all. What? Why are you smiling?"

Richard's smile broadened. "You forget how well I know you, Jack. And look," he added, pointing forward, "the tour is over, and judging by my son's gleeful skip, it went well. That's reason enough to smile, I'd say."

CHAPTER 16

Twilight was well advanced when Jack Brengle knocked on the door of Regis House. The door was opened by Miss MacAleer, who looked him up and down sternly, clearly undecided whether he met with her approval. "Yes?" she demanded. When Brengle removed his uniform hat, the woman's expression softened. "Ah, I know you. You're Captain Brengle. You came here with Captain Cutler a few days ago looking for Miss Lucy."

Brengle inclined his head. "That is correct, madame. That is exactly what I was doing, just as I am doing now. I believe the lady is expecting me. Might I trouble you to announce my arrival?"

Miss MacAleer cast a furtive glance over her shoulder before stepping outside and closing the door behind her. "Of course I will tell her you are here, Captain Brengle. She is very much looking forward to seeing you. I have rarely seen her so animated as she has been today. Nonetheless, I feel that I must caution you."

"Caution me?" he said in alarm. "About what?"

She held his gaze. "I fear she is ill. It may merely be the result of what she has endured recently." She paused, perhaps hoping for Brengle to offer details about that, but he remained silent. "She seems uncommonly tired much of the time, and she has developed a persistent cough. I advised her to forgo seeing you this evening and go to bed instead. But she would not hear of it. You are sailing tomorrow, she told me, and nothing could prevent her from seeing you tonight. I am speaking frankly to you, and, I trust, confidentially. She would not appreciate my interference."

"Of course," Brengle said. He swallowed hard, recalling Lucy's intermittent fits of dry coughing the day before. Try as she might to stifle them, she could not. And her face had lost much of its healthy glow by day's end. He had extended the invitation for supper tonight contingent on her feeling up to it, but she assured him she was fine. The landlady's news stirred feelings he had not known he had.

"I will inform her that you are here," the proprietress said brusquely when Brengle offered nothing further. She turned to go back indoors but turned back around when Brengle said, "A moment, if you please, Miss MacAleer."

"Yes, Captain?"

He eyed her closely. "You truly do care about Lucy, don't you?"

"I should think the answer to that is obvious," the woman harrumphed, clearly offended. "I shall miss Lucy when she leaves my establishment, which, alas, I expect she will do shortly. Come inside, if you wish."

Several minutes later, Lucy walked slowly down the front stairway, her eyes fixed on Jack Brengle looking up at her. Despite the relative warmth of the evening, she was wearing an ankle-length cloak lined with fur. From her wrist hung a small, embroidered silk purse. When she reached the bottom step, Brengle bowed deeply, took her right hand in his, and brought it to his lips. He felt a sudden stab of concern at her flushed complexion but said only, "You look beautiful, Lucy. I will be the envy of every man in Boston this evening."

"And I, of every lady," Lucy countered. "Surely you know what they say about a naval captain's dress uniform?"

"No. What do they say?"

"It sends a lady's heart aflutter and melts her resolve."

"Well, then, I'm off to a good start. The evening looks more promising by the minute!" He offered her his arm, and she took it, laughing quietly.

"What's funny?"

"You didn't see the look on Miss MacAleer's face when you said that," she whispered. "She is quite strait-laced, you know."

"Apparently so. Well, the older generation has different ways," he said flippantly.

Lucy laughed again as she slid her left hand into the crook of his elbow and gripped his forearm. "A good evening to you, Miss MacAleer," she called out to the landlady standing by the open door. "Please don't wait up for me!"

"That's odd," Brengle said. "I didn't see Miss MacAleer just now. I could swear she had already gone inside."

Lucy smiled. "You might not see Miss MacAleer, but I assure you, Miss MacAleer sees you. Nothing gets by her, especially when a gentleman comes calling!"

"I consider that a good thing, considering you are a beautiful young woman living alone in a big city. Does your mother not approve?"

"She would, if she were here. My mother died several years ago."

"I'm so sorry, Lucy."

She squeezed his forearm. "Not to worry. As I said, it happened several years ago. I remember her fondly and always will. But I have learned to live with my loss."

"What took her?"

"Cholera was the official cause of her death. But I shall always believe it was a broken heart. When my father left his law practice and sailed to the Orient as director of Cutler & Sons, my mother begged him not to go. She feared she would never see him again. But my father went anyway. He was a stubborn man. Duty, and all that. As it turned out, my mother was right. My father was lost at sea. My mother never knew. She died before that sad news was delivered."

Brengle tipped his hat to an elderly couple passing by, then gently pressed her arm to his chest. "Losing both your parents in such a short span must have been very traumatic for you. Did you blame Cutler & Sons?"

"I did at first," she admitted. "It affected my relationships with the rest of the family, and I was wrong to let it," she said somberly. "But can we forget the past and talk about the present? Or even the future? The present and future are things we can influence. The past is not and is best left there."

"The past is important, Lucy," he said quietly. "What you did back then defines who and what you are today."

"Exactly my point, Jack. Perhaps I will tell you about it later, if you still want to hear it."

"I will," Brengle promised her. "Whenever you are ready to tell me. There is nothing about you I don't want to know."

They walked the remaining three blocks to Union Street in silence. When they entered the restaurant, the maitre d' bowed low before leading them to a corner table draped in a snow-white linen tablecloth and set for two. She was touched to see a vase containing yellow roses and a small silver candelabrum at its center. After taking Lucy's cloak and seating her, the maitre d' said to Brengle, "May I bring you a bottle of wine for this special occasion, Captain? I can recommend a fine one to complement any dish."

"No doubt you can," Brengle remarked. "And we will take your recommendation. But first, if my lady approves, we will start with a glass of your best Madeira." He looked at Lucy.

"Your lady approves," she said.

The maitre d' nodded approvingly. "Excellent choice. A dry one, might I assume?"

"You may."

"Excellent."

As the maitre d' hurried away from the table, Lucy remarked, "You have been here before, I take it, Jack."

Brengle nodded. "Yes, I have."

"In the company of a beautiful lady?"

Brengle smiled. "Only tonight. I have been here only once before, and I was alone. I came in yesterday afternoon to secure this table for this evening. Why do you ask?"

"The maitre d' seemed quite deferential to someone he has never seen before."

Brengle grinned and leaned forward. "Which confirms that a captain's uniform has a purpose beyond sending a woman's heart aflutter."

Lucy's laugh turned into persistent coughing. Apologizing more with her hands than with words, she pulled a small white cotton handkerchief from her purse and covered her mouth with it until the coughing subsided. As she was returning her handkerchief to her purse, she noticed, for the first time, bright flecks of red on the white linen. She bundled it up and thrust it back inside quickly before Jack could see it.

"I'm sorry, Jack," she said when she had taken a sip of water and recovered her voice. "Please excuse me. I seem to have caught a chill."

"Are you sure you are all right, Lucy?" Brengle asked with concern. "Shall I take you back to Regis House?"

"Not if you value your life, Jack Brengle! I wouldn't dream of cutting this evening short. I am quite all right; really, I am. And I shall have months to recuperate before you return." She smiled brightly. "Ah, here comes our Madeira. That will help soothe my throat more than anything."

The deferential sommelier poured the Madeira, and the two young people clinked glasses, toasting each other with "Santé" before they drank.

As they sipped the golden liquid, their conversation became more relaxed and more animated. Both agreed that their supper of creamed codfish served on a bed of mashed potatoes and accompanied by squash and peas and freshly baked bread was perfect. To their mutual delight, they discovered they had much in common, small things and larger, more important things. To Brengle's relief, the alcohol did seem to have a restorative effect on Lucy. She didn't cough again, and her complexion took on more color. When she finally steered the conversation toward the hidden shoals of her turbulent past, however, she seemed to lose ground.

"You needn't explain anything to me, Lucy," Brengle said, reaching across the table to squeeze her hand. "You have told me some of it, and the rest of it I do not need to know. If you must tell me, let it wait until I return and you are feeling better."

"But I want you to know everything about me, Jack. I have done things of which I am . . . not proud. If we are to be . . . together . . . If you see me as somebody you may want to be with, even as a casual friend . . ."

He gave her a meaningful look. "Lucy, we have known each other for only three days, and I believe that we are already more than casual friends," he told her. "I think you agree."

She looked down and nodded.

"You have already told me enough about yourself—and I have already observed enough about you—to know that the rest is immaterial. And by the bye, what you may not know about *me* is that I too lost my mother at a young age. I understand how such a loss can affect someone. Richard and the Navy pulled me out of a bitter downward spiral into drink and self-loathing. So, let's agree to put all that behind us, at least for now. The only thing that interests me this evening—the only thing—is the woman I see sitting across from me. Do you know her? She is an exceptionally intelligent and fascinating young woman whose affections I wish for but do not deserve. My most devout wish is that what I am experiencing at this moment will last a long, long time."

He paused while she studied him seriously. "There," he breathed at length, "I have said it. I have played my hand earlier, much earlier, than social conventions and common sense allow. So be it. I care little about social conventions. What I *do* care about is you, Lucy. I care for you in ways I cannot fully express. And tonight, neither of us has the luxury of time on our hands. I am sailing tomorrow morning. So, what I needed to say tonight has now been said."

"Thank you, Jack," she said softly. "Thank you for saying that. No one has ever said such things to me."

Aware that patrons at nearby tables were casting curious glances in their direction, Lucy decided she didn't care. She reached out and boldly took his hand in hers. "I feel the same way about you, Jack. I do. Which is why this may be the perfect time to tell you my big news. I have told no one else. I wanted you to be the first to hear it."

Brengle arched his eyebrows. "Well, by all means out with it."

Lucy's laugh triggered another round of dry coughing that she quelled with a generous sip of wine. She leaned forward in her chair. "This afternoon I was summoned to the office of Mayor Quincy on Beacon Hill. He is asking me to serve as an official spokesman for the anti-opium committee my uncle Thomas is serving on!"

"That is wonderful news, Lucy! Congratulations! The mayor has chosen wisely."

"Do you think so? I expect he's giving me a chance to atone for my manifold sins and wickedness. But I suppose you are right. Who better to preach against the perils of using opium than one who once advocated it? He offered to pay me a small stipend, but I refused to accept it. I told him that I still have the money Harlan Sturgis paid me for promoting *his* services. The mayor had a good laugh over that."

"I'll bet he did. Good for you, Lucy." He squeezed her hand. "I'm proud of you. Very proud."

She ducked her head, then smiled into his eyes. "Once again, it's been a long time since I have heard words like that directed at me."

"Well, they're well deserved." He scanned her face, suddenly alarmed. "But why suddenly so glum?"

She looked down at the tabletop, still clutching his hand. "Just when I believe I have found what I have been seeking all these years, and just when someone I care for starts putting things to rights for me, he up and sails off to distant shores. I hardly know you, Jack Brengle. I've been hearing about you for a long time, but I have actually known you only three days. And yet, somehow, it's enough. I don't want to remember what my life was like before I met you. Whatever may happen to us in the future, I will always be grateful for these three days, and I will forever be badgering poor Richard for news of your illustrious career."

"That will hardly be necessary, my dear girl. Do you not know that when my duty in Batavia is over, I will be resigning my commission in the Navy and joining Cutler & Sons? I will likely be living in Hingham, so you won't have to ask Richard about my career. You can ask me. Perhaps right here at this very table."

"I had heard it mentioned, but during these past few days I have not allowed myself to believe it. Is it true, Jack? You are leaving the Navy?"

"It is. You have my word on it." He leaned in closer and spoke in the hesitant tone used by those who fear that a newfound joy will suddenly vanish. "Look, Lucy, I have no better sense than you about what the future holds for us. And yes, I agree, this has all happened very quickly. But I have long held that when it comes to affairs of the heart, things *should* happen quickly. The heart knows the truth, and I listen to mine very carefully. Not always wise for a naval commander, perhaps, but it has always been my practice."

She bit her lower lip. "What is your heart telling you now?"

"It's telling me that whatever my future may hold I want you in it."

"Thank you, Jack," she whispered. "That pleases me more than you could possibly imagine. It gives me a reason to live, to hope."

"I should hope so," he said, puzzled by her choice of words but grateful to hear them, nonetheless. As the effects of alcohol wore off, Lucy began stifling yawns as well as coughs. His plate was empty, but hers had barely been touched. He signaled the waiter for the bill.

"Not yet, Jack," she protested. "I don't want this evening to end. Not now."

"Nor do I, sweet Lucy," he said fervently. "But end it must. I need to get back to my ship, and you need to get to bed. Nothing ends here. To the contrary, this evening marks a glorious beginning."

* * *

Eighteen miles to the southeast, on the second story of a newly refurbished house near the intersection of South Street and Lafayette Avenue, Anne Cutler rolled onto her right side and draped her left arm over her husband's chest. A puff of warm, humid air, a rarity for this time of year, billowed the lace curtains at the open window.

"Heavenly," she murmured. "Just heavenly." She inched closer to him. "Dear God, how I am going to miss you these next few months."

Richard drew the fingertips of his left hand lightly up and down her arm. "And I will miss you, my love. But I'll be back before you know it. And this will be my last voyage. Henceforth, my place will be here in Hingham with you and our children."

"God be praised for that," she said fervently, then sighed, "I do understand why you must go."

"Then I am a fortunate man. Not many wives would be so understanding."

"I do have one boon to ask, however. And I am quite serious about it."

"Ask it."

She lifted her head from his chest to look into his eyes. "I ask that you do not involve yourself in any fighting on this trip. If fighting must be done, let it be done by those going over there to fight."

"Jack, for instance?"

"Yes, Jack. And the others in Jack's squadron. It's not your responsibility, Richard. Not anymore. It's not the reason you are going to Batavia. You are going as a passenger, as director of Cutler & Sons' international operations. Which means you are no longer the captain of a Navy frigate. Agreed?" When her husband merely hummed, she prompted him, "Are we in agreement, Richard?"

He kissed her forehead. "We are, to the extent I am able. What I can promise is that I will devote myself to my duties as director and avoid becoming involved in matters unrelated to them. Does that satisfy you?"

"Not entirely. I believe you have cut yourself a length of slack with that promise. But it will have to do. And thank you for making it. I will rest a little easier." She lightly massaged his chest. "On another subject, I think it's best to leave Sydney here with Rachel tomorrow. She's too young to understand leave-taking. She would likely be inconsolable if she saw you sailing away from her."

"And Jamie?"

"Oh, Jamie," she laughed. "He wouldn't miss it for the world. He fancies himself an admiral commissioned to see you off properly. He has been practicing his salute for a week."

Richard grinned. "Good for him. I'm going to enroll him in the new Naval Academy as soon as I get back." He rolled onto his side, facing her. "And you, Anne? How will you fare tomorrow?"

Her response was quick. "You know very well how I will be. To everyone present I will be the dutiful Navy wife. Some may even think me cold, uncaring, and detached. But you know better. When your ship has sailed out of sight, I will return to Hingham, see to the children, and then come in here, close the door, and put quill to paper. You know why."

* * *

At that same moment, in her room in Regis House, Lucy Cutler Seymour sat before the mirror on her vanity table staring at the image staring back at her. Her heart boiled with emotions, and her brain was unable to offer hope or a way out. Jack's embrace and endearments as he said goodbye at the front door continued to play sweet music in her ear. She clung to those words as to a lifeline tossed to a drowning sailor. But would they, could they, stem the tide of despair that had washed over her tonight? There really was no future for her, no hope of a life with Jack. The end seemed inevitable, and it was drawing nigh. And while her resolve might still be up to the struggle, her strength no longer was. How, at a time like this could God be so cruel as to offer her hope, a road to salvation, only to take it away?

"Jack, my sweet Jack," she whispered. "I am so sorry I couldn't tell you the truth." She slowly undid the buttons of her blouse. When she reached the bottom button, she wrenched the shirt free, threw it aside, and glared into the mirror, searching for hope, her eyes bright with defiance. To no avail. The tiny pink dots on her chest above her breasts were not only still there, but there were also now many more of them.

CHAPTER 17

SUNDA STRAIT, INDIAN OCEAN
February 1848

"Good morning, Richard. You slept well?"

"I did indeed, Jack," Richard Cutler said, stepping onto the quarterdeck. "The executive officer's quarters in this ship rival any captain's cabin on any other ship of my acquaintance. I have slept well the entire voyage." He turned to the broad-shouldered man standing by the helm. "And I reckon you can't wait to boot me out of there, eh, Mr. Redfield? Well, your chance will come soon enough."

"Not at all, sir," Redfield replied smoothly. "I am in no hurry to reclaim my bed."

"Mr. Redfield was honored to offer you his cabin on this cruise," Brengle assured Richard.

"I hope that's true. But as I recall, it was not Mr. Redfield who extended the offer."

Redfield merely smiled.

Brengle noticed Richard scanning the waters ahead. "Look familiar to you, Captain?"

Richard nodded. *Chippewa*, sailing under steam and a small press of canvas fore and aft, was approaching the narrow, often choppy funnel of water that separated the palm-fringed islands of Sumatra and Java and connected the Indian Ocean to the Java Sea. The Sunda Strait was notorious for the pirates that infested its waters. And its waters did indeed look familiar. Several years earlier, he had sailed them in *Suwannee* with Jack Brengle as his first officer, Jonathan Montgomery as one of his eight midshipmen, and Anne, who was pregnant with Jamie. Just there, off to port, between the small islands of Krakatau and Sanglang, *Suwannee* had chased down two pirate vessels intent on plundering a Spanish merchant brig. Her guns had made short work of the brigands' vessels, he remembered proudly. Today, those same waters were unruffled and empty.

Other memories rushed in as well: tortured images of the wreck off that far off island known as New Zealand, which was still hundreds of sea miles off to starboard; his last sight of his wife before the fateful wave struck, washing so many members of his crew to their deaths and others onto the white sandy beaches.

He shook his head. Despite the pain of remembrance and the central role he played in inflicting that pain, he had grown to love New Zealand and its people, *pakeha* and Maori alike. He again toyed with the notion of sailing to Sydney and Auckland on the pretext of securing new markets for Cutler & Sons while at the same time rekindling old memories and burying whatever ghosts might be lingering. It was fantasy, of course. Securing new markets in the Orient was the purview of Pieter De Vries and Ben Cutler. And good memories did not require rekindling. As for ghosts, best to leave them be.

"Take the wheel, if you please, Mr. Mathews," Brengle said to the sailing master. "We will anchor in the Bay of Banteen and make for Batavia in the morning. Too many currents and shoals along the coast to risk passage at night. Mr. Fletcher!"

"Aye, Captain!" A dark-haired young midshipman stepped forward and saluted.

"Advise Mr. Swenson to furl all sail when she comes into the wind and ready stations to drop anchor. We will proceed henceforth under steam alone."

"Aye, aye, sir!" Fletcher saluted and strode forward, calling out to pass the word to the burly, square-jawed Swede whom the crew referred to as "the Viking" behind his back.

"You have the deck, Mr. Redfield," Brengle said to his executive officer. "Mr. Cutler, if you would please join me in my cabin in fifteen minutes."

"Of course, Captain," Richard affirmed.

A quarter hour later, Richard Cutler stepped down the aft companionway to the gun deck and the captain's cabin to his right. He returned the salute of the blue-coated Marine sentry standing at the door. The sentry stepped aside to allow Richard access to the cabin without a formal invitation from the captain. Only the captain's personal steward was otherwise granted that privilege.

Brengle was at the far end of the cabin, seated before a modest work table laden with neatly stacked papers.

"Come in, Richard," Brengle greeted him, standing up from the table. Noise from the deck directly overhead signaled the evolutions of sails being doused and furled. Two decks below, the twin seven-hundred-horsepower engines sputtered and coughed. The gratifying roar of the engine rumbled through the fiber of the ship as the massive wheelhouse blades churned the waters of Sunda Strait.

"We made it, Richard! Look out there," Brengle urged, pointing at an oversized porthole on the cabin's starboard side. "If my navigation is correct, which of course it is, that is the fabled island of Java. A welcome sight, eh?"

"You are right, Jack, and you have every reason to gloat. Save for that storm off Cape Verde, this cruise has run like a well-tuned clock. Congratulations. Your longest voyage as captain is behind you, and it went with hardly a hitch. Doubtless you will henceforth be known as 'Lucky Jack,'" he teased.

Brengle shook his head dismissively. "Fact is, Richard, I *was* lucky, and you know it. The Fates and the weather were with us on this cruise. We hardly needed to engage the engine till we raised Cape Town. And you helped me in ways only a commander can fully appreciate. My thanks for your stewardship."

"Stewardship? I have done nothing since leaving Boston but sit back and enjoy the breeze on my sun-burned face. A new and delightful experience for me."

"Yes, quite," he said dryly. "Aside from taking your leisure, your work with the guns and small arms was exemplary. Peter and Bull"—referring to Peter Sayres, chief gunnery officer, and Bertrand "Bull" Chase, captain of Marines—"believe that the crew is ready for anything, at any time, and I tend to agree with them. So do the men. They're restless. They want action."

"Can't blame them. We've been at sea for more than two months without much for them to do beyond the drills. For men trained to fight, anything is better than inaction. Still, there's more training to do. And I'd advise keeping the men aboard ship as much as possible when we make port. Their pent-up energy could spell trouble ashore."

"My thoughts exactly," Brengle said. "Let's pray we see action soon. We should raise Batavia by noon tomorrow. If *Columbia* and *Richmond* are there as planned, our stay in Java could be short. That will be up to Terence Neale and the British commodore. Certainly there's not much to gain by waiting. Every day we delay gives the enemy another day to prepare his defenses."

Richard nodded. "By now, they must know our intentions. The pirates have a decent spy network, and it's often hard to distinguish friend from foe just by looking at them. They've already had ample time to gather their reception committee."

"Just as we have had time to plan our assault," Brengle countered. "But you needn't concern yourself with that. You're here for a different reason and have a different job to do, though I will sorely miss your company and your wise counsel when we go on the attack. So will the men."

* * *

The next morning, after a quick wardroom breakfast, Richard Cutler slung a long glass across his shoulders and went topside. He stepped up onto the starboard mainmast channel and swung himself onto the ratlines leading up. Holding fast to twin hempen shrouds, he climbed steadily to the spot where in years past the fighting top would have been. Today, a sturdy plank placed there anchored two sets of shrouds, the one on which he had just ascended and another, to which he now clung, narrower set that led up to the foremast peak. As he neared the peak, he stopped climbing and worked his arms through the ratlines. Once secure, he unlooped the long glass and raised it to his right eye.

What he saw made him smile. Batavia was familiar territory to him. The former Dutch colonial capital was in sight and fast approaching. Already he could make out the rise of masts in the harbor and glimpse the Dutch architecture above the city's old defensive wall. The small islands protecting the harbor entrance were as he remembered them: low-lying, untamed, and uninhabited, and so many of them that even the fiercest seas posed no serious threat to those anchored within the harbor. Far ahead, slightly off to port, he could just make out the majestic volcanic peaks of Borneo, a biologist's mecca, the largest island in Asia and the third-largest in the world—or so the Royal Academy of Science had recently decreed.

A glance down at the weather deck revealed tiny twigs of men looking up at him. He also noted the ominous dark shape of a mammoth hammerhead shark swimming lazily in the turquoise water alongside the frigate. Several members of the crew had spotted the beast and were pointing excitedly at its dorsal fin cutting through the calm waters. Richard swallowed hard. He hated sharks. Haunting images of mangled bodies washed up on the beach near where *Suwannee* was lost, their eyes glazed, their mouths frozen open in silent shrieks of horror, continued to plague him. As he held his breath and descended to the deck hand under hand on a backstay, black-headed terns wheeled and screeched overhead, either in welcome or warning.

As *Chippewa* steamed under reduced power into Batavia Bay, off-duty sailors and Marines, at sea for weeks beyond the sight of land, assembled on deck for a glimpse of a land of which they had heard much but knew little. They scanned the harbor and waterfront for clues of what awaited them. There was not much to go on. *Columbia* was there. *Richmond* was not. There was no sign at all of the Royal Navy. The waterfront was largely deserted, and Richard was happy to note that the squalid tenements formerly clustered outside the western wall of the city had been replaced by a neatly cultivated field.

"Stations for dropping anchor!"

The harsh cry from the boatswain was unnecessary. The sailors on anchor duty had been in place since *Chippewa* entered the bay. As the frigate rounded into the wind and cut power, the one-ton, cast-iron hook was cut from its fittings and plunged into the depths, its rode clattering out of the hawse hole. The outbound voyage was over.

As *Chippewa's* crew secured the ship for a layover of indefinite duration, Midshipman Henry Hall, junior deck officer, stepped up and saluted Brengle. "Sir, *Columbia* has lowered her cutter. I believe her captain is intending to come over to us." He handed over his long glass.

Brengle extended the glass and brought it to his eye. Hall was right. That was Terence Neale stepping aft to the stern sheets, no doubt about it. Neither he nor Richard had seen Neale since *Suwannee's* maiden voyage to Batavia five years earlier, but his form and bearing were unmistakable.

Brengle collapsed the glass. "Prepare a side party, Mr. Hall. We shall welcome Captain Neale aboard *Chippewa* with full honors. Handsomely, now!"

"Aye, aye, Captain!"

"Mr. Beasley!"

The second midshipman on the quarterdeck, a chubby teenager with a ruddy complexion, stepped forward. "Sir!"

"Advise my steward that I shall require an assortment of spirits in my cabin in fifteen minutes. Then join the side party."

"Aye, aye, Captain!"

As *Columbia's* cutter approached *Chippewa*, a side party of four midshipmen, two quartermaster's mates, and two boatswain's mates assembled at the port entry in two parallel rows five feet apart. Against the bulwarks on the opposite starboard side of the deck, Bull Chase made ready a squad of five Marines, the polished steel of their rifles gleaming in the sun. Despite the length of their voyage from Boston, their uniforms were as crisp and clean as though never worn, and they kept their eyes front and center as they stood at ramrod attention.

Richard Cutler appeared from below, where he had hastily changed into his captain's uniform.

"Your timing is impeccable," Brengle said as Richard adjusted his bicorne uniform hat on his head. "Shall we greet our distinguished guest?"

When the ink-blue uniform hat of Terence Neale appeared in the open space of the port entry, at a signal from the boatswain, the side party broke into a cacophony of pipes, fifes, and drums. The clamor ended abruptly when Neale turned to his right and doffed his hat in salute to *Chippewa's* quarterdeck. He then continued forward to where Richard and Brengle stood waiting to greet him.

"*Marines, present arms!*" Bull Chase bellowed. The five Marines held out their sea-service rifles stiffly before them.

"*Marines, make ready!*"

The Marines took aim at the sky.

"*Fire!*"

Five shots rang out in unison, an explosive *feu de joie* that sent a frenzy of sea birds squawking in protest and flapping their wings in a wild effort to get aloft.

"*Stand down!*"

The five Marines, in perfectly synchronized timing, banged the butts of their rifles on the deck and resumed their rigid stance.

Terrence Neale saluted Richard Cutler, the senior officer present, and then Jack Brengle before warmly shaking hands with both. "My God!" he exclaimed. "I'm honored indeed to be so generously piped aboard a ship and greeted by not one but *two* captains! Thank you, gentlemen. Tell me: who's in charge here?"

Richard answered straight-faced. "I believe you are, Commodore."

Neale grinned. "Quick with the words as ever, eh, Captain?"

An unspoken communication passed between them. Although Richard and Terence Neale did not always see eye-to-eye when it came to naval strategy and tactics, when it came to both friendship and seamanship they were of one mind.

"Shall we go below?" Brengle suggested. "I'm afraid it's no cooler down there than up here, but at least we won't have the sun in our eyes."

Neale nodded. "As you wish, Captain."

"Dismiss the men," Brengle called out to his executive officer.

Each of the eight oversized portholes in Brengle's cabin had been hinged open to allow entry to the harbor breeze. The captain's steward, dressed almost entirely in crisp white cotton, stood by a finely polished mahogany side table that bore an assortment of wines and spirits. The sunshine filtering in through the ports caught the bottles and reflected on the bulkheads and furniture in multicolored circles and triangles.

The three men took seats at the cabin's worktable. "Before we begin," Neale said to Brengle, "I want to welcome you and your crew to Batavia, and I want to extend an invitation to you and your officers to join me and my officers for supper tomorrow evening, after you have everything squared away. Richard, you are most welcome to join us, although I understand from Mr. Ben Cutler that you bear the status of a sorry lubber on this sally. America's great loss, sir!"

"On behalf of my officers, I accept your gracious invitation," Brengle replied. "And the following evening, Wednesday, I hope you will allow us to reciprocate here in this cabin." He glanced up at his steward. "You are up to the task, Mr. Taylor?"

Taylor bridled. "Of course, Captain," he replied stiffly.

"Excellent. Now, gentlemen, what is your pleasure?" Brengle swept an arm toward the side table. "May I suggest a spot of Macallan's? It's a heavenly scotch, and perfect for toasting our safe arrival in Batavia."

"That will do nicely for me," Neale said.

Brengle held up three fingers to the steward. Naval protocol suggested that the host follow the lead of his guest on such occasions.

"Is there any word of *Richmond*?" Brengle asked when the whiskey had been poured and distributed.

"Yes," Neale replied grimly. "We have received word, and I'm afraid it is not encouraging."

"How so?"

"She is in dry dock at the British naval base in Hong Kong. Her engine gave out during a routine patrol, and teredo worms—or whatever they call those little bastards out here—have gotten into her hull despite her copper bottom. For the past month she's been going through an extensive refit."

"How much longer will the repairs take?"

Neale shrugged. "An excellent question, Richard. The honest answer is, I don't know. The Royal Navy bases out here are understaffed. It will be a while."

"Can we afford to wait for her?"

Neale snorted. "The question, unfortunately, is, can we afford *not* to wait for her? I'm afraid the news gets worse." He looked expressionlessly at his two colleagues. "It seems the British will not be joining us on our expedition to the Dai Nam border."

Richard and Jack looked at one another and then back to Neale. "Why not, in God's name?" Richard finally said.

"I don't know. You'd have to ask Lord Palmerston or Viscount Russell, or whichever lordship in Whitehall is setting policy these days. The decision was made, and it was made in London, not here. Rumor has it that even Admiral Brathwaite had no say in the matter. In fact, I understand he's been recalled to London from Sydney. And that, my friends, is a shame. Not only does he understand the geopolitics in this part of the world as well as any European can, but he also understands naval strategy better than most of my acquaintances."

A palpable depression settled over the cabin.

"Do we abort the mission?" Brengle finally asked Neale.

"How can we?" Neale said passionately. "The British may have pulled out the rug from under us, but we cannot abort the mission. Most of the sailors the pirates are holding are Americans. If we pack up and go home, we will leave those poor sods to their fate. Once the pirates understand that there is no ransom coming, the captives are dead men. We must rescue them before that happens. In any case, we have no orders to abort. It goes on."

"So we are on our own," Richard said softly.

"We are on our own," Neal confirmed. Then, with confidence real or pretended, he added, "But chin up, gentlemen. We will prevail." After a silence, "We have no choice."

CHAPTER 18

BATAVIA, ISLAND OF JAVA
February 1848

Two hours later, Richard Cutler and Jack Brengle, still stunned by England's betrayal, were rowed ashore. Their destination was Cutler & Sons' headquarters. Midshipmen Samuel Hallowell and Robert Beasley had been sent ahead to formally announce their arrival. Although word of *Chippewa*'s arrival had already reached Cutler & Sons, the midshipmen's announcement sparked a flurry of activity within the offices and private chambers of the three-story building. Pieter De Vries called everyone together—cooks, servant girls, gardeners, maids, and security personnel—to put into motion the well-rehearsed welcome.

"You all know your duties." De Vries told an assembly that included Ben and Daisy Cutler as well as Jonathan Montgomery. Standing at her usual place on such occasions, a bilingual Javanese woman translated his words to the staff. "They are perhaps an hour away, and Mr. Cutler and I expect everything to be in proper order. After Captain Cutler and Captain Brengle arrive, local dignitaries will be joining us for luncheon. Remember: So long as he is here, Captain Cutler is to be obeyed and afforded every courtesy." He looked at Ben Cutler. "Anything you wish to add?"

"No," Ben Cutler said. "I have every confidence that our people will perform their tasks in their customary exemplary fashion."

De Vries clasped his hands together. "Very good," he said. "We all have work. Let us do it."

Amid the fanfare that greeted the new arrivals, Montgomery found it difficult to have a private word with either Richard Cutler or Jack Brengle. The joy of their reunion was apparent nonetheless. Richard gave his former midshipman in *Suwannee* a firm handshake followed by an embrace. Montgomery's reunion with Jack Brengle was no less emotional, to the satisfaction of all those aware of how these three men had managed to stare down death and survive the dangers of the Antipodean wild. Daisy Cutler stood there taking it all in, enjoying the easy camaraderie among the three brothers-in-arms.

"You are looking well, Jonty." Richard said before correcting himself. "Pardon me, Lieutenant. I meant to say 'Jonathan.'" The three Americans were in the library, having excused themselves after the luncheon was concluded.

"If you please, Captain," Montgomery returned. "Not many people call me Jonty nowadays. Daisy alone is afforded that dubious privilege."

"I think Jonathan is most appropriate," Brengle said fondly. "You're a man now. And a damn fine one. I hardly recognized you. I was very impressed by the confidence with which you delivered your toast," he added. "I was proud of you."

"Thank you, sir," Montgomery said. "The person I am today is largely the result of what you and Captain Cutler made of me yesterday."

"That is kind of you to say," Brengle said, "though I believe such praise is unwarranted."

"I agree with Jack," Richard said. "You have matured nicely, Mr. Montgomery! It's no wonder that Ben's daughter, Daisy, was hanging on your every word. I imagine all the young women around here are equally smitten by your looks and manly charm," he teased.

Montgomery blushed and waved away the compliment. When he spoke, his voice had an edge. "I wouldn't know about that, Captain, and frankly I wouldn't care. Miss Daisy Cutler is the only woman I look at, and the only one I ever will look at."

"I see," Richard said quietly.

"I pray you do, sir. I intend to marry her. If I may go further, I—we—are hoping that you will officiate at the ceremony. And if he is willing, I would like Captain Brengle to stand up with me."

Richard and Brengle exchanged glances before Richard said to Montgomery, "How does Daisy feel about that?"

"She agrees," Montgomery said firmly.

"She loves you as well?"

"She does, sir."

"She wants to marry you, then." It was not a question.

Montgomery nodded.

"I assume Lucy's father is agreeable?"

"He is, sir."

Richard smiled at last. "Well, I am delighted to hear it. And I am delighted to be among the first to congratulate you, Lieutenant. Perhaps most of all, I am delighted for Daisy. You two are a fine couple."

Montgomery exhaled in relief. "Thank you, sir."

"Have you set a date?" Brengle asked.

"No, sir. Not yet. It will depend on several factors, not the least of which is the timing of our attack on the pirate lair."

"Hold on," Brengle said. "Surely you have no notion of participating in that operation?"

The answer to that question was written boldly on Montgomery's face. "I do indeed, sir."

"What about your arm? I understand you are all but crippled."

"I was for a time," he said quickly. "But my arm has healed. Observe." Montgomery slowly lifted his left arm, held it out horizontally, and then raised it above his head. He held that position until his arm began to tremble from the strain. Still he stood firm. "See?" he said at last, with an audible effort. "My arm is as steadfast as the rest of me."

Richard picked a small book off a table. "Here, catch this." He tossed it underhand toward Montgomery's left side.

Montgomery lunged at the book, missed catching it, and grimaced, massaging his arm and staring down resentfully at the book on the floor.

"Sorry, Lieutenant. I had to do that. You are doing remarkably well, I must admit. Nor am I surprised by your progress. You have a heart of oak, and I wish that we could include you. But to my mind, you are not quite there yet."

Montgomery's hurt was obvious. "Perhaps not to fight, sir, but my arm has healed sufficiently to put me back on *Columbia's* quarterdeck. I can do that job. If I am denied, I will find it hard to live with having shirked my duty."

"We'll see," Richard concluded. "In any event, the decision is not mine to make. Nor is it Jack's. Captain Neale will decide, and whatever he decides is what you will do. Are we in agreement on that, Lieutenant?"

Montgomery hesitated, weighing options that did not exist, then nodded ruefully. "We are, sir. You have my word."

* * *

At that moment, fifteen hundred miles to the north, Ben Stokes shuffled over to his shipmates sitting next to the wall of the dank, musty room that smelled rankly of the privy. He sank down beside them and leaned against the rough wooden wall. "It's no use, Russ," he said to Russell Crain, *Boston Maid's* second mate. "The captain eats practically nothing. If we don't eat, we die, and this food is all we're likely to get. It ain't half bad, really."

As if to prove his point, Stokes dug his short wooden spoon into the wooden bowl he was holding on his lap and brought a bite of soggy rice mixed with bits of fish and greens to his lips. He ate hungrily, careful to keep his free hand under the spoon to catch any morsels that might drop off.

"It's not the food, Ben," Noah said. "You know that. We're treated well enough, all things considered. At least we're alive. It's the shame he feels for losing his ship, for being thrown into this godforsaken prison and being left here to rot. It breeds despair. Food don't help that."

"'Tis the same for all of us," Crain said. "We all feel it, especially him. He's been here longer than any of us." He pointed across the room to the skeletal man in rags who sat alone against the wall, staring into space. It was hard for any of them to imagine that the tattered old man could ever have been someone of consequence. Yet why would he be here otherwise? "I can't remember seeing 'im eat much of anything."

"Aye," an able-rated seaman agreed, rubbing his thin, grimy face against his tattered sleeve. "Poor bastard. What he must be thinking, day after day after day in this stinking hole I can't begin to imagine! At least I don't have a family and young 'uns to fret about. I'm amazed he ain't half-mad by now."

"Mebbe he is," another scruffy-looking sailor remarked.

"You can't blame him or Captain Walsh for any of this," foretopman Noah Wright said, not for the first time. "We let the ship down, pure and simple. Captain Walsh goes below for a little rest, and then what happens? The watch was caught napping. We let them pirates run over us quick as you please and seize our ship. How those sneaky bastards managed it I still can't fathom. But sure as hell they did, and it wasn't the captain's fault."

"I don't see how the bastards could have snuck up on us like that either," a second able-rated seaman groused, shaking his head. "We never saw, 'em, we never heard 'em, yet there they were. And here we are."

"For the love of God, Matthew," Ben Stokes said irritably, "there's no use in pounding that drum over and over again. We've been through all that a thousand times, and where has it got us? What happened, happened. Hell's bells, let it be, will you? I'm going over to try to get that poor bastard to eat *something*, or at least to *say* something. He has no one else. He must have lost all of his crew when his ship was taken."

"Good luck," Ben Stokes said. "Even Captain Walsh can't get a response from him."

The living skeleton flicked a lifeless glance up at Stokes as he walked across the room, then shifted his gaze downward to the bowl of uneaten rice beside him. Either he did not see Stokes approaching or he chose to ignore him.

Thirty-seven other prisoners were scattered across the floor. Most were Americans, though the group included a handful of British sailors and men from other nations. Narrow slits of windows admitted feeble sunlight during the height of day that allowed the prisoners to peer out. What they could see was not encouraging. Thick vegetation on two sides would block a rescue attempt from inland. The river that flowed past on one side was too shallow and rocky to admit ships' boats, and the endless sea of sawgrass on the other offered no traction for anyone foolish enough to attempt a frontal assault. Through the window slit, far out to sea on the southwestern horizon, they could just make out the rise of hills on the island of Hainan.

Nevertheless, despite the obstacles, the prisoners were convinced that deliverance was in the works. Either the ransoms the pirates must be demanding would finally be paid, or a rescue party would come. It was simply a matter of holding out until then.

"We can't give up," Stokes whispered to the filthy, emaciated man. "We'll get out of this somehow, mark my words. You need to build your strength and your spirits. Please eat, sir."

The skeleton shook his head. "Bah!" he spat contemptuously, the first sound Stokes could recall hearing him utter.

CHAPTER 19

Days rolled by, becoming weeks that threatened to become months. To military officers determined to rescue their imprisoned countrymen and knowing they possessed the wherewithal to do it, the forced inaction was excruciating.

The wait for repairs to restore *Richmond*'s steam engine seemed interminable. To make matters worse, it was winter, the rainy season, and nearly every afternoon a cloudburst spread gloom across the island, from buildings ashore to ships in the harbor, slowing progress and fraying nerves. Already *Richmond* had been in dry dock for weeks at the Royal Navy shipyard on Kowloon. Everyone understood that the delays, however frustrating, were unavoidable. The parts needed to reconstruct her engine were hard to come by, as were the skilled technicians needed to install them.

A sudden stroke of good fortune eased the frustration. Commodore Finlayson of America's East India Squadron finally responded to Terence Neale's appeals for additional naval assets to support the attack on the pirates' lair. Although he repeated his lack of resources, Finlayson nonetheless agreed to send Neale *Saratoga* and *Dexter*, both with full complements of Marines. Furthermore, he offered a starting date for the expedition, suggesting a rendezvous in Hong Kong in mid-April after the rainy season had ended. By then, Finlayson wrote, the repairs on *Richmond* would be completed and Neale would be commanding five frigates, a naval squadron equal in number and strength to his own, sufficient to do the job and get the captives out and to safety.

"Thank Christ!" Neale sighed after reading the dispatch to Jack Brengle. "Now we have a fighting chance. The guns and Marines on those two ships will give us the edge we need. Mid-April gives us a month. Assemble the officers here in my cabin in, say, two hours, and we'll start planning."

"I'll tell Hallowell to pass the word," Brengle said.

"Good. Oh, by the by, Jack, a stack of letters arrived for you in that last dispatch pouch. Most are from the Navy Department, of course, but one, judging by its handwriting, originated elsewhere." He handed over the letters.

Brengle flipped through them until he came to that one letter. He caught his breath at the sight of the small, elegant script. The handwriting was unfamiliar, but he knew in a heartbeat whose it was. He looked up at Neale, who smiled and motioned toward his personal dining cuddy on the aft port quarter.

Brengle went directly to it and closed the door. Without taking his eyes from the letter, he drew out a chair, sat down at the table, and opened the folds of delicate blue paper.

55 Brattle Street
Cambridge, Massachusetts
19 December 1847

My Dear Jack:

You will not read this letter for months, and when you do, you will be far away on the outer edge of the world. I pray your voyage to Java was uneventful.

I wish I had better news to tell you. It seems that your intuition and concern for my well-being were prophetic. My physician informs me that I have contracted a form of typhus, God knows where. It hardly matters now. Although the symptoms are very unpleasant, I am well cared for here in my grandmother's home. She is an excellent nurse, and family members are looking in on me at all hours of the day. Truly, my life is blessed, and I am ashamed that I have learned that only now that I am sick. Sometimes, when

I think of the burdens I put on everyone, I am overcome by guilt. When I consider your kindness to me at a time when most men would have walked away, I want to weep. I do not deserve you, Jack. But please know that your care and concern helped to save me. To my dying day I shall faithfully follow the path you have laid out for me.

There is much more to tell you, and I will write again as soon as my health improves, which please God it soon will. I just wish to say now that I am thinking of you. We are making progress in our war against opium here, as I trust you are there. I am proud that you and I are fighting the war together.

There is hope, dear Jack, and we must both believe that. For myself, I miss you more and more as Christmas draws nigh. I will light a candle for you.

Always think well of me, and pray for me as I pray for you. Take good care of yourself and come home, when you can, to those who love you.

With deep affection,
Lucy

Brengle took a moment to digest what he had just read before going back out to the main cabin. Terence Neale was seated at his desk reviewing some papers.

"Is your surgeon available?" Brengle asked abruptly.

Neale looked startled. "I believe he is. Why do you ask?"

"I'd like to have a word with him, if you please."

"Is something wrong?"

"I don't know. That's why I need a word with him."

"Very well. Sentry!" Neale called out.

The cabin door opened a crack. "Captain?"

"Pass the word for Doctor Hanrahan, Corporal."

"Right away, Captain."

The cabin door opened several minutes later to admit the ship's surgeon. Unlike many of his medical contemporaries serving in naval vessels, Stephen Hanrahan presented a professional appearance in a crisp pair of brown trousers and a pressed beige coat. His reddish head, beard, and mustache had been meticulously groomed, and his kindly eyes shone with a confidence born of his excellence in his craft.

"Good morning, Captain," he greeted Neale before shifting his gaze to Brengle. "And a good morning to you, Captain. What can I do for you gentlemen?"

Brengle said, "I am the one who had you summoned, Doctor. I would like to ask you some questions."

"Ask away."

"How serious is typhus?"

Hanrahan eyed him curiously. "You look healthy enough, so may I assume you are not the patient in question?"

"That is correct. I am inquiring after an acquaintance in Boston. A young lady."

"I see." Hanrahan stroked his beard thoughtfully. "Your question is not easy to answer without more information, Captain. I cannot examine her, of course, and although the disease has been a plague on humanity for a long time, not a great deal is known about it. There are several variants, some of which can be quite serious. Do you know the patient's symptoms?"

"Not in detail. Only that they are painful and unpleasant."

"Typhus is indeed that. Symptoms involve, among other unpleasantries, extreme fatigue, vomiting, and dysentery."

"Is there a cure?"

"It depends on several factors. The form of the disease, of course, and the physical condition of the patient, not to mention the medical treatment she is receiving. Prior to contracting the disease, was the lady in good health, do you know?"

"I believe she was."

"And is she now in good hands?"

"The best, Doctor. The best medical attention that Boston and a loving family can provide. That said, I must ask you one last question, and I beg of you an honest answer. Is it . . . can the disease be fatal?"

Hanrahan looked him squarely in the eyes. "It can be, and often is. I'm sorry to be vague, but that is all I can say with precious little to go on. Recovery from a serious medical condition such as that depends on a variety of factors, not the least of which is the patient's will to live. If she has the constitution of your Lieutenant Montgomery, I would say her chances for a full recovery are excellent. On the other hand, if she is prone to buckle under stressful circumstances, I would not be as optimistic. Again, as with most serious medical conditions, physical recovery depends on one's mental attitude."

Brengle nodded. "I understand, Doctor. Thank you for your counsel and your time. You have been most helpful."

"Your servant, Captain." He was making to leave the cabin when Neale said, "Speaking of Lieutenant Montgomery, Doctor, I have a decision to make regarding his status. You know the issues involved. So, I ask you: In your medical opinion, after having observed Lieutenant Montgomery twice a week in recent weeks, should he be allowed to sail with the squadron to China? My question refers only to his physical ability to command."

Hanrahan answered without hesitation. "Let him sail, Captain Neale. If you were to beach him now, after all his hard work and improvement, it would do him great harm. Let him seek his destiny. Let him sail."

Neale nodded but did not reply.

"It's a risk for him," Hanrahan conceded, "and I don't understand why he wants to take it. In my book, he has no further need to prove himself. I suspect his desire to accompany you is tied to his loyalty to you both, as well as to Captain Cutler. Not to mention to his country. And perhaps his conviction that a woman such as Daisy Cutler deserves a warrior for a husband, not an invalid."

Brengle arched his eyebrows. "Montgomery told you that last bit, Doctor?"

"In so many words, yes. Look, gentlemen, you both know the lad far better than I do, and I suspect you agree with me." He looked at Neale. "My prescription in this case is to trust your instinct, Captain. It will not fail you. Now, if you two will please excuse me . . ."

* * *

As preparations for the squadron's departure intensified, Richard Cutler faced several dilemmas. Since arriving in Batavia two weeks earlier, he had immersed himself in the business operations of Cutler & Sons' Far East operations. The ledgers he scrutinized portrayed a company with diverse revenue streams, an impressive return on investments, and an acceptable alignment of revenues with expenses that had allowed the opening of offices in Kuala Lumpur and Manila. He had expected the ledgers to reveal such progress. It had been the norm since the days of Philip Seymour and, before him, the legendary Jan Vanderheyden, the first director. More than anyone, Vanderheyden deserved credit for building Cutler & Sons into a commercial power in the Orient. Thirty years of successful operations had built a solid financial base sufficient to cover all projected expenses during the next five years. Yet, despite these strengths and the prospect of continuing prosperity, the ledgers, studied in a certain light, also revealed weaknesses that foretold trouble ahead if they were allowed to fester.

What troubled Richard most as he worked through the numbers was the large percentage of current annual revenues generated by a small group of customers. Unlike in North America and Europe, where widely dispersed and relatively small-scale customers often purchased the full array of Cutler products, in the Orient, large conglomerates were not buying traditional Cutler sugar, molasses, and rum. In fact, many of them were not buying anything at all. They were instead renting the holds and sailors of Cutler merchant vessels to transport their own goods to their own customers, an unsettling number of which had recently taken root in Japan and China, two substantial markets that Cutler & Sons had yet to successfully penetrate. Cutler management might know what the competition was doing, but they were less clear on what to do about it. Richard had several ideas brewing, and he intended to discuss these ideas with Pieter De Vries and Ben Cutler as soon as he finalized his report. Time, he realized, was not on his side. Time was the enemy. Unless certain conditions were brought under control, Cutler & Sons could end up competing against itself while the competition seized market share and the United States fought other nations' battles in a part of the world that held limited strategic importance for it.

Perhaps, his thoughts continued, the British had reached similar conclusions. Was that why they had withdrawn from the battle arena despite the overt threat the pirates continued to pose to their own prosperity and sailors? He recalled a conversation with George Bancroft in which the Navy secretary had warned that nations, like men, are motivated by greed and self-interest. Whatever the bases of an alliance between nations, geopolitics dictates that if one nation sees an advantage outside of the alliance, that nation will exploit its advantage and leave its ally in the lurch, despite promises to the contrary. Why else would the United States be constructing forts along its east coast?

Richard looked away from the ledgers at the sound of a commotion out in the front hallway. Going out to investigate, he saw a *Columbia* midshipman in full undress uniform standing by the front doorway with the strap of a thick leather dispatch pouch slung over his shoulder. Richard began walking toward him just as the midshipman began walking toward Richard.

"It's all right, Siti," Richard said to the young servant who had opened the front door. "I know this young man."

The midshipman strode confidently up to Richard, saluted him, and said, "Two dispatches for you, Captain, just arrived." He reached into the pouch and produced two letters. As soon as the letters were in his hands Richard recognized their origins. One was from the Department of the Navy. The other was from Anne.

"Thank you, Mr. Sears."

"Sir!" The midshipman saluted a second time, then strode back down the hallway toward the front door.

Richard walked back into his office, closed the door, and put both letters on his desk. He sat down and read Anne's first. It was thick and was dated 29 October 1847, several months earlier.

33 Lafayette Avenue
Hingham, Massachusetts

My Dearest:

More than a week has passed since you set sail from Boston. Although it seems like a far longer passage of time, I am comforted by the thought that when you read this letter you will be in Batavia, and that soon, please God very soon, your work will be finished and you will be returning home. You know I understand how important that work is. You must also understand that I would do nothing to interfere with what you must do. Just know that the day you arrive home in Boston will be the happiest day of my life.

Though there is much to tell you, I know exactly where to start. As the French delicately say, Je suis enceinte encore! *Yes, my love, we are going to be parents once again, soon after you return to Boston. I had a notion before you sailed, but I wanted to delay writing to you until my condition was confirmed. Now it has been. I am planning to tell both your family and mine after I send this letter off to you.*

Would you consent, if the babe is a boy, to our naming him John? It's my father's name, as you know, and the name of your cousin. As we have often discussed, there is yet another man in our lives named John whom we both wish to honor. You do understand, don't you, my darling?

Richard paused to read that last paragraph. He pursed his lips and nodded slowly. Were it not for Captain John Shilling of the Royal Navy and what he did in New Zealand, neither Richard nor any member of his family would be alive today. Anne would know that he could not object to that name.

He continued reading the rest of the letter. What followed were accounts of the children, the kind of correspondence that only a parent would take to heart. Then some further good news.

We have received the final contract from Little, Brown. Mr. McDonough has suggested some changes in the manuscript, mostly in word usage. I am inclined to accept all his suggestions. I am certain you will agree when you read the final manuscript, otherwise I would have waited for your return. It's amazing to me how a publisher can work such magic with text which I thought already perfect and make it better. The contract stipulates that the book will be published in six to twelve months. Otherwise, the terms are more or less as we discussed. So we will have yet another reason to celebrate upon your return!

There followed some news concerning Harlan Sturgis, none of it good for him. Two of his henchmen had been persuaded to turn coat as state's witnesses, and a number of women had defied social norms by coming forward to testify that Sturgis had blackmailed them into prostitution. Due in large measure to Lucy's written testimony, charges of abetting prostitution had also been filed against the Chinese couple who owned the building in Boston that had harbored Sturgis's opium den.

Odd, Richard thought as he perused the letter again, Anne had not mentioned Lucy's illness, which Jack had recently confided in him. Perhaps she had not known about it when she wrote. Or Lucy may have downplayed her condition.

The letter went on with words of endearment that ended:

> *Be well, my beloved husband. My warmest regards to Jack, Terence, and, of course, Jonty. My prayers to all men who are called upon to fight and die for their country. My love, always, to you.*
>
> *Anne*

A roll of thunder distracted his thoughts as he reread the letter for a third time. A distant flash of sheet lightning visible through the open window confirmed that a late-season thunderstorm was brewing. He placed the letter on his desk and picked up the dispatch from the Navy Department. As expected, it contained standard-issue correspondence between the Department and one of its captains overseas. The postscript marked "Confidential," however, was not standard:

> *I cannot and I will not order you to do anything, Captain Cutler. That was our agreement, and I respect the burdens of management currently placed upon you. However, should the need arise, you have my authority to do whatever you deem necessary to assist Commodore Neale. I realize you and he have not always seen eye to eye on naval tactics, but I'm sure you would agree that he is a good man and a fine naval commander. In assisting him you will have my gratitude and the gratitude of our nation. I shall leave it to you, as the ranking naval officer in Batavia, to determine if, when, and how such assistance should be rendered.*

The dispatch was signed by the signature and seal of Secretary of the Navy John Y. Mason.

Eight days later, Jonathan Montgomery and Daisy Cutler were dining alone in the garden behind Cutler headquarters at a small table on which two servants had placed several platters of simple food and a carafe of Beaujolais. The day was drawing in, and a chorus of birds serenaded the sunset in the trees surrounding the garden. Twilight had sketched the western sky with streaks of pink, orange, and amber against a backdrop of pale blue. A gentle breeze carried the now-familiar scents of tropical flowers. The two serving girls lingered discreetly on the fringe of the garden until Daisy dismissed them.

"Are you not hungry, Daisy?" Jonty asked into the evening quiet. She seemed lost in thought as she stared expressionlessly at her plate. "You have hardly eaten anything, and you haven't touched your wine." He failed to mention that he hadn't done much better. "Captain Neale has been so generous in granting us this time. I want our last evening together to be one we shall always remember."

"Do you think for one moment that I don't want that, Jonty?" Daisy answered him. "But what I truly want for this evening has nothing to do with food or wine."

"What, then?"

She looked up. "I believe you know."

"Do I?" He flushed when he saw the longing in her eyes and averted his gaze. "Yes, I believe I do."

"And?"

He shook his head. "This is not easy for me, Daisy," he told her quietly. "To be so close to you during the day, and often during the night, and not be allowed to act on my desires is torture. Exquisite torture, to be sure, but torture nonetheless. We have discussed this. I will not marry you until I return from China. You know why I am so adamant about that. I thought you understood."

Daisy bit her lower lip. "I do understand," she said, "and I am forced to accept that. But I am going to miss you more than I can say, and I need you to love me before you go. You must know what I am talking about. Have I shocked you?"

He paused, again avoiding her gaze. The birds in the trees had gone silent. "What about your father? For God's sake, Daisy, how would he feel, knowing we are together in that way just a few feet down the hall from him."

She shrugged. "My father is not like most parents, Jonty. He tends to flaunt social conventions." He could barely see her wry smile in the darkness. "If he didn't, how could he tolerate living with me? Likely he would turn a blind eye and a deaf ear, with a glad heart. You know how he feels about you. How he feels about us. My father wants me to be happy, and he knows I am very happy with you. Do you understand?"

"Yes, I do," he had to admit.

"Well, then." Daisy stood up, came around the table, and dropped to a knee beside him. She took his hand in hers and placed it over her heart. It was beating in wild rhythm with his own, as was the pulse he could see throbbing in her exposed throat. He felt the hard rise of desire.

"Daisy!" he gasped, knowing that he was losing the battle with his conscience.

"Please, Jonty," she whispered urgently, "Please be mindful, but please take me upstairs! Now!"

When she awoke the next morning, he was gone. There was only a hollow in the pillow to show he had spent the night in her bed.

CHAPTER 20

OFF GUANGDONG PROVINCE, SOUTH CHINA SEA
April 1848

The gales of the previous day had blown eastward into the Philippine Sea, leaving calm seas and clear blue skies in their wake. The six vessels of the American squadron—five frigates and the supply ship *Savannah*, doubling as a hospital ship—were steaming westward along the Guangdong coast. *Columbia*, the flagship, led the way, followed in a far-flung but orderly diamond pattern by *Chippewa*, *Richmond*, *Saratoga*, *Savannah*, and *Dexter*. Ahead and off to starboard lay Macau, a small land mass connected to the mainland by a narrow strip of land. Portugal's toehold in the Oriental trade and the oldest European possession in China, Macau was an important outpost of European imperialism. It managed a vast wealth, garnered in part by its strategic location and in larger part by controversial trade agreements signed three centuries earlier between emissaries of the Ming emperor and King Sebastian of Portugal. Local authorities from time to time allowed the American East India Squadron to drop anchor in Macau's well-fortified harbor and temporarily conduct business from there. It was a tenuous arrangement at best, since the United States, while needing secure bases for its ships, sought to avoid entanglements in Chinese internal affairs save for when American interests were threatened.

The sun's brilliant rays reflected off endless ripples of seawater on both sides of *Columbia*, creating a glare so strong that sailors had to shield their eyes when looking anywhere but down. It was with difficulty that First Officer William Bowen, in command on *Columbia*'s quarterdeck, noted that flags were being hauled up the signal halyard of *Saratoga*, the frigate farthest to the north and therefore closest to the Chinese mainland. David Marston, the junior officer of the deck and the senior of the three midshipmen stationed on the quarterdeck, pointed them out eagerly.

"I can see the flags, Mr. Marston," Bowen said curtly. "What I need is confirmation of what the flags are telling us."

"Aye, aye, sir," Marston acknowledged. He raised his glass to study *Saratoga*'s port signal halyard, lowered the glass long enough to consult his signal book, then raised the glass again. Satisfied that he was reading the signal correctly, he reported: "Four vessels sighted to windward, sir. Junk-rigged. No markings or other distinctions."

"Hmm," Bowen mused. "Junk-rigged with no markings. That would appear to eliminate government ships. Could be pirates shadowing us. What do you think, Mr. Marston?"

His opinion requested, Midshipman Marston freely offered it. "The enemy already knows we're here, sir, and they know why we're here. So why would they shadow us? I'm thinking these are coastal traders out of Canton and the Pearl River making for Macau or Hainan."

"Could be," Bowen mused, not sounding convinced. He pondered a moment, then: "Go below and advise the captain that he is requested on deck. Then find Lieutenant Montgomery and advise him of the same. He's off duty, so you're likely to find him in the wardroom."

"Aye, aye, sir!"

After going below to the gun deck and informing the captain of Bowen's request, Marston continued down the aft companionway to the berthing deck. From the orlop, one deck lower still, he could hear the muffled rumblings of the steam engines, the thrum of the paddlewheel, and the slosh of seawater, comforting sounds signifying power. Most enemy warships in these waters continued to rely strictly on wind, giving *Columbia* the edge in any battle.

In the wardroom, located aft directly under the captain's quarters on the gun deck, Marston found the off-duty commissioned officers and senior warrant officers taking their ease. The surgeon, Stephen Hanrahan, was in an armchair reading a book. A hotly contested game of whist was being played at a large circular table, pitting Marine captain Jason Albright and a Marine lieutenant against Second Officer Charles Cadwick and Third Officer Jonathan Montgomery. Lyall Dean, the sailing master, was watching the proceedings from a comfortable nook, sipping coffee from a mug provided by the wardroom steward, Jeremy Cook. Judging by a grunt, a curse, and a slap of cards on the table as Marston approached, the two Marine lieutenants were being hard done by.

Marston strode to the table and saluted Montgomery: "Sorry to disturb, sir," he said. "Mr. Bowen sends his compliments and requires your presence on deck."

Montgomery stood from the table. "Very well, Mr. Marston. I shall follow you. Gentlemen," he said to the three remaining players, "we'll pick up where we left off. Charles, the winnings are substantial and are ours for the taking. Keep a sharp eye on the kitty while I'm gone."

"Dream away, Lieutenant," Albright laughed. "That money is ours. A timely exit, I'd say!" he added.

On the quarterdeck, Terence Neale and William Bowen were conferring by the helm where a team of quartermaster's mates worked the wheel. Montgomery approached, kept his distance, and waited. When Neale noticed him, he waved Montgomery over.

"We have spotted four junks to the north, Lieutenant," Neale said, pointing in the general direction. "Probably nothing of consequence, although I agree with Mr. Bowen that we need to verify that. *Columbia* is breaking formation to have a closer look. You have the most experience sailing in these waters, and no one has a better knowledge of the difference between a merchantman, a government vessel, and a pirate junk. Light aloft, if you please, and tell us what you see. Mind that arm of yours. Take no risks, you hear me?"

Montgomery saluted and a minute later was climbing the ratlines in the starboard foremast shrouds. The going was slow. He found he could not reach up with his left arm and hold it there for any length of time because the pain in his shoulder and upper arm was too acute. Instead, he grasped an upper ratline with his right hand and pushed himself up with his left. In due course, he reached a height where the shrouds narrowed leading up to the truck and he could command a broad sweep of the distant shoreline of Guangdong Province.

As *Columbia* jogged slightly to port to further aid his view, he entwined his legs and right arm through the ratlines and around the shrouds. He steadied himself, peered through the glass, and brought the distant images in closer. Yes, there they were: four junks sailing one behind the other on a westerly course approximating the course the squadron was following. At first sight he could see nothing suspicious or out of order. Then he noticed that none of the junks had an anchor hanging a short way down from the prow. This Montgomery found unusual. Coastal traders often had to drop anchor at a moment's notice to avoid being swept onto a lee shore, and most kept their anchor ever at the ready. If these vessels were not coastal traders, they could be either government ships or pirate ships. Either way, they would be armed. Since Montgomery could not see over the ships' transoms, he could not determine if they carried guns. What appeared to be gun ports were closed. Nor could he see anything of note above the transom—no superstructure or cargo. The upper deck of each vessel had been stripped clean of everything save the masts. This, too, was unusual, but in his opinion neither observation warranted sounding an alarm. No doubt these anomalies could be explained. In these waters, most merchantmen carried guns to discourage piracy.

Boston Maid's guns had not been enough to protect her, he mused, lowering his glass. For almost a year, Captain Walsh and his crew had been rotting in a prison in Guangxi awaiting payment of a ransom that would never be paid. On this issue, the United States government was adamant. Since the atrocities along the Barbary Coast a half century earlier and the administrations of John Adams and Thomas Jefferson, American policy dictated that under no circumstances would America treat with any entity demanding ransoms. Such demands would be met with American steel and shot, and American blood, if necessary. But never with American treasure.

Montgomery continued to study the junks as they sailed on a course parallel with *Columbia*'s. These were not government war junks, he decided. Chinese government vessels made their identity known to friends and foes alike. Threatening or in any way interfering with one constituted a capital offense punishable by death. Many carried red and gold banners slung between the mainmast and the much shorter after mast to emphasize their identity. No such banners fluttered here; nor did they display any other symbol of imperial authority.

There were other clues. The differences between a pirate vessel and a merchant vessel were not always clear cut. Unlike Western ships, whose features revealed their function, most Chinese junks were rigged and constructed in a similar fashion. Nonetheless, there were differences, however subtle. Size was one. War junks tended to be larger and beamier than merchant junks, in large measure due to heavy batteries mounted on their weather decks. But that was not always true. Smaller and swifter war junks had their place in Asian naval engagements, filling the same role as frigates in Western engagements when serving as the eyes of the fleet and reporting on enemy movements. No, Montgomery concluded, the only sure way to determine a junk's purpose was either to board her or feather up close enough to her to survey her deck from above. But he saw no reason to recommend doing so. The four junks, now less than a mile away, looked innocuous enough. The fact that they were altering course to the north, closer to the shallower water and menacing shoals and skerries of the Guangdong shoreline, was likely attributable to xenophobia triggered by the sight of an American naval squadron with unknown intent closing fast from the south.

Montgomery climbed down to the quarterdeck and made his report. Neale listened to Montgomery's observations and conclusions, then nodded and turned to the quartermaster's mate at the helm. "We shall return to station," he said, "and resume our original course."

The matter was settled.

* * *

After several hours on their original course, the high interior hills of Hainan loomed directly ahead. China's largest island, long considered a tropical paradise by Westerners, had few permanent residents. Instead, it served as a place of exile for government officials who had fallen out of favor with the emperor. Located at the entrance to the Gulf of Tonkin,

Hainan and its craggy hills afforded protection from prevailing north-easterly winds, and the myriad deep-water inlets and bays on its coasts offered vessels refuge from storms—and enemies. The island also offered an excellent staging ground for an assault on the similarly indented mainland coast visible to the north. Although details remained sketchy, the British and Chinese intelligence services had determined that American sailors, including the captain and crew of *Boston Maid*, were most likely being held captive in one of these coves and inlets. Back in Batavia, Richard Cutler had argued caution, predicting that the pirates had sensed the looming attack and moved the hostages further inland toward the Li or Gui Rivers as bait to lure the American rescuers into a trap. Jack Brengle had supported Richard's argument, to no avail. Terence Neale would not budge. As he had done before, the "by the book" commander relied on his orders to counter any difference of opinion on how the attack should be conducted.

"Orders are orders," he had insisted during a rare display of pique over disagreement among his officers, "and our orders are explicit. They are open to neither negotiation nor interpretation. We know where the captives are being held, and we must get them out, whatever the cost, and then get out of China. If American merchants still choose to take their chances in the Oriental trade after this," he added, "so be it. But they must assume the risks and not expect deliverance from the U.S. Navy."

Richard could not dispel his intuition that something was wrong. While orders were to be followed to the extent possible, a field commander must have the authority and flexibility to modify tactics—and even the orders themselves—to fit the circumstances and to achieve the stated objective. It was what Napoleon Bonaparte had famously referred to as "creative soldiering," and in all his great battles he had allowed his marshals that flexibility. To Richard's mind, the principle applied equally to leadership in naval and land engagements. But he saw no point in challenging Neale further at this stage.

* * *

Early in the evening, with the sun hovering on the western horizon, the squadron settled at anchor off the southwest coast of Hainan. With their frigates anchored in the lee of what had become a northeasterly of note, five captains, in company with Richard Cutler, were in the commodore's after cabin in *Columbia* reviewing the next day's battle plan while enjoying a large and elaborate meal. Similar quantities, if not qualities, of food were being served in the wardrooms and berthing decks of *Columbia's* four sister ships. By this time tomorrow, Richard mused somberly, after the assault on the mainland, many of these men would be dead.

The strength of the plan, Neale stressed to his officers, lay in its simplicity. Intelligence had confirmed that the captives were being held in a prison on the mainland across the Qiongzhou Strait near the Gulf of Tonkin. The prison was accessible by land only during a dead low tide. Low tide tomorrow was at four bells in the morning watch. The five frigates would therefore get under way at the change of watch at four o'clock and steam the twelve miles to their destination, reaching it an hour later. A naval bombardment targeting an immaterial area down the coast would commence at three bells to provide a distraction and a cover for the squadron's ten boats. Two boats from each frigate would be manned by Marines and sailors, with enough room in the boats to convey the freed prisoners out to the American ships. The landing site and invasion route had been chosen to avoid the broad, grassy marshes that almost surrounded the target. The assault of the stronghold would begin as soon as the bows of the boats hissed ashore.

The great unknown was the state of the defenses they would face. This they would not know until the assault began. Regardless of what the defenses might be, Neale was confident they could be softened by a barrage of six-pounder cannon fire, an array of howitzers, and volleys of canister shot, each volley with the effect of a giant shotgun blast. Only when the beachhead was softened would the Marines storm the defenses with antipersonnel explosives, including shrapnel-filled grenades, and make short work of any pirates left standing, most of whom, Neale predicted, would flee inland at the first salvo.

The ships' officers had finished their deliberations and were enjoying a last brandy before returning to their ships to snatch what sleep they could. They were in for a long day tomorrow.

* * *

Captain Neale and the other officers were bolted awake early the next morning when a series of cries erupted from aloft and the deck shuddered under the stamp of running feet.

"Captain! Captain!" an urgent voice called down the aft companionway.

Terence Neale hurried on deck. Richard Cutler and the senior officers followed close behind. When they looked in the direction where those on deck were pointing, what they saw confused them. Out of a heavy mist rolling down from the high hills of Hainan loomed a series of masts, their identification, as yet, unknown. They were still a ways off but were picking up speed in the freshening breeze.

"What the hell!" Neale demanded. Then it dawned on him. "Sweet Jesus in Heaven!" he exploded. "How could this have happened?"

As the sun rose higher in the morning sky, dissipating the mist and affording greater clarity of vision and understanding, four junks, the very junks they had spotted yesterday, bore down on the American squadron from around the southern tip of Hainan. Two junks were in the vanguard; the other two kept pace a short distance behind. As the Americans stood transfixed, the upper deck of the lead junk burst into flames. In the next instant, the tophamper on a second junk similarly broke into flames that rampaged up its lateen sails, rigging, and spars. The other two junks began to catch up with their burning sisters. Together, in a jagged line of offense, the four junks—two in flames, two not—bore down on the anchored American frigates.

"*Fire ships!*" Neale cried out, his voice laced with something Montgomery had never heard before from him: fear. "All hands stand by to fend off!" Neale remained where he was, rooted to the spot by this fiery vision of hell.

CHAPTER 21

OFF THE ISLAND OF HAINAN, SOUTH CHINA SEA
April 1848

Richard snapped up a speaking trumpet. "Belay that order!" he shouted. "Start the engines! Stand by to cut the anchor cable! Look lively, men!" To Neale, more softly, "Sorry, Terry. I'm assuming command!"

Neale did not protest.

To the sailing master Richard shouted, "Turn the helm over the moment we are under way, Mr. Dean! Bring the port batteries to bear!"

To the flag midshipman: "Signal the squadron to follow our lead, Mr. Marston! Quickly, dammit! We've not much time!"

To the boatswain, who had hurried on deck: "Clear for action, Mr. Reeves!"

To Jonathan Montgomery: "Advise the gunner to ready the port batteries. Then report back here!"

"Aye, aye, Captain!" Montgomery shouted.

Reeves and Montgomery hurried off to obey Richard's orders.

Richard glanced astern. The four junks were closing fast. A warning flashed through his mind: Why were only two of the junks engulfed in flames? Was it so the other two could pick up their comrades after they had abandoned ship? He doubted it. As far as he knew, the Chinese didn't seem to put much value on life. No, something more sinister was at work here. But what?

Just then he saw an astonishing sight. Perched high up at the tiller of the lead junk, on the port side, a squat, gray-bearded man was pumping his fist in the air as though cheering on a team in a match of some sort.

He was steering into almost certain death, about to take many good men with him, and he was, of all the damnable things, grinning!

"Think this is funny, do you?" Richard snarled. With a swift motion, he withdrew his revolver from its holster, flipped off its safety catch, and took aim. "See if you find *this* amusing!" He squeezed the trigger, the pistol discharged, and the helmsman fell onto the deck. Another pirate jumped up to take his place at the helm.

As *Columbia's* steam engines coughed and sputtered to life and Reeves prepared to sever the anchor cable with a downward slice of a cutlass, squads of pirates in all four junks, hidden until now behind the vessels' high bulwarks, rose and took aim with long-barreled, old-style muskets and let off a volley that peppered the quarterdecks of the American frigates with shot. Cries and curses and splashes of seawater confirmed multiple men down.

The American sailors and Marines, struggling to respond to the sudden and unexpected onslaught, managed to get off a few rounds. Some of their bullets found their mark, but most did not. Nonetheless, the water surrounding the ships filled with floating and thrashing bodies and became red with blood.

Dexter, the smallest of the frigates at 213 feet, 10 guns, and 3,400 long tons, was the first to come around and train her guns on the approaching junks. She opened fire on the closest junk with four 12-pounder guns on her port side. One shot struck the junk amidships at the waterline, the impact igniting a stentorian explosion that instantly disintegrated the junk and created a blast wave that sent men on all the vessels, friend and foe alike, reeling and sprawling onto a hard deck or into the dark waters. Thunderous echoes resounded off the high hills of the island's interior, one after another in a macabre symphony until the sound gradually faded away, to be replaced by silence broken only by the pitiful moans and pleas of broken and drowning men.

As the three remaining junks came on, Richard Cutler gazed about at the grisly scene. On the quarterdeck, Neale, Bowen, and Dean were down, whether wounded, dead, or temporarily stunned he could not determine. Forward, it was no better. Bodies were everywhere. Some men were laboring to get up, to make sense of what had just happened.

Others lay deathly still. Suddenly it came as a sickening blow to Richard what the pirates were about. He struggled to rise but found he could not. A sharp pain in his left thigh prevented it. He looked down to see blood oozing from a ragged hole in his left trouser leg.

Grimacing, he crawled forward to the large rectangular opening amidships, gripped the coaming with both hands, and with a mighty heave hauled himself to his feet. A thick rivulet of blood ran down his leg.

"Masters," he managed to yell down to the gunner on the gun deck, "aim for the junk not on fire. Got it? The junk *not* on fire!"

The gunner raised his right arm in acknowledgment.

Columbia was finally coming around, but too slowly. The remaining fireship would be upon her before her guns could be brought to bear. What remained of the junk's crew fired a final volley of musketry and began leaping overboard into the frothing South China Sea, apparently preferring their chances with sharks to certain death on the junk. Richard was closing his eyes to the inevitable when the harsh report of great guns sounded nearby. He looked shoreward to see the aftermath of *Chippewa*'s discharge.

"Everyone down!" Richard cried. "Grab hold of something, anything. Steady, men, steady!" His gravelly warning went largely unheeded. There was too much commotion on deck for his parched voice to carry.

It happened quickly. Again a mighty explosion; again the deep rumble of thunder rolling off the hills and valleys of Hainan and on into the far distance; again the instant disintegration of a pirate junk; and again an aftershock of such violence it burst eardrums and sent Richard and other men over the side into the sea.

Jonathan Montgomery had not heard his captain's warning, but he and everyone else knew by now what payload that junk was carrying. He knew the drill. Moments before *Chippewa*'s great Dahlgren guns had opened up, he had lunged toward the base of the mainmast and clung to it for dear life, his stomach and face pressed down against the wooden planks of the weather deck. After the savage hot blast had passed over him, he lay still, taking stock of his four limbs, one at a time, testing for pain or weakness, relieved to feel only the ever-present pain in his left arm.

Slowly he raised his head and glanced astern. The acrid stench of smoke and sulfur was clearing along with the smoke, and he saw only a few men stirring. One of them, a Marine, was kneeling as if in prayer, his hand using his rifle as a crutch in an effort to stand. Another man, a tough and normally sharp able-rated seaman, had managed to stand on legs as unsteady as a drunkard's in a pub. His face was smeared in black. Shell-shocked, he was looking around stupidly, disbelievingly, as if searching for something to do or for someone to go to. Several other men were crawling on the quarterdeck as stray bullets pinged and whined around them. Behind them, not far away, the blazing mast of a fireship rose above the frigate's stern rail. *Columbia's* engine had stalled, and she was now drifting helplessly into harm's way.

Montgomery looked to where Richard Cutler should have been but was not. He looked up and down the deck without spotting him. He inched his hands up the mainmast and gradually pulled himself to his feet, then waited a few moments before taking small steps toward the center hatchway. Searching around the opening, he again saw nothing of Richard, or of Captain Neale. Only then did he look where he feared to look: over the side into a sea foaming with blood.

Cutler was in the water on his back, his legs spread-eagled to keep his body afloat, conserving his strength and moving his arms and hands just enough to maintain buoyancy. Jonty saw a thin trail of blood floating around Richard's left thigh.

"Lower the boats!" Montgomery yelled. "You men, there!" he shouted at two sailors and a Marine coming toward him. "Give me a hand with this." He gestured to the system of ropes and pulleys set on the mainmast boom to lower the boats earmarked to convey Marines ashore. "We have to get the captain and everyone else out of the water!"

"Sharks, sir!" a second Marine cried out in warning.

Montgomery hurried to the starboard rail. To his horror, he saw a vast school of sharks, dark forms prowling beneath the surface ripping meat from bones, feasting on a banquet of human flesh. One of them, a huge monster with narrow dark stripes running crosswise down the length of its back, was coming at Richard with smooth, powerful sweeps of its tail. The shark's dorsal fin broke the surface of the water as it knifed toward its prey, now only a few feet away.

Spotting a rifle abandoned on the deck, Montgomery grabbed it, checked that it was loaded, and took aim at one of the shark's black eyes, and squeezed the trigger. A hit! The shark convulsed, curling its body and thrashing its tail in a wash of water rapidly churning a bright red. Other sharks, drawn by the fresh blood, rushed to feed on one of their own. Richard Cutler was granted a reprieve that lasted but a few heartbeats before another shark, equally mammoth, left the feeding frenzy and came at him.

"Give me your knife, Kincaid!" Montgomery shouted to the able-rated sailor, who handed over a rigging knife with a six-inch serrated blade. As Montgomery took the knife and dove into the sea, the fire ship slammed into *Columbia*'s stern with an almighty crash. Grappling hooks were tossed over from the junk, securing one vessel to the other. The pair turned in time to the wind, tide, and current in a gruesome dance.

Montgomery surfaced a few feet from Richard and started swimming the short distance between them.

"Jonty!" Richard rasped, spluttering water. "Get away! What in thunder are you doing?"

"Returning a favor," Montgomery replied without taking his eyes from the large dorsal fin now circling them. When the beast came in close, he lunged with the knife, striking its snout and drawing blood. The shark darted away leaving a trail of red behind it.

"Get the hell out of here, Jonty!" Richard demanded, his voice little more than a croak. "Save yourself! That's an order, Lieutenant!"

"Sorry, Captain! I can't hear you!"

"The hell you can't!"

Montgomery jabbed at another shark, then another and another. Their sandpaper-like skin was tough, but the prick of a knife's point was enough to drive them off. Someone screamed nearby, another victim of the savagery. Even closer, a garbled scream was suddenly cut short. Montgomery glanced up. A pair of Marines on *Columbia*'s burning deck had delivered a merciful *coup de grace*.

"Help is on the way, Captain! Hang on, sir!"

The voice came from above, on *Columbia*'s deck, where two battles were being waged. One battle pitted the ship's Marine guard against what was left of the small but determined crew of the fire ship, who were driving back the Americans coming to aid their fallen officers and crew and to throw buckets of seawater on the flames consuming the frigate's mizzen mast and afterdeck. The clothes of one pirate had caught fire, but he fought on as though that was but a minor inconvenience. A Marine stepped up and fired his rifle. The pirate flew backward before slumping down onto the deck.

In another battle, Marines and sailors were firing down on the schools of sharks. Keeping their aim well clear of shipmates struggling in the sea, *Columbia*'s crew, those who could stand and shoot, pumped round after round of shot into the exposed backs and heads of the silent maneaters, creating a witches' brew of sudden death that lured some sharks away from stricken shipmates. But it did not lure away all of them.

"Ahoy, Captain," another voice called out, much closer. "Ship oars!" the voice commanded. "Port side, stand by to bring the captain and lieutenant aboard. Starboard side, fend off with oars!"

Desperately treading water, Montgomery stabbed at shark after shark as *Chippewa*'s clinker-built gig glided in and came to a stop with a backing of oars. Farther away, he could see an armada of ship's boats coming to the rescue of their shipmates, dead and alive, in the water. Montgomery slid his left arm under Richard's chin and side-stroked to the gig, where waiting hands reached out and gripped him beneath his arms.

"No!" he commanded. "The captain first! Take him first!"

The sailors complied. Slowly, painfully, Richard Cutler was pulled aboard the gig. The other oarsmen pummeled any shark coming within range. Exhausted beyond measure, Montgomery jabbed frantically with his knife until it was his turn to be hauled up.

"Here, Lieutenant!" a voice called urgently. "Grab hold of this here oar! We'll pull you over!"

Loath to turn around, Montgomery kept his back to the gig and a firm grip on his knife.

"Drop the knife, Lieutenant," an exasperated voice called. "Take the oar. We'll pull you over!"

Montgomery turned his head to see the blade of an oar edging toward him. Reluctantly, he released the knife and took hold of the blade with both hands. As he felt himself being pulled to the gig's side, he saw Jack Brengle on *Chippewa*'s quarterdeck watching him through a long glass. On an impulse, Montgomery raised his right arm to wave to him but felt his grip on the oar with his damaged left hand slip.

Hands gripped his shoulders. "Here we go, Lieutenant," an oarsman urged. "One, two, three, *up!*"

Two men grabbed Montgomery's left arm and made to haul him aboard. Montgomery pulled away from the jolt of pain in his injured shoulder and splashed back into the water. He recovered quickly and tried to hoist himself up on his own. As he draped both arms over the gig's gunwale and kicked hard with both legs, a sudden jolt of lightning-hot pain ran down his leg and he was shoved against the side of the gig.

He fought against the excruciating pain of teeth sinking into muscle and bone, the metallic stench and taste of brine mixed with blood—his own—and the panicked feeling of drowning in the back of his throat.

"Captain!" he managed to gurgle. Richard saw the helpless terror in Montgomery's eyes and lunged weakly to reach him. They clasped hands briefly, but another vicious tug pulled Montgomery away from him.

"*Jonty!*"

Their eyes met, and in those final heartbeats a host of memories, hopes, and dreams passed between them. Another vicious swirl of white water exploded at boat side. Richard saw a flash of white underbelly, a mammoth open maw with twin rows of savage, flesh-tearing teeth, and a moment later, Jonty Montgomery was gone.

CHAPTER 22

BATAVIA, ISLAND OF JAVA
April 1848

Richard Cutler and the other seriously wounded sailors and Marines left the next day in *Saratoga*. When he reached Batavia, he ordered transportation to take him to Cutler & Sons, and Daisy.

She was waiting for him in an anteroom on the first floor, seated on a high-backed blue settee, her hands folded in her lap and her eyes downcast. Her white muslin dress matched the paleness of her skin. Her hair hung lank and disheveled about her shoulders. For a moment he could only stand and look at her, searching for the right words that would not come. When she would not lift her eyes to look at him, he brought over a teak chair and sat down close to her.

"Sweet Jesus, Daisy!" he said, shaking his head. "I'm so sorry. So very sorry."

She nodded but did not look up or show any emotion. Her hands were clasped together so tightly that the knuckles had turned white.

Silence, save for the rhythmic tick-tock of a mantel clock. Moments elapsed. More silence. When he spoke again, she shook her head ever so slightly, a signal, he inferred, that she was not yet ready to allow him to speak of the brutal reality that had ripped her life asunder. It was as though she had thrown up a breakwater and had walled herself in against the inevitable torrent of emotions.

After several more minutes of silence, Richard said hesitantly, "Daisy, I loved Jonty too. He was like a son to me. I loved him for all he was, for all he meant to me and to my wife and family. And to my ship and my crew. And to you especially, my dear Daisy. I understand your pain, I really do!"

She nodded acknowledgment but kept her head bowed. "What happened out there, Captain Cutler?" she finally asked in a faint voice. "No one will tell me. No one will tell me anything. Not my father. Not Mr. De Vries. Not even the lieutenant sent ahead from *Saratoga*. I know he knew," she said accusingly. "He was *there!*"

Richard winced and swallowed hard. "I will tell you what happened, Daisy, though it pains me more than I can say. Jonty sacrificed his life to save mine. And it was not for the first time."

"How did he . . . die?" She could barely utter the word.

Again Richard swallowed hard. He could not divulge the morbid truth, that he had seen Jonty savaged and then pulled under by sharks. "He died in the line of duty, as did many brave men that day."

"Where is . . . his body? Did you bring it back so that I can at least say farewell to him?"

"He is buried at sea, Daisy. It's traditional in the Navy."

With that, the dam threatened to break. "My God! I can't bear this!" She buried her face in her hands, but the dam held. Tears did not come. "He was so good and kind, and so strong. He didn't deserve to die. He shouldn't have gone! And I loved him *so!* We were to be married when he returned!"

"I know, my dear," Richard whispered raggedly.

Her bloodshot eyes went to his. "You were going to marry us!"

"I know," Richard reiterated.

She shook her head, as if to deny her grief. Unable to bear her suffering, Richard left his chair, sat down beside Daisy, and put his arm around her shoulders. When he did, the dam burst. She collapsed against him as great gulping sobs shook her. There was no consoling her, nothing he could say or do but hold her against him and wait for the storm to abate.

"I'm sorry, Uncle Richard," she said at length, sniffling. "I'm so sorry. I didn't mean to cry. Please forgive me." She pulled away from him, struggling for composure. "I can see you have suffered too. Terribly." She accepted the kerchief Richard offered, wiped her eyes and blew her nose, then sat up straight.

"Jonty would not want me to act like this, would he? He would think he was undeserving of such fuss and bother." She sighed deeply and said stoically, "However sad this is for me and families of the many others who died, I know I must be brave and return to my duty."

"What duty is that?" Richard asked, surprised as much by her resolute tone as by her words.

When Daisy did not respond, Richard said, "Perhaps it would be better to stop trying to do your duty, Daisy, and start taking care of yourself." When she merely looked at him, he added, "You must give yourself time to grieve, my dear. Ignore what others tell you and ignore what you believe society expects of you—what anyone expects of you—and grieve to the extent you must, for the young man you loved and who loved you in return. And not least of all, for the life you two had planned together. Only by doing that can you find peace in your heart and in your mind. Trying to push aside your feelings will only increase the length and intensity of your grief. Trust me on this, Daisy," he soothed. "I have the benefit of hindsight, of personal experience."

Richard gently withdrew his arm and rose from the settee. "Daisy, you and I have things to discuss in the days ahead. Some very important and, I fear, very unsettling decisions must be made. For better or for worse, I am the one charged with making them. Trust me to do so with your best interests in mind. Do you trust me?" he asked, looking into her tear-stained eyes.

She nodded. "Of course. Jonty trusted you. That's enough for me."

"Good."

He patted her knee paternally, then made to leave the room. Before he reached the door, she called him back. He turned to face her.

"Yes, Daisy?"

"Thank you, Uncle Richard. Thank you for what you said and thank you for caring. About me and about Jonty."

He smiled at her. "You are most welcome, my dear," he said, adding poignantly, "you are not just a member of my family, Daisy; you are also the woman Jonty loved." He walked out the door, leaving her to the solace of her tears.

When Richard Cutler walked into the first-floor parlor where Pieter De Vries and Ben Cutler were waiting for him, the mood was somber. One look at Ben Cutler's face told Richard of the twofold pain his cousin was suffering: the pain of his daughter's tragic loss and his own loss of a young man he had looked forward to calling his own son. Richard hoped what he was about to propose would bring him and Daisy some comfort, although he was far from certain it would.

The three men sat around a highly polished mahogany table bearing pots of coffee and tea and silver platters of sandwiches and fruit. No one appeared particularly hungry.

Ben Cutler opened the conversation. "Before we begin discussing your agenda, Richard, I must ask, how was my daughter when you spoke with her? I overheard you talking, and I heard her weeping. As painful as it was to hear, I was relieved. She has been so stoic, so controlled."

"I found her as I would expect to find someone who has been told that the young man she adored and planned to marry is gone forever. Her life and dreams have been shattered. She needs time to work through this horror the best way she can. She'll make it, of that I am certain. But it will take time. Time and the love you give her. She is a strong and resilient young woman. That and her sense of duty will carry her through this."

"God knows she is resilient," Ben Cutler agreed. "And stubborn. Jonathan was an excellent match for her. She brought out the best in him, and he, the best in her. Dear God, he will be missed," he choked, turning away to hide his face.

"Yes, he will," Richard agreed, waiting for Ben to continue.

Ben Cutler turned back. "I wish there was something I could do to help ease her pain. Waiting for her to work through her grief is not enough."

"I believe there *is* something you can do," Richard countered, "something we can all do for her and for the family as a whole. In fact, that is why I asked you and Pieter to speak with me today. What I am about to say may sound radical to you, but I am convinced it is essential to the future of the Cutler family and to those, like Pieter here, who have tied their destiny to ours."

"You have our full attention, Captain," De Vries said. "Please continue."

Richard cleared his throat and allowed several seconds to elapse. Then: "I think we can all agree that our first priority here in Batavia continues to be the release of our sailors held captive in China. We don't know how many are there—and we don't know for certain *who* is there—but we know the number is substantial. They are Cutler & Sons personnel, most of them, and we must get them out. To allow further delays would be intolerable!"

De Vries and Ben Cutler exchanged looks.

"We of course agree with you in principle, Richard," De Vries said after a pause, "but how do you propose we do that? Beyond what we have already done? What are you suggesting? That we launch another attack on their stronghold?"

"I am suggesting nothing of the kind. I never supported that strategy, and I don't support it now. We can never get them out by attacking their prison, no matter how many times we try. It's a futile waste of men and resources."

"How do we do it, then?" Ben Cutler asked in a rare display of exasperation.

Richard's voice was firm. "We do it by paying the pirates the ransom money they are demanding. There is no other way."

Ben Cutler and Pieter De Vries looked at one another and then back at Richard in shock.

"We can't do that, Richard," Ben said condescendingly, like a parent explaining something basic to a child who should know better. "Your government is adamant on that point. The United States has stated over and again that it will not pay ransom money to any party, for any reason. For you to even suggest such a thing to your State Department could mean the end of your naval career. You do realize that, don't you?"

"I do realize that. But it won't matter. I have already resigned my commission. I signed the papers on the voyage here from Hainan. Captain Brengle is working on his resignation as well and will send both letters to Washington when he returns from Hong Kong next week."

"I am very sorry to hear that, Richard," Ben Cutler exclaimed. "Ending a long and illustrious career is a very serious change. But you still have not answered the central question. If we agree that paying ransom is the only way to secure their release, who will pay it? The United States government will not, do you agree?"

"I do."

"So who, then?"

"*We* will, of course."

Ben Cutler's jaw dropped. "I don't think I heard you correctly. Did you say *we* will?"

"Yes, we. Cutler & Sons. We have done it before. In Barbary. We paid the dey of Algiers a king's ransom to free my great-uncle Caleb and the crew of his ship *Eagle*. The ransom demanded then was greater than what is being demanded now, and Cutler & Sons had far fewer resources to draw on. So we did it once, and we are about to do it again."

Ben Cutler shook his head in stupefaction. He made to speak, but no words came out. He looked to De Vries.

"Richard," De Vries said, his voice strong, "this is all very interesting, but making such a payment will all but bankrupt Cutler & Sons' operations here in Batavia. What then?"

Richard's voice in reply was equally adamant. "What then, Pieter, is that we enter negotiations to sell our business in the Orient. If we can't find a suitable buyer, we cease operations here and sell off our assets piecemeal."

"Dissolve? Sell?" De Vries threw up his hands in frustration. "Richard, you are like family to me. *Mijn Gott*! Ben and I understand that you have suffered the most horrific trauma in China. I doubt I could function after witnessing such a thing, let alone act so normally. We do not wish for a moment to scoff at you or add to your burdens. But my dear friend, have you taken leave of your senses? What you are proposing is impossible! We cannot walk away from everything your family has built here, everything we *have* here!"

"What, exactly, *do* we have here, Pieter?"

The question threw De Vries. The answer seemed obvious. "Why, just look around you, Richard. What do you see?"

Richard made a show of looking around. "I see an attractive building, well-appointed rooms, a loyal staff, our merchant ships in the harbor, and the promise of what could be."

"You no longer wish to pursue that promise?"

Richard shook his head. "Not here. I have studied the books, Pieter, and I can see that we are making money. Good money. For the moment. But I also saw things in those books that trouble me."

"Trouble you? What troubles you?"

"For one thing, the fact that we are making most of our money not from selling our products but by selling space in our holds to clients who seek to transport and sell *their* products. That part of our business is being threatened by other companies from other countries. For Cutler & Sons to compete and sustain profits in the Orient, we would need to fundamentally change what we do and how we do it.

"Before we can even contemplate doing that, though, we must rescue our sailors. They have already sacrificed too much. And for what purpose? So that we can sell space in the holds of our merchant ships? Damn it, Pieter! Is that worth the investment we have had to make in treasure and blood?"

When there was no immediate answer, Richard said more calmly, "Please hear me out, gentlemen. When my family sailed from England to the colony of Massachusetts nearly a century ago, they had dreams of building a mercantile empire using the lucrative trade routes from America to Europe, and from Europe to the West Indies. Those trade routes were already well established by that time. What made them profitable, for us, were the products my family produced, which in those days was limited to sugar and molasses. We hadn't started making rum yet. But we made money selling high-quality sugar and molasses—plenty of money, enough to sustain every member of the Cutler family. No one suffered. No one went hungry. We all prospered.

"Ben, you can verify everything I just said. Your father and uncle on Barbados were two of the beneficiaries. And it was your mother, Julia, who introduced us to the Mount Gay families on Barbados. That was a boon to the Cutler family if ever there was one. It got us into rum production, the most profitable segment of our business, then and now."

Despite himself, Ben Cutler nodded.

"What I am now proposing," Richard went on, "is to take the family business back to its roots. It worked well for us in the past, and there is no reason to doubt that it would work well for us in the future, at far less cost. Ben, you are welcome to join me in America. Cutler & Sons always has a need for a good administrator. The director of our Boston office is soon to retire. You could take over from him. His shoes will be difficult ones to fill, but if there is one man who can do it, and do it well, that man is you."

Ben Cutler blinked. "That is quite an offer, Richard," he said at length. "Food for serious thought, certainly. But remember: I have a daughter to consider."

"You do, and I just met with her. I did not want to tell her this without first speaking with you, but I will be encouraging her to accompany me and Jack in two weeks' time when we sail for Boston. As you know, I have a large family there—it is her family too, after all, and yours—and any one of us would be delighted to take her in until you could join her. And most important, I believe this is what Jonty would want for Daisy."

Ben Cutler sat in silence, rubbing his chin and considering. Richard looked at De Vries.

"As for you, Pieter, you may want to consider acquiring our assets in the Orient. You have excellent business instincts, and given a free hand you can set this ship to rights, just as Jan Vanderheyden did many years ago after Jack Endicott was lost at sea. What is more, you have all the right connections. If you are interested, we can negotiate favorable terms. Perhaps we can still find a way to do business together in the future. What do you say? Will you think about it?"

De Vries was staring into space with his hands clasped in his lap, as if weighing his options or already running the numbers. He nodded slowly. "I will," he promised.

"I'm glad."

After a period of silence, Ben Cutler asked, "How will your family react to all this?"

"I don't know, Ben, but I believe the benefits of what I am proposing far outweigh the costs. My job now is to sell this concept to my family. I think I can do it."

"I think you can, too," Ben Cutler said.

"We'll see. For the moment, as part of this plan, I do have questions about logistics, such as how best to contact the pirates and arrange for a transfer of funds."

"Leave that to me," De Vries said. "As you just said, I have the right connections, and those connections include getting inside the pirate camp and the pirate mind, insofar as that can be done. It shouldn't be too difficult, and it shouldn't take too long. Once those brutes smell lucre, matters tend to progress."

"That is good to hear, Pieter. I shall leave this matter in your capable hands. You have my proxy to do whatever you think is necessary to get those men released. The ships to bring them back here are already in Hong Kong."

* * *

Three days later, Richard walked to the wharves by the harbor, having received word from an orderly that Jack Brengle's ship had been sighted steaming into Batavia Bay. The two men met at a local pub that was a favorite of sailors of many nations. The exotic food was delicious, but what drew patrons was the selection of hard-to-find European beers and ales. Both men ordered a slug of Grolsch beer. After the waiter had been paid, Richard asked, "A good voyage, Jack?"

"An excellent voyage, Richard, all things considered. But I'm looking forward even more to our upcoming voyage home."

"I'll drink to that. Tell me, how is Terence? He took quite a blow. He must have lost a lot of blood."

"He'll pull through. But I think that like his ship *Columbia*, he will forever be a shadow of his former self. Still, he's doing a far sight better than either Dean or Bowen. Those poor fellows didn't make it."

Richard heaved a sigh. "Yes, I know. What of the rest of the crews? Those who came out alive?"

"Like us. Looking forward to going home." He paused, then blurted, "We should never have been there. We were on a fool's errand, and too many good men paid the ultimate price for a bad government decision, Jonty first among them! I'm sure that the sorry sods held prisoner in China would agree with me."

Richard nodded solemnly. "I suspect they would, Jack. But don't blame our government for what happened. Blame me."

"You? In God's name why?"

"I should have stepped in much sooner than I did. I had the authority. I should have done something to stop the madness."

"What could you have done? You had your orders, and you had your duty to consider. My opinion? Taking command of *Columbia* when you did saved many lives. The real threat was the bomb vessels, not the fire ships, and it was on your order that our gunners concentrated on them. Terence would be the first to agree with that. In fact, he already has."

Richard said nothing further until the waiter placed two steins of foamy beer on the table. Richard raised his stein and held it out. "To Jonty," he said solemnly.

"To Jonty," Brengle returned. They clinked steins. "And to home." They clinked steins a second time.

"Speaking of home," Richard said after a respectful interlude, "I brought something with me that you may find interesting."

Brengle perked up. "Oh? What is it?"

"A letter." Richard fished in a coat pocket. "Hang on. It's here somewhere. Where is the damn thing? Ah, sorry, here it is." Out came a letter written on delicate blue paper. "It arrived soon after we sailed for Hainan. Took its time getting here."

Brengle's eyes went wide. He took the letter and smiled down at the familiar handwriting on the outside.

"I received a letter from Anne at the same time, so I have a sense of what you're about to find in that letter."

Brengle broke the red wax seal, unfolded the letter, and began to read, his face expressionless at first, then becoming increasingly animated as he read on. When he finished, he looked away, ostensibly at the paintings of ships and seascapes decorating the walls, before returning to the letter and rereading it.

"Good news?" Richard carefully probed.

Brengle's eyes remained trained on the letter. "Yes," he replied so softly Richard had to lean in to hear him. "Very good news. The best news possible. Lucy is going to live! She says she is still in pain and will be for some time. The doctors have put her on medication that is keeping her weak. But with Lucy's strong spirit, the doctors see nothing to prevent her from living for many years to come." Brengle pounded a fist on the table in glee. "However much time Lucy may have left, if she and God are willing, she will spend it with me! I will take good care of her." Brengle again banged his fist on the table, this time so hard it rattled tableware and caused patrons at a nearby table to look over and gawk at him. "Lucy is going to live!" he explained to them in apology. "She's going to be all right! It's a goddamn miracle!"

"I'm happy for you, Jack. Very happy for you and for Lucy. I wouldn't let her go to a less deserving man."

Brengle said nothing further. He collected himself as he stared down at the letter. "She's going to be all right," he whispered.

"You'll be happy to know that we'll be shoving off as soon as we finish provisioning *Chippewa*," Richard said to lighten the mood. "By the way, Daisy will be joining us on the voyage."

"Do say!"

"I *do* say. What's more, her father is going to join her in Hingham. Ben is going to take Charles Henley's position as director of our Boston office. He'll be sailing for Hingham in one of our merchant ships as soon as he has helped to finalize arrangements here in Batavia."

"What arrangements do you mean?"

"There is much more to tell you, and I'll get to all that just as soon as I order another round of beer for us! It's time to lift our spirits, Jack!"

CHAPTER 23

BOSTON, MASSACHUSETTS
September 1848

Boston Harbor was alive with activity. Much of it was commercial, but recreational craft—rowboats, single-masted sloops, and two-masted ketches—with families on board for a day's outing on one of the thirty-odd small islands that dotted Boston Harbor flitted about in the warm late summer sun and gentle northwesterly breeze. Other small craft were there simply to observe at close hand the sleek two-hundred-fifty-foot steam frigate and escort her down the deepwater channel between Deer Isle and Long Island, and from there on to her anchorage in the inner harbor by the commercial juggernaut that was Long Wharf.

"What do you think of Boston so far, Daisy?" Jack Brengle asked. He was standing with her and much of the ship's officer corps on *Chippewa's* quarterdeck, all excited to be taking in the sights and scents of homecoming.

Daisy Cutler was smiling, to Richard's immense satisfaction. She had rarely smiled on the voyage from Java. Worse, at times she had seemed unbearably unfocused, as though unwilling or unable to structure a life without Jonty in it. Despondency and uncertainty seemed to be her constant companions, despite everyone's best efforts to lift her spirits. And yet she had begun to show a change as they neared Boston.

"It's nothing like I have ever seen before," Daisy replied in wonder. She pointed off to port. "What is that island over there? It looks intriguing."

CHAPTER 23

"That's Thompson Island," Richard said. "As a boy, I scoured those hills and glades in search of Indian arrowheads."

"Did you find any?"

"A few. It's high tide now, but at low tide you can walk there from the mainland out to the island on a sandbar. You needn't have a boat."

"How marvelous!" she blurted out excitedly. "Can we do that, Uncle Richard? Oh please, can we?"

"If you would like to, of course we can."

"I would love to!" Daisy enthused. Then she went suddenly quiet, as she had often done during the three-month voyage, presumably, Richard thought, because she was thinking how delightful it would have been to cross that sandbar with Jonty.

Long Wharf was drawing closer. The arrival of a naval steam frigate was an infrequent event in Boston, and citizens and shopkeepers and children came running to Long Wharf to witness the evolutions of anchoring as *Chippewa* rounded into the wind. Richard nodded with satisfaction. He knew well that all this commotion would prompt Charles Henley to alert a master and mate of a Cutler packet boat that a voyage to Hingham was likely imminent.

Applause and cheering broke out when Richard and Jack stepped up from the captain's gig onto Long Wharf, followed by Daisy Cutler wearing her one good summer dress and favorite straw hat with a long blue ribbon tied fetchingly beneath her chin. Once on dry land, she continued to clasp Richard's hand tightly. After so long at sea, her legs were wobbly and she had to work to maintain her balance.

"Why the applause, Uncle?" she asked as she looked around at the people watching her from a respectable distance.

Richard grinned. "The good citizens of Boston are welcoming a beautiful young lass," he said, squeezing her hand. "As they should."

Daisy shook her head. "You, sir, are the consummate flatterer!"

Brengle stepped up, his sea bag slung over his shoulder. "I'm off, Richard," he said. "I see a carriage for hire over there on State Street, and I'm going to take it before someone else does. *Chippewa* is in good hands with her exec. See you in a couple of days."

"All right, Jack. Good luck with everything."

238

Brengle leaned in close. "Thank you. God willing, she will accept my proposal."

"God is willing, my friend. Trust me."

The two men each took one step back and saluted in formal fashion. Richard then took two steps forward to embrace his lifelong friend and ally. After the embrace, Brengle tipped his hat and bowed to Daisy. He turned on his heel and was soon swallowed up by the crowd, which by now was beginning to disperse.

"I want to take you to meet Mr. Henley, the director of our Boston office. His office is right over there." He pointed. "I'll have a word with him, and then we will be on our way. Mr. Henley, remember, is the man your father is going to replace. We shan't say anything about that now, however."

"I understand," Daisy said.

An hour later, a brisk breeze was pushing along their thirty-foot packet boat on a broad reach. The afternoon sun cast golden lights on the bright green grass of the harbor's protective islands and their deciduous trees, leaves painted ever so delicately with autumn harbingers of amber and russet. Richard and Daisy said little to each other on the hour-long sail. Daisy was absorbed in the delightful sights passing by her, and Richard was thinking of his family, wondering if Anne had received his last letter, sent in an official dispatch the day after he returned to Batavia from Hainan. If she had received it, all would already have been revealed to her. If not, he would have some explaining to do during the next several days.

Daisy was enjoying the boat's motion and the sun on her face, and was close to nodding off when Richard nudged her. "See that island yonder?" he said, pointing ahead to a low-lying island coming up to port. "Just beyond it, to starboard, is Hingham Harbor."

Daisy nodded.

"That's Grape Island," Richard said, adding, "it's my favorite of the harbor islands. It happens to be where my naval career began."

That brought Daisy fully awake. She shot him a curious look across the cockpit. "There? On that little island? How?"

"A lot of shells end up there. The currents, I suppose. In any event, as a boy I used to row out and engage in epic sea battles. Mussel shells served as naval vessels, clam shells as merchantmen and supply ships. It was great fun. I even got friends in Hingham to come over with me and join in."

"Did you win many battles?"

"My dear, I won them all!"

They shared a laugh, joined by the boat's master, a grizzled old seaman who had been in the employ of Cutler & Sons for many years, and his mate, a tall, well-proportioned, blond lad of twenty or so years who clearly knew the ropes of seamanship. He had introduced himself to Richard and Daisy as Trevor. Throughout the brief voyage he had cast appreciative glances at Daisy, who did not seem to mind his attention. Richard smiled inwardly.

As the sloop creamed into the harbor and approached the wharf at Crow Point, the mate hauled in the jib and main sheets to slow her down. As the bow feathered up to the dock, the helm was swung hard over, bringing the sloop into the wind and to a virtual halt, sails flapping impotently. They drifted the short distance to the dock. The mate jumped out and secured the bow and stern lines to cleats. He helped Daisy out and took the baggage from Richard. "Please excuse me, Miss Daisy," he said respectfully, "I must locate a carriage for you and Captain Cutler. It shouldn't take but a minute."

"Thank you, Trevor," Daisy said graciously.

"My honor, Miss Daisy." Young Trevor smiled at Daisy, and she, blushing, smiled back at him.

A short time later, their carriage pulled up in front of the Cutler home on Lafayette Avenue. Richard got out first, took the two large bags and placed them on the ground, then handed Daisy down before offering a double-eagle coin to the driver.

"T'won't be necessary, Captain," the burly, bearded driver said. "This trip's on me. Welcome home, sir."

"Thank you kindly," Richard said and took Daisy's hand. "We'll leave the baggage here for the moment, Daisy. Come."

A gentle knock on the front door was answered by a young woman well known to Richard. "Captain Cutler!" she gasped, her hand to her mouth, "you're home!"

"I am, Rachel. And this time it's for good!" Richard kissed her fondly on the cheek. "Rachel, this is my niece, Daisy Cutler. She will be staying with us until she gets settled."

Rachel looked at Daisy. "So nice to meet you, Daisy," she said sincerely. "We all welcome you here."

"Where's my wife?" Richard asked pointedly. "And the children?"

"In the lounge. All four of them."

"All *four*?" It took a moment to register. "The baby . . ."

Rachel smiled. "Little Jonty is a healthy, bonny lad, as you are about to discover for yourself."

Her words met empty air. Richard was already striding eagerly toward the parlor. He softly opened the door and peeked inside. What he saw convinced him that the decisions he had made had been the right ones.

Anne was seated on the camelback sofa reading a book to their tow-headed young son and their wee daughter half-hidden within the folds of her mother's voluminous gown. Young Jamie was giving the story his full attention, while Sydney was drowsing and contentedly sucking her tiny thumb. Nestled in the crook of Anne's arm was the baby she had given birth to and nurtured all those months Richard had been away. As he gazed at this heartwarming tableau, Anne looked up, their eyes met, and in that brief, tender, moment he knew he was, truly, home.

The End

EPILOGUE

The signal fire built two weeks earlier at Pemberton Point on the tip of Nantasket Peninsula was first spotted shortly after daybreak at an observation post on World's End in Hingham. Minutes later, the steeple bells of First Parish Church began tolling. One after another, the churches in villages along Boston's South Shore picked up the toll, which ultimately reached into inner Boston itself. By midmorning, citizens of seaside communities were hastening by foot, coach, horse, and boat to Long Wharf to witness history in the making.

There were historic precedents for such a gathering on the Boston waterfront, one of which involved the Cutler family. At the end of the previous century, the schooner *Falcon*, captained by Agreen Crabtree, had sailed across the Atlantic from Algiers to Boston carrying the long-imprisoned crew of the Cutler merchant brig *Eagle*. Prominent among those former hostages was Caleb Cutler, of the second generation of Cutlers in America, the first Cutler to hold the formal position of director of Cutler & Sons. That time, it seemed that most residents of Boston and the South Shore had turned out to welcome home the native sons of New England.

Today's turnout would not be as grand. The United States was no longer the disrespected plaything of more powerful nations on the world stage. Its Navy was as formidable as any in either hemisphere, and the reach and dominance of its merchant fleet were unparalleled. America's honor was today no longer as easily offended as it had been fifty years earlier. Too, the United States was not at war. The so-called Opium War was strictly a British affair. America had played only a peripheral role in the conflict. Its beef was with the Chinese smugglers and pirates operating illegally in China, not with the emperor. The United States government was not out for territory, opium, or prestige in the Orient. It simply wanted to free American citizens taken prisoner and brutalized while engaged in legitimate business. And now, those hostages were free and in Boston Harbor, just a few feet away from a sea of excited spectators.

As *Saratoga* slowly approached the long open space prepared for her at Long Wharf, she cut power as her crew and a dock crew made ready to warp her in. To the delight of the crowd, the Boston Brigade Band, a local reed and brass ensemble of some note, launched into a stirring rendition of "Home Sweet Home." By this time, the frigate's port railing was lined shoulder to shoulder with its passengers, who were responding gratefully to the applause and cheers of the hundreds of onlookers crowding the dock. The afternoon was sunny and cool, a typical day for early spring in Boston, but no one seemed concerned about the weather.

The man the crowd had assumed would be first off the frigate was indeed the first one off. He stood at the entry port, staring at a crowd that was growing larger by the moment and pushing against the cordon of constables and against each other for a better vantage point. The man wore a loose-fitting woolen overcoat and a woolen hat against the chill. The long beard was gone now, but he had yet to fully regain the weight he had lost. Yet his eyes sparkled with the intensity of youth.

When he hesitated at the wide gangplank leading from ship to shore, a lieutenant came up to offer a hand. His offer was politely refused. Placing both hands on the parallel railings on the gangplank, the man hoisted himself up and started walking down the inclined passageway. His footing was unsure, his legs wobbly despite the strength he had garnered during his convalescence in Batavia and the long voyage home. But his gaze held steady ahead with a fierce determination.

When he stepped onto the wharf, a reception committee was there to greet him. He recognized them all—Richard and Jamie, William, Thomas, Diana, Zeke, and others—all of them blood members of his family, save for one. But it was the young woman standing in their midst who continued to hold his attention. Now that woman came forward.

"Welcome home, Father," she choked, unable to say more. When his emaciated arms enfolded her, she hid her face in the folds of his overcoat. The crowd of onlookers backed off and maintained a respectful silence, aware of the fragility of the moment.

"Lucy," the man whispered hoarsely. "My dearest, dearest Lucy. How are you, my sweet daughter?"

She looked up at him with welling eyes. "I am well, Father." A smile slowly spread across her face. "At the moment, I am exceptionally well!" She turned and held out her hand to the small cluster of individuals standing close behind her. The one who stepped forward to take her hand was the one man in the reception committee Philip Seymour had not recognized.

"And who have we here?" he asked quizzically.

"Father," Lucy said, her voice bolder, more confident, "may I introduce my husband and Cutler & Sons' newest employee, Jack Brengle?"